T0357117

Mrs. Lilienblum's Cloud Factory

Also by Iddo Gefen

Fiction
Jerusalem Beach

Mrs. Lilienblum's Cloud Factory

IDDO GEFEN
TRANSLATED BY
DANIELLA ZAMIR

Astra House **∧** New York

Originally published as מפעל העננים של גברת לילנבלום in the Hebrew language, by Kinneret Zmora-Bitan Dvir

For information about permission to reproduce selections from this book, please contact permissions@astrahouse.com.

Astra House
A Division of Astra Publishing House
astrahouse.com

Printed in the United States of America

Library of Congress Cataloging-in-Publication Data

Names: Gefen, Iddo, 1992- author. | Zamir, Daniella, translator.
Title: Mrs. Lilienblum's cloud factory / Iddo Gefen ; translated by Daniella Zamir.
Other titles: Mif'al ha-'ananim shel geveret Lilenblum. English
Description: First edition. | New York : Astra House, 2025. | Summary: "A comic novel about a tech startup that turns sand into rain clouds"-- Provided by publisher.
Identifiers: LCCN 2024048376 (print) | LCCN 2024048377 (ebook) | ISBN 9781662600876 (hardcover) | ISBN 9781662600883 (epub)
Subjects: LCGFT: Satirical fiction. | Novels.
Classification: LCC PJ5055.22.E3483 M5413 2025 (print) | LCC PJ5055.22.E3483 (ebook) | DDC 892.43/7--dc23/eng/20241214
LC record available at https://lccn.loc.gov/2024048376
LC ebook record available at https://lccn.loc.gov/2024048377

First edition

10 9 8 7 6 5 4 3 2 1

Design by Alissa Theodor

The text is set in Granjon LT Std.

The titles are set in Neue Haas Grotesk Display Pro.

To Neria, who was there from the beginning; and to
General Luciano Rodríguez Ancelotti III,
for adventures best left untold

Mrs.
Lilienblum's
Cloud
Factory

There she was, sitting in the middle of the desert in a burgundy bathrobe, holding a half-full cocktail glass—a sight so uncanny the poor Dutch hiker who crossed her path could only ascribe it to sunstroke, courtesy of the sweltering southern summer. Such was his panic that he immediately called for extraction via satellite phone, then sat down a hundred feet from her, clutching his last water bottle, drinking as sparingly as possible until the black rescue jeep finally arrived.

The driver stepped out and wavered at her, ignoring the petrified Dutchman, who had only then realized the woman was no mirage.

"Ma'am, are you okay?" he asked.

She nodded, leaned back in her white deck chair, and took a sip of the clear liquid. A wide-brimmed straw hat and round sunglasses hid much of her face.

"What are you doing out here?"

She didn't answer.

The man swept his gaze across the sand, spotting a small mound in the distance and a half-hidden ravine behind a cluster of low bushes.

"What's that?" He jutted his chin toward her glass.

"Martini," she replied. "I've had better."

He eyed the tiny beads of condensation trickling down the glass. The martini was ice-cold. The perplexed rescuer took another step in her direction.

"What's your name, ma'am?"

Taking off her sunglasses, she peered at him with a pair of green-gray eyes.

153
DAYS
TILL
RAIN

O nly one fact appeared indisputable—Sarai Lilienblum turned up three days later, in the heart of the large crater, a few miles from the desert ski village where she lived. Her son, Eli, received the news of her whereabouts shortly after nine A.M.

"They found her," his father exclaimed over the phone, waking him from a deep sleep. "In the crater, in a burgundy bathrobe."

"Burgundy?" Eli croaked. "Really? They found her?"

"Yes, and yes," his father said. "They're taking her to the ER at Soroka. It's probably no more than a mild case of dehydration, but just to be on the safe side."

Eli sat up in bed. "Did she say where she's been? What happened . . ."

"No, no. We'll know more when they let me see her."

"Good, good," Eli repeated, attempting to cement the news, help it strike roots in the world. He wondered whether he was supposed to feel happier. A car horn blared from the phone. "So you went to see her?" he asked.

There was a brief silence. "You were asleep, Eli, and there was no time. I left in such a hurry I even forgot to put on socks . . ."

"Right, no, yeah," Eli replied, "the important thing is that they found her."

"Yes, that's the important thing," his father echoed softly. "And I need you at the lodge today. Someone has to make sure the Icelander doesn't burn the place down."

"Burn the place down?" It took Eli a moment to realize that his father had reverted to his goofy, joking self. Which meant it had to be true, his mother really had been found; there was now a specific location in space and time to point at and say—then and there.

He lay back staring at the ceiling, trying to visualize his burgundy-robed mother in the desert. The image was blurry. As a child he had often felt gripped by the strangest notion: that there were places erected only moments before the first visitors arrived; that half an hour prior, in what appeared to be a small Tuscan town, someone would announce, "Let's go, guys, pull a few houses, a road and a vineyard out of storage, they'll be here any moment," and lickety-split, all the extras would be bused in to take their positions. Walking up and down the streets, casual and confident, as if the town had been standing there since time immemorial. And once the tourists left, the crew would quickly pack the town up again and move on to the next one. He remembered confiding this to his mother, throwing in the word "maybe" a few times. Crouching to his height, she looked around surreptitiously, then asked, "How did you know?" Said she used to work for the very company in charge of all the tourist towns. He believed her for three whole years, until he told a girl he loved that Paris wasn't a real city and she laughed. As payback for lying, he gave his mother the silent treatment for two weeks. But some ideas aren't easily discarded, which is why even now, at twenty-two, whenever he arrives someplace new, he takes a good look around, to see if maybe one of the buildings is slightly askew, or a street sign in the wrong language. And as he lay in bed after hanging up with his father, a strange possibility crossed Eli's mind—that maybe, just maybe, his mother had spent the past three days in a traveling town; that perhaps, after all the roads and houses had been boxed up and stored away and the crew and extras gone back home, she decided to stay on a little longer.

A n hour later, as Eli peered into the gaping fridge, waffling over what to put on his toast (butter or jam), Naomi Lilienblum burst through the door.

"She's gone completely off the rails," his big sister announced with a hug, then plopped her backpack and suitcase in the corner of the kitchen before downing three glasses of tepid water at the sink. The twenty-three-hour voyage from Silicon Valley to the Lilienblum residence on the cliff of the large crater had taken its toll—the sloppy bun, the creased black shirt, the sheen of sweat filming the rocking horse she had impulsively tattooed on her nape a few years back and that was often kept stabled under a collar.

"Why couldn't she have shown up two hours ago and let me shower at home in Tel Aviv like a human being?" she said, pulling a tub of cottage cheese and a tomato out of the fridge. "Here, this is healthier," she said. "Now tell me exactly what happened."

He sliced the tomato and told her.

"It started at the dinner party." Three days earlier, they had hosted a dinner to celebrate his mother's accomplishment—her students' third-place victory at the regional robotics competition. Six guests, including the head of the council, had arrived to see the invention that had nabbed them the prize: an automated, self-opening sensor-controlled umbrella that deployed a split second before the first drop of rain, or, in reality, a slightly larger than average red umbrella with a thermometer and small antenna taped to the bottom of the handle. The judges claimed that if not for the high manufacturing cost and small safety matter of the umbrella unintentionally popping open whenever the temperature in the room dropped below sixty-four degrees Fahrenheit, it might have taken the crown.

"Why are you telling me about umbrellas? When did you realize she was missing?"

"When I went upstairs to tell her the guests were here." He had assumed his mother was still holed up in her study—where she spent most evenings working on her inventions—oblivious to time. Eli and his father knew that when Sarai was up there, time became *Sarai's time*, and there was no imposing on *Sarai's time*. His father once said that if there was a UN office in charge of the world's time zones, they would be sure to have at least one report on the unique phenomenon by which "in the northern hemisphere, on 4 Ha'arava Street, on the second floor, in a room to the left, time bends to Ms. Sarai Lilienblum's will."

But when Eli went up and opened the door, she wasn't there. They weren't immediately worried, but half an hour later, when they tried her phone for the third time and found it resting on her nightstand, they began to wonder.

"Oh god, please don't tell me he did that dumb meditation thing of his in front of the guests."

"That's exactly what he did," Eli laughed. A decade ago, their father had gone on a three-day meditation retreat and returned with a breathing exercise he practiced whenever he felt panicky, even though he was never quite sure whether it was two breaths in, one out, or one in, two out. Eli said that at first he thought his father was completely overreacting, that she would turn up any moment. But by midnight, long after the last of the guests had gone and still there was no sign of her, even he admitted there was cause for concern. He told his sister that their father woke up the whole neighborhood, and the following morning police officers and search and rescue volunteers went out to canvas the area.

"A rescue team with a track record of zero rescues, you mean."

"Don't be such a hater, I'm sure it's just a matter of a decade, two tops, until they find McMurphy," he said. She laughed at the inside joke. It never ceased to amaze him how they could be so different and yet have such a similar sense of humor.

"So it took them three days to find her?"

He nodded.

"And why did she disappear in the first place?"

"I honestly have no idea," Eli said.

"Okay, so that's you, but the cops don't either?" Naomi sighed, a grating sigh that meant if she had been called in, she would have cracked it in no time. Even more annoying than her condescension was knowing she usually wasn't wrong.

"Did you go through her study?"

"Of course we did, Naomi. We turned the place over. There's nothing in there."

"Maybe not thoroughly enough," she muttered, and before he could protest she was already halfway up the stairs.

He followed her into their mother's study, where the sanded, white-washed walls and light parquet floor stood in stark contrast to the dark, rough wooden beams from which the houses on the cliff were erected. As befitting a robotics teacher, the room was a clutter of gadgetry, most of which she had fashioned with her own two hands. Among the jumble he could make out an old computer screen and small fan next to an electric pencil sharpener and microphone; but the rest eluded clear definition—a hodgepodge of lightbulbs, cables, wires, and mirrors so tangled it was impossible to tell where one object ended and the other began. Every time he stepped into his mother's study, Eli was struck with the same stumped awe that he had felt on his one and only visit to a modern art museum. While his sister poked around the room, he followed suit, mimicking her movements. On their mother's green desk, he spotted a pocket-size broom tied to a red toy car.

"Wow, this was mine," Eli said, reaching for the car. As if on its own accord, the tiny vehicle took off, speeding every which way, leaving the desk in a further state of disorder. Naomi continued to rummage through the room, then paused to point at an oddly triangular outlet on the opposite wall. "Why does it look like that?"

From what Eli understood, it was a special power outlet their mother had built for devices that ran on more than 240 volts.

"It's a miracle the place hasn't caught on fire—yet," Naomi replied, brushing her hand over a few of her mother's strange brainchildren, triggering a robotic arm holding a toothbrush, and restarting a counterclockwise clock.

"I'm not sure she'd be thrilled by us tinkering with her stuff," Eli said.

"Then next time she should think twice before taking off," Naomi said, and plucked a black remote from the shelf.

"Wait, it's not ready!" Eli warned, but his sister had already pulled the trigger. A stirring noise sounded from the ceiling and a cloudburst of stinging ice-cubes landed on her head. As she took cover, Eli snatched the remote and turned it off. Once the pelting ceased, Naomi looked up and saw a large metal duct emerging from the ceiling.

"What is going on with that woman?! What's she building now?"

"It doesn't have an official name yet," Eli said, shrugging a few ice cubes off his shirt. "She's been calling it a universal AC."

"A what?"

"It's an air conditioner that's supposed to set the temperature by country, or something like that, don't ask me." He showed her the remote. Next to every button there was a small sticker of a flag; he recognized Sweden and China, and was fairly certain the one in the corner was Mexico. "You press a button and the device whips up the same weather as in that country," he explained. "Or at least it's supposed to."

Naomi gave it another try, but this time nothing happened.

"Like eighty percent of her inventions, it's not entirely there yet," Eli added, knowing that ninety would be a fairer estimate. Naomi placed the remote back on the shelf. Just then the ceiling shook with a soft whir and a thin trickle of sand poured from the duct onto the floor. Eli diverted some onto his palm. "She brought the desert into the house. Nice." He grinned.

A third press of the button, and the rivulet of sand only picked up, a layer of thick powder slowly sheeting the room. "Stop it, Naomi," he said, but the buttons refused to respond. The sand was swallowing up the floor, and in less than two minutes they were standing on a small stretch of beach, the air around them grainy and thick. Struggling to keep his eyes open, Eli started to cough.

"Oh, for fuck's sake," Naomi grumbled and stomped out. Fumbling his way through the blinding fog, Eli collided with the table before limping out into the dusty hallway to find his sister waiting for him; she slammed the door shut, and the room belched out a thin trickle of sand from under the doorframe.

"This sandstorm will continue forever," said Eli.

"We'll give it some time, her supply has to run out at some point," Naomi said. "But where the hell is it coming from?!" She gestured toward the ceiling, trying to guestimate the path of the interior duct line. Storming the laundry room, she hopped onto the dryer, tilted her head up, and listened to the low purring coming from above. She hopped off, marched down the hallway, leapt onto a chair, and poked at the ceiling panel. "Where is this shit coming from?"

"Ask Morgenstein," Eli said.

The name Morgenstein was etched in the minds of every child in the village, the mythic mustachioed, pipe-chewing Swiss architect whose innovative technique for building ski chalets in the Eastern Alps earned him the Bauhaus Prize. After devoting three years of his life to adapting his construction methods to the hot desert climate, he could show off the fruits of his research: affordable wooden houses more durable and eco-friendly than any viable alternative on the planet. Town lore had it that rulers of the Sahara begged him to grace their land with the first desert ski village, if not sell them his modular secrets, but prodded by his Jewish father to help the poor Jews with their fledgling state, he settled in Israel. Specifically, the cliff over the large crater. It was rumored that Minister Sapir traveled to Switzerland on a clandestine mission to secure the blueprints; that later Morgenstein flew in for three grueling weeks in the middle of the Israeli summer to oversee construction, and that on the day the last brick was laid in the new town square, Prime Minister Ben-Gurion himself attended the inauguration ceremony and wrote in his journal that thanks to this Morgenstein mensch, the Jewish people could desert-dwell once more.

Over time, the residents of the cliffside community discovered that hidden behind their identical exteriors, each house offered up its own secret crevices, some of which had gone undetected for years. "Morgenstein alcoves," they called them. One woman was surprised to find a serviceable bathroom while drilling a hole in her bedroom wall, while a neighboring family stumbled upon a hidden door under their sink during a kitchen makeover. As for the Lilienblum family, they chanced upon their own "Morgenstein alcove" while replacing a light fixture, exposing an inlet in the ceiling leading to the laundry room. Initially the cliffside residents attributed the alcoves to Morgenstein's dazzling brilliance, his unparalleled ability to create an "avant-garde living experience"—the masterwork of a true genius. Some speculated that the cryptic compartments were designed to cool the homes on hot summer days, while others believed they were Morgenstein's tribute to the Dead Sea sinkholes. But the passing of time and a year-round average of 90°F in the shade had wrought their worst on the timber and the houses gradually lost their luster, much like the Swiss architect's reputation. As far as the younger generations were concerned, Morgenstein was no architect extraordinaire but the culprit behind a mounting number of irreparable malfunctions, a name tossed around whenever a new problem arose.

Why is the roof leaking?

Ask Morgenstein.

Why do the doors swell in the summer?

Why does the sink keep clogging?

Why hasn't it rained around here in three years?

Why did Ruthie leave Victor for a Slovenian tourist?

Ask him, ask Morgenstein.

Thousands of defects, oversights, and existential quandaries were still waiting to be addressed by the architect, waiting for Morgenstein to appear and address all the questions and claims with his soft European accent, to finally sort out the mess.

"Okay, head over to the lodge. Dad texted me that he needs you there. I'll take care of this," Naomi volunteered, to her brother's great relief. His mind looped back to the day she had taught him to ride a bike. He was six years old and got the hang of it quickly enough, peddling down the street all by himself; but at the first crosswalk he squeezed the hand brake for dear life, and suddenly his sister materialized between him and the traffic. He'd never forget that reassuring feeling of having someone act as a buffer between him and the untamed world.

3.

The lodge stood on the southern edge of the Cliff, on the lip of the crater. Much bigger than most houses, it was the third largest structure in the village, dwarfed only by the rec center and the Bialika mansion.

Just outside the lodge, to the left of the entrance, stood a wooden ski slope a few feet high—a remnant of the original 1950s plan to turn the lodge into a tourist attraction. Two refrigerator trucks were hired for the grand opening to haul in snow from the Safed mountains, but on the long, largely unpaved journey from the Galilee to the Negev the snow became jagged, mutating into a giant ice sculpture that took three days to melt. Then came the attempt at artificial snow, for which a few industrial iceboxes were procured from a defunct ice cream factory. After months of trial and error they squeezed out a vat of plush ersatz snow, just enough for a small mound that would melt clear away before another batch could be served up. Over time, the ramp and lodge behind it remained the lone evidence of the great scheme. Only years later, when a bus full of Canadian tourists broke down nearby, the idea of turning the lodge into a hostel came up. Boaz Lilienblum, a young tour guide from Haifa at the time, was using the abandoned space as a makeshift sleeping quarters. When the council head caught wind of the group of squatting hikers, he immediately saw dollar signs; instead of shooing them away, he asked Boaz to set up a hostel and small visitors center on the premises—an offer that led the Lilienblum family off the verdant Mount Carmel and onto the cliff over the large crater.

Eli had been working at the lodge for almost a year, since his army discharge. He wasn't an official employee, but came by for a few hours a day. Instead of hiring employees, Boaz made due with volunteers who didn't overstay their welcome. What was mainly for lack of funds in the first few years later became a matter of convenience; he was a stickler who preferred people not sticking around long enough to have a say. For better or worse, the local council members kept out of it. When Boaz ran himself into debt the first few years, the council did little to help, but when he managed to double the number of tourists on the Cliff—through truly Herculean efforts—they basked in his accomplishment. Eli could never understand why his father insisted on working such long hours, living in a constant state of stress, but Boaz wasn't one to ask for assistance, so Eli made sure he wouldn't have to. At first he came by the lodge for an hour here and there, emptying trash cans and tidying up, but slowly he began to assume more responsibilities. Not all spurred by goodwill, it was also an attempt to anchor himself, perhaps even find purpose. His military discharge had left him feeling adrift, and the work in the lodge gave him something to hold onto. Over the past year he had rarely seen his friends, most of whom were very long plane rides away, sending him photos from Himalayan mountain peaks or Aztec temples he knew he would never see with his own eyes, photos that only made him burrow deeper into the familiar cliff. The outside world loomed dark and muffled, and the thought of venturing out there made his chest constrict. Naomi, by contrast, did everything within her power to get away—enrolling in a boarding school at fourteen, and never looking back. It was as if for every year his sister spent away from the Cliff, he sent his roots another inch into the ground.

Eli entered the lodge to find two tourists battling it out at the ping-pong table and a third perched in front of the TV, eating a yogurt. Sitting down at the paper-strewn table that served as the front desk, he saw a note from the Icelandic volunteer saying they were out of milk and he'd be back in the afternoon. After his and his father's three-day no-show, he was pleasantly surprised to find the place more or less intact; he didn't think the Icelander had it in him. Eli skimmed over the reservation list before going on the local news website. The headline about his mother's disappearance was still there. He thought about the yawning discrepancy between the words that appeared on the screen and the events that were already behind them. He texted his father (*there yet?*), swept the front porch, emptied out the trash cans, and restocked the toilet paper in the bathroom. Then he sat back down at the desk, threw his feet up, leaned back, and closed his eyes.

The desk bell jolted him out of his repose; a freckled, brown-eyed young woman was smiling at him. "Do you have flip-flops for the shower?" she asked in Spanish-accented English.

He heaved himself up and shuffled to the storage room. Nestled in the bottom of the closet were a pair of blue flip-flops beside a note in his father's sloppy handwriting, "Must be returned!" He placed the flip-flops on the desk and checked his phone for messages. No word from Boaz. He turned to the computer and hit refresh; the article about his mother was stubbornly still there—as was the woman, trying to read the screen upside down.

"Anything else?"

"It's about the search, the article?"

He nodded.

"About McMurphy, right?"

He considered her again, this time with a more discerning eye. Hair tucked under a beige bucket hat, she wore a white scarf knotted loosely around her neck and a thin, retro jacket—incongruous in the desert— with large triangles in pink, gold, and white.

"Where did you buy that hat?"

"The flea market in Tel Aviv, you like it?" she asked, part serious, part cynical.

She was a typical McMurphy tourist, as the Cliff dwellers called the travelers who boarded planes and then traversed the country by bus in search of the tourist who had gone missing over a decade ago. Every year someone stumbled upon some old object instantly attributed to McMurphy, rekindling the preposterous yet persistent rumor that the Irishman might still be alive, holed out in the desert. The McMurphy tourists took selfies knee-deep in the ravine or squatting behind a hill at sunset, before moving on to a new destination the next day. Instagram was filled with photos hashtagged #searchingforMcMurphy. Every new photo drummed up more tourists, and Eli had a low tolerance for all of them—including the young freckled woman standing in front of him.

They were all drawn there by a dumb urban legend, instead of the beauty of the desert. It was like scaling Everest just to see what flag was stuck on top. Boaz didn't like the trend any more than his son did, but often said that if it wasn't for the McMurphy *miracle*, he'd be paying back the loan for the lodge well into his eighties. "I'll join them if it pays the bills." Which is why he encouraged the search tourism, collecting all the supposedly McMurphy-related left-behinds over the years, from torn T-shirts to single papers from frayed notebooks, and even turning one of the rooms in the lodge to a makeshift McMurphy museum.

Eli had neither the energy nor the motivation to explain that McMurphy was no more than a fairy tale, and that it was his mother who'd been found, so he went along with the farce.

"How did you know it was about McMurphy?" he asked, narrowing his eyes in mock suspicion. "How long have you been on the Cliff?"

"Since yesterday," she replied.

"And you already worked it out? Those are some instincts you've got!" He woo-hooed.

She deposited the flip-flops on the counter for a moment and smiled, his cynicism evidently lost on her. "So they searched for him all this time?"

"It's hard to say," he said in a whisper. "They keep a pretty tight lid on it, even from us residents."

"*They?*"

"The village rescue team. They're top-notch, world famous. If anyone can find him, it's them."

The door jangled open and three tourists with big rucksacks walked up to the desk.

"I'll come back later. I'd love to hear more," she said, and he nodded, already taking a check-in form out of the drawer. He showed the tourists the shared rooms and communal showers, and when he returned to his desk she was no longer there. He checked his phone again and this time there was a message from his father: "I saw her, seems fine." He called, but Boaz didn't pick up. He texted him (*Healthy? Where was she? With who? Pick up!*). Boaz texted back (*Later*). After a few moments he received a text from his sister (*A fucking martini!!! What's gotten into her??!!*) and was piqued by the fact that once again she'd managed to be in the know before him.

That afternoon, he received another text from his sister (*Come home. She's here*).

Instead of taking the main road that bisected the village, he opted for the longer, scenic route home, walking along the lip of the crater. As the sun slowly sank into the horizon, he paused a few times along the way, taking in the view. At the bottom of the crater lay a thick blanket of mist he hadn't noticed in years, even though there was certainly ample opportunity—it was almost always there. As he approached the house, the lights flickered on all at once, illuminating his father's white Mazda parked outside. The door was open. He stepped in expecting to see his mother on the couch with a cup of green tea—lemon wedge on the side.

"Mom?" he called out into the dark living room.

He heard his father's voice coming from the kitchen, "She has to see someone, Naomi, we can't handle this on our own." His father and sister were standing at the counter, Naomi chopping cucumbers.

"Where is she?" Eli asked.

Wearing an exasperated expression, Boaz pointed at the ceiling beneath the bedroom. "Went to bed. She was exhausted."

Eli was ashamed of his overwhelming relief.

"Did she say anything?" he asked, to which Naomi retorted, "What's there to say?"

"A lot," their father muttered.

"But why do you have to know right now, Dad, why can't it wait?"

"What are you arguing about?" Once again, Eli had been kept in the dark.

Naomi slid the cucumbers off the cutting board into a bowl filled with tomatoes, dressed the salad with tahini and olive oil, and took a seat at the table.

"Dad thinks we should send her to a psychiatrist. And I think it'll only make things worse."

Boaz drummed his fingers on the fridge. "I didn't say psychiatrist, Naomi, I said someone who can take a look and tell us how she's doing, for god's sake."

"She's doing great. Looks perfectly normal to me."

"Were you not listening to her? She said she saw McMurphy," Boaz exclaimed, his voice and hands shaking.

"She said what?" Eli hoped he had misheard.

"It wasn't like that, she was just kidding."

"Sounded awfully serious to me, Naomi."

"Oh, come on, Dad, you're building an entire theory on two bad jokes she made in the car. Let's give her at least a week before we decide to start calling her mentally impaired."

"Before *we* decide? You'll be here to decide?!" Boaz blustered. Eli couldn't remember ever hearing his father so contemptuous. He had a softness about him, an innate equanimity that accommodated a diversity of thought and opinion.

"What did they say at the hospital?" Eli asked.

"Nothing. According to the doctors her tests all came back normal," their father said. "But they did say it was unlikely that she'd actually been in the desert this whole time. Her vital signs were too good when they brought her in."

"What does that mean, *unlikely*? What did she say when you asked her where she'd been?"

Naomi glanced at her father, who sighed and plunked himself into a chair. "She didn't. She's acting completely normal, but when you ask her anything about the past three days, nada, she just clams up."

"Okay, that is a little strange," he admitted, to which his father threw his hands in the air and said, "See? Your brother also thinks she's batty!"

"Not as a person, just this specific behavior . . ." Eli clarified.

"My brother mostly thinks you're overreacting," Naomi determined. "We all just need to take a deep breath and—"

"That's enough, Naomi, you can't do this," Boaz huffed.

"Do what?"

"Dump the responsibility on others and walk away," he said, staring at the table's broken leg. "With all due respect, tomorrow you'll be returning to your fancy hi-tech life in Tel Aviv while I stay here." Looking at Eli, he quickly corrected himself, "We. *We* two is barely enough as it is. We have the lodge to run. We can't do everything on our own."

Naomi waited for Eli to chime in, but he seemed unsure of what to say. She picked up her empty plate and lowered it into the sink.

"You know what? You're right." She took her car keys out of her pocket, then put on her shoes.

"Nomi'le, I didn't mean it like that. I appreciate you coming, I do. All I'm saying is that I'm going to handle this as I see fit."

But Naomi already had her hand on the doorknob and one foot out the door by the time Boaz begged, "Don't leave like this." Less than a minute later she reappeared with a backpack. Marching up the stairs with her suitcase, she announced, "I'm not leaving you with all this." She disappeared, and the next sound they heard was a door slamming shut upstairs. Boaz gave his son a quizzical look. "She's staying?"

"Looks like it . . ." Eli replied, relieved at the realization that he wouldn't be spending the next few days alone with his parents. He took a pot of sweet potato soup out of the fridge and heated it up. Boaz declined a bowl but Eli poured him one anyway, topping both servings with a good glug of coconut milk. Slurping a spoonful, Boaz *mmm*ed, after which they were quiet for a while; genetics saw to it not only that their silences were similar, but that each rested a hand on their foreheads when tired, or laughed in that slow, easy way. He enjoyed knowing he was the continuation of his father's movement in the world.

Eli warned his father not to enter Sarai's study, told him about the sand spill of unknown origin. Boaz laughed, said he'd given up on trying to find all the Morgenstein alcoves in the house long ago. He told his son how years earlier, when they had just moved in and he was still young and determined, he would call the Swiss embassy twice a week, pestering them for Morgenstein's blueprints. He had figured that somewhere in the Alps there had to be a museum, or at least an archive, dedicated to the work of the genius architect, and that somewhere amidst all the documents and sketches, he would find the blueprint of their house indicating the exact number and location of the alcoves.

"Did the pestering pay off?" Eli asked.

"Yes, the embassy sent me a bunch of blueprints of the houses he designed on the Cliff, but they didn't make much sense," Boaz said. "Morgenstein's blueprints are a pretty dubious matter, unreliable at best."

"How come?"

"It's rather a long story," his father said, and took another spoonful of soup. "What I did learn from all those documents was that Morgenstein wasn't exactly an architect."

"Meaning?"

"The truth is he was distinctly *not* an architect." His father snorted. Apparently, the representative of the Swiss embassy who'd helped him locate Morgenstein's documents was a real architecture buff. He had taken on the task of tracking down the blueprints not only because Boaz was a royal pain in the butt but because he was curious to learn more about this revered Swiss architect he'd never heard of. A quick online search only left him more mystified—there were barely two hits on this person who was allegedly among Switzerland's premier architects. A lengthier, more thorough investigation led the embassy official to a small architecture museum in Basel, where he unearthed not only Morgenstein's blueprints but information regarding his credentials, or rather lack thereof, information that had come to light after the collapse of one of his buildings. "After serving a short prison sentence, he moved as far away from Switzerland as he could, bouncing from one lesser-developed country to another, wherever he could land a project. Which is how he found himself in Israel, building the houses on the Cliff," Boaz said with a shrug. "He managed to pull one over on some poor shmuck at the Ministry of Construction and Housing, making them believe they were getting the work of a genius at a discount rate."

"And no one in Israel had any idea?" Eli quaked. Just like that, a bubble had burst.

"I don't know if they did or didn't," his father replied. "What I do know is that it's a lot easier to explain to people that their roofs leaked because of some architectural whimsy and not because someone hired an unlicensed loon."

After clearing the table and doing the dishes, father and son went upstairs, Boaz taking a left at the landing and Eli a right. Eli glanced at the opened bedroom door and caught the back of his mother's neck peeping out from the blanket. His father shut the door before he could make out her face.

Eli went to his room and lay down.

"Did Dad go to bed?" Naomi's voice rang out loud and clear, as if she was right there on the bed beside him. It was one of their mother's most recent novelties, utilizing the small Morgenstein alcove in the ceiling above their bedrooms to test a new inter-room communications network. An invention that was supposed to have an off button.

"Yeah," Eli said, then added, "Thanks for sticking around."

"Don't get used to it. I'll wait until the dust settles and then I'm out of here," she said. "This whole business is already costing me three vacation days as it is."

The fact that his sister would translate their family crisis into monetary units annoyed him. Staring at the ceiling, Eli racked his brain trying to recall whether his mother had ever hinted at wanting to disappear.

"Remember the time we went to see *The Lion King*?" he asked Naomi. After a few silent moments she said, "When you ran out in the middle? You were six?"

"Right. Remember that Mom ran out after me?"

"Eli, honestly, I'm beat, you can tell me tomorrow—"

"She found me standing outside the theater crying hysterically, and didn't even hug me. Just stood there quietly."

"God, so she waited for you to calm down, the horror! You're just making up traumas. Go to sleep."

"When she finally did open her mouth, she said that wherever she goes, she always looks for escape routes."

"What does that even mean?"

"That whenever she went someplace new, a restaurant or a doctor's waiting room, her first instinct was to figure out escape routes. The door, the window, even the sewer. Map out the exits."

"She just said that to calm you down."

"No, no. It wasn't that. It was something that weighed on her. She needed to unburden it."

"She needed to unburden herself on her crying first grader? And at six years old you possessed the cognitive and emotional know-how to make that observation?"

"The memory was always there. The understanding came much later."

"Okay, and your point is . . . ?"

Eli bit his lower lip. "I was hoping you'd know."

"I can tell you what I make of it," his sister said.

"What?"

"That even back then our mom was already a few fries short of a Happy Meal."

"Yeah, right?" He laughed.

4.

Naomi's snoring woke him from a fogged-up dream. That's what he called dreams he couldn't remember, dreams that left their emotional traces without any visuals. He got up to pee. Intimations of morning filtered in through the windows; he guessed five, maybe five thirty. He didn't want to check. For some time now, he had felt the world was too readily known, the answer to every question just a keystroke away, every destination within an image search. He washed his hands and face and headed back to his room, but his sister was snoring so loudly there was no point trying to sleep. Walking down the hallway, kitchen-bound, he saw his mother through the slightly ajar door to her study. His body tensing, he inched it open. Sarai was standing in the middle of the room with her back to him, a headlamp strapped to her forehead illuminating a small mound of sand. Her hair, which always came to her shoulders, stopped at her chin, and her body was wrapped in the infamous burgundy robe. With her shoulders slumped and a blow-dryer held limply in her right hand, she seemed to be vaguely contemplating the triangle-shaped outlet on the opposite wall. Flecks of sand were still swirling down from the ceiling in places, joining the others on the mound.

"Mom?"

She spun around, blinding him with her headlamp. "Eliush," she said and smiled, quickly switching the light to a softer mode. She walked over and hugged her son, and he hugged her back, tighter than he had in recent memory.

"I see you tried to turn on the air conditioner," she said. "Didn't work too well, did it?"

"Oh, I'd say it worked too well. Don't worry, we'll clean it up."

She laughed. When he was little, she used to tell him they were both made from the same stuff. Just as there were different blood types, she explained, there were also different substances that made up a body, and although she could never point out the differences at a molecular level, she could always tell if the person in front of her was made from the same matter as her. Over the years he often wondered whether she genuinely believed this, or whether it was just one of those things mothers told their children. He considered her now, and still wondered. She seemed the way she always did—sane and strange.

"What are you doing here?"

"I woke up and couldn't fall back asleep. And I didn't want to wake your father."

She even sounded like herself, as if the past three days had left no mark on her.

"Mom. Where were you?"

"Oh, just here and there."

"Here and there where?"

She didn't answer. She was tinkering with the blow-dryer cord. Looping it around her hand, she deposited it in the corner and headed for the door.

"Where, Mom?"

"Everything is fine now," she said. "Believe me, everything is all right."

He did believe her. Her voice, words, body language. Maybe the two of them really were made from the same stuff, but either way, he knew his mother, could read her, see she wasn't lying. She seemed fine. A little tired, but all in all, just fine.

"You'll explain it to us at some point, though, right?"

She stroked his arm. "You know perfectly well that I could never hide anything from you." She removed the headlamp, tossed it onto her desk, and walked out.

5.

Naomi and Eli spent the morning bucketing sand out of the room. After two hours of strenuous labor the pile finally seemed to thin out, revealing several of Sarai's inventions that had been buried underneath. One by one, Eli ferried them outside to dust them off and line them up along the wooden deck and grass. The low fence surrounding the house just barely concealed the mosaic of gadgets and gizmos from passersby. In the afternoon, Sarai stepped out of her bedroom onto the balcony looking over the lawn. As she swept her gaze across the display, Boaz called out from below, "We'll move everything back inside in a few minutes." Sarai considered the lawn for another moment, said, "Just leave it there," and retreated back into her room.

Over the next few days, she emerged from her bedroom only to eat or read the paper in the living room, never staying downstairs for long, and showing no interest in the exhibit of her inventions spread across the lawn. "There's nothing to worry about, I just need a little more time," she said during one of her brief excursions to the kitchen. Naomi consulted with a psychologist friend who said the smart thing to do at that point was not interfere, but that some fresh air or family meals wouldn't hurt, if she could be coaxed. The Lilienblums made sure to remind each other that in certain respects Sarai's behavior couldn't even be called abnormal. "Summer stupors" was a term they'd come up with in Sarai's first years of teaching, as she spent her summer breaks lazing in bed with a book, sometimes even just staring at the ceiling. She said it wasn't a much-needed rest from the hubbub of the school year, but a necessary phase in the process of her inventions. She had once thought the moment of invention was when she began hooking up the wires, but over time realized that her best ideas came in moments of idle contemplation. For every hour of work, she had to spend a few hours of complete inactivity.

But Eli was restless. After his mother went missing, he had hoped that finding her would solve the mystery and put all their questions to rest. But the opposite was the case: After the earthquake came the quiet, and that quiet turned out to be even harder to handle.

He spent the next few days dividing his time between shifts at the lodge and home, while Naomi cordoned off part of the living room for a makeshift work station. She told her boss she had a family medical emergency and would be working the next two weeks from her parents' house, and since she was running a team of Ukraine-based engineers, she was in effect working remotely whether it was in Tel Aviv or the desert. Over the next few days, the house was abuzz with the sound of her conference calls. Eli was ignorant of the technical—and often nontechnical—terms in her conversations, but he was jealous all the same, often lingering in the kitchen after a meal to eavesdrop. He had always favored the corporal world over that of computers, proclaiming more than once that "nothing is more miserable than a life spent in front of a screen." His whole life he had heard his father insisting that a man has to choose between money and happiness, and he had believed him; but ever since Naomi started working in hi-tech, this belief had been shaken. It happened the summer of his high school graduation, during a day trip to Tel Aviv to visit his sister in her new workplace. From the polished parquet lobby and vanilla-scented hallways, to the front desk secretary's offer of citrus- or cucumber-infused water, he was charmed by it all. At lunchtime, Naomi told him they could eat at the Italian or Mexican canteens but said he didn't have to choose, they could do both if he wanted. More than anything, what took his breath away was the overwhelming abundance of *choice*.

He had by no means grown up poor. Like most families on the Cliff, the Lilienblums were middle class, but to achieve that status his parents had had to bend over backward. The loans they took out to get the lodge going had plunged them into a pit of middle-age debt. This was around the time Naomi had taken off to boarding school and Eli remained alone with his parents, serving as firsthand witness to their slow, strenuous climb out of the financial mire. It was hard work. For years choice wasn't on the menu—there was no this vacation destination or that, this restaurant or that, this store or that. And even after they had dug themselves out, the understanding could never be unetched from Eli's mind—in this life, you can't have both. You could go to the movies, but couldn't get the popcorn. You could never take your foot off the pedal, because financial hardship was always just around the corner. He had thought he loathed the luxury of choice, but touring his big sister's office, he discovered he coveted it. Wanted to be part of it. The people in those offices didn't look at all as miserable as his father—while putting in a twelve-hour workday—said they were. The realization that people only a few years his senior—kids basically—were earning more than his parents ever would drove him crazy, made his blood boil. This world of plenty in which his parents had no place—he would stay outside the gates of this techno promised land, this club that would not have his parents as members. He wouldn't betray them for a complimentary spa beverage like his sister had. He vowed to pave himself a different path in the world, one closer to home. To the known knowns. But now that Naomi was filling the house with her hi-tech talk, these thoughts looped back into his mind, sending him into a tizzy all over again. So he tried to spend as much time as he could at the lodge, and to let other things ruffle his feathers, like the fact that they were dangerously low on toilet paper, or that the Icelandic volunteer had elevated laziness to an art form.

In the evening, Eli returned to the lodge to onboard a new volunteer. In exchange for room and board, the volunteers were expected to work for a period of no less than three weeks. This volunteer was late. Waiting at the front desk, Eli browsed the local news site, relieved to discover that the story about his mother's disappearance had finally been taken down.

"Why didn't you say it was your mother?" the Spanish tourist asked with a smile, tossing the blue flip-flops onto the counter.

"You're the new volunteer?"

"I asked first."

Wiseass. "Let's keep this professional," he countered in a half-hearted warning. But her expression remained unfazed.

Walking her through the ropes of the morning shift, Eli showed her the list of checking-out guests and where the kettle and coffee jar in the kitchenette were kept. He instructed her to charge two dollars for a croissant and a dollar for a piece of toast with butter and jam. He handed her the keys, and she took them, pausing for a moment as the back of her hand touched his. "We good?" Eli asked, reaching back his hand.

She nodded. "Difficult few days?"

"It's behind us now," he announced. She asked whether she should open the McMurphy museum in the morning and he said no, he didn't want anyone trying to sneak out memorabilia. He saw that his answer was met with disappointment, but he remained unfazed.

"You know, this whole McMurphy business, you're looking for something that's not there."

"What do you mean?"

"It's impossible to survive in the desert on your own. There's no happy ending there." He told her he had only been kidding when they spoke the other day, that the search team had stopped looking for him ages ago.

"Then why a museum? What's the point?" she asked impatiently.

"Because a good disappearance story means tourists, and tourists mean money."

"A real startup nation."

He snorted. "Startup nation is in Tel Aviv. We're a different kind of nation."

6.

When Eli was eight, his mother told him she was afraid of him; since then he had wondered whether all mothers were afraid of their children. He had come home from school to her sitting in the kitchen, peeling a tangerine. She seemed sad, so he asked if she was okay. After a few moments of silence, she said it scared her how perceptive he was. She meant it as a compliment—his sensitivity, his kind eyes, but the word *scared* had stung, leaving a scar on his body even after his brain had caught on. She tried to explain herself, said she was used to being alone with her thoughts and feelings, and that after he was born, she realized there was someone who would come to see her more clearly than anyone else.

"It's just a little strange, you know? Your whole life you're used to being invisible, and suddenly you're not."

They didn't talk about it again, and out of respect for the boundary he felt his mother had set, he had since done his best not to see through her.

Even in the days following her return from the desert, he stuck to the pledge he had made to himself so many years earlier. Naomi would ask him what he thought was going through their mother's mind, and he would say he didn't know, tried his hardest not to guess.

Unlike Naomi and Eli, Boaz objected to the idea of simply letting Sarai reacclimate at her own pace. One morning, a week after Sarai's reappearance, Eli found his father standing under the balcony with a bouquet of flowers and a small model rocket kit. Sarai's penchant for ballistics—which would later find expression in her studies of aeronautical engineering at the Technion—was a fondness that came about by accident, on her fifteenth wedding anniversary, when Boaz surprised his wife with a weekend at a secluded Japanese-inspired B&B in the desert. Just as the owner of the charming retreat was proudly pointing out the small Zen fountain, the first in a succession of deafening missiles flew over their heads. As they soon learned, in a rather unfortunate turn of events, their first romantic getaway in years had coincided with a large-scale missile-testing operation at the nearby air force base. Two minutes later Boaz was already repacking their overnight bags, ready to up and leave, but when he stepped back out he found his wife crouching between a pair of bonsais, squinting into her binoculars. Eighteen missiles were shot that night, and she eagle-eyed every one of them, Boaz sitting patiently at her side plugging his ears. And now Boaz was standing two stories below her feet with a cardboard box containing a DIY rocket. Sarai looked at the gift with curiosity, and went down, appearing on the lawn. She accepted the bouquet and took a small sniff while eyeing the box.

"Black Basalt 2," Boaz said. "The aerospace industry launched a new version two months ago, a special collector's model."

She tore the box open and dumped all the plastic and metal out onto the grass. Together, his parents began to sort the parts in an order whose logic Eli couldn't follow. Every so often their hands brushed up against each other, and Eli wished the moment would last forever.

Boaz's rocket was a success. After Sarai finished assembling it, she picked up where she had left off before her disappearance and returned to her old inventions, hauling them out onto the lawn and toiling under the sizzling mid-summer sun. In addition to a big parasol and fan to shade and cool his wife, Boaz brought out an extension cord with ten outlets, and even replaced the sprinklers with a drip irrigation system so the water wouldn't spray her gadgets. His father's love was always grounded in action—he found it easier to build Sarai a workshop in the backyard than tell her he had missed her, easier to handle her hospital discharge forms than admit it had been awful without her. When he wanted to patch up a small hole in the fence through which the neighbor's cat kept padding into their yard, Sarai not only vetoed the idea but built the furry interloper a motion-activated drinking fountain, a project wedged between her work on a toothbrush with built-in dental floss, and a mirror with a weather forecast display.

Naomi suggested calling an electrician to fix the wires in her study, but Sarai said she liked working in the sun. It seemed that the life of the Lilienblum family was almost back to normal, and Naomi said she'd give it a few more days and if there were no more incidents, she'd head back home to Tel Aviv.

"Without knowing what happened?" Eli asked. She replied that sometimes one needed to know what not to know.

7

The email concerning the first king of Haiti arrived some two weeks after Sarai's return. The ugly-fonted, poorly spaced letter declared Eli not only to be the great-great-grandson of King Henri Christophe the Great, but, by a singular stroke of luck, his closest living blood relative. To ease his mind, the writer assured Eli he was writing in his capacity as a prominent, well-respected lawyer in his country. As a man who had dedicated his life to the pursuit of justice, he considered it his civic duty to ensure that the king's great fortune—valued at approximately 8.6 million dollars—made its way to its rightful beneficiary. For a modest seven percent fee—the legal minimum—it would be his pleasure to see to all matters pertaining to the transfer of funds into Eli's account within thirty days. Eli read the email to Naomi while she lay on the couch, staring at the ceiling.

"'Dear sir, time is of the essence, please send me your bank account information as soon as possible. This financial matter must be resolved before corrupt officials in the Haitian government learn of this sizable fortune and get their hands on it . . .' My god, who writes this crap?"

"You have to admit it's pretty creative." Naomi giggled. "And besides, if there are people out there who bother to send out these emails, there are people who write back."

"The great-great-grandson of the king of Haiti?! If someone went to the trouble of writing this they could at least have hatched a less ridiculous premise."

"You're wrong," she said, and sat up. "That's just it. People are yearning for the implausible."

Eli was adamant that no one ever fell for these email scams, but Naomi held her ground, positing that out of a group of a hundred at least three would write back. "It's simple statistics. You just have to cast a wide enough net."

Years of arguing with his sister had taught Eli that she was invariably right, and yet, not even five minutes later, a bet was made—Naomi would compose the most implausible letter she could think up, an email so outrageously absurd it would likely be reported as spam, and Eli would send it to a hundred recipients of his choosing. "If even one of them sends back a serious reply—you win."

Hola Madam,

My name is General Luciano Rodríguez Ancelotti III.

I know what you're thinking—what are the chances the author of this email is indeed a real general and not a ruthless swindler hunting for gullible prey? Madam, fear not. I am not interested in your money, or any other earthly possession. I have enough wealth of my own, such that I do not have to work another day in my life. However, this wealth has not brought me happiness in this cruel and bitter world. Distant acquaintances—former naval officers in the great Israeli army—once told me about your compassionate heart. They said when crisis comes, anyone in the world could reach out to you and you would serve as their light-house. Well, crisis has come, and so I am writing to you, perhaps because I have nothing left to lose. All that I ask is to share with you both my life story and great wealth, for life has condemned me to loneliness.

Please! If you can find a small measure of kindness in your heart, write back!

And if you cannot, consider yourself exempt from replying to this morose letter.

Adios, au revoir,
Yours in friendship and faith,
General Luciano Rodríguez Ancelotti III

Hannah Bialika sent back a seven-word reply:

I'd love to hear your story.
Hannah.

Hannah Bialika was probably the last person on Eli and Naomi's list they expected would answer. Having moved to the Cliff some years back, she seemed to actively avoid the locals. It wasn't only her standoffish ways that turned the villagers against her, but mainly the gift she had received from her husband for her seventy-fifth birthday—the most lavish residence in the village, a mansion overlooking the majestic view from the Cliff. The house was built into the very tip of the Cliff, a rare geological goosebump etched three hundred meters into the crater and the original reason the village was established there in the first place. The Cliff resembled a long, wide corridor opening to the large, glorious, all-encompassing crater. Not long after setting up the lodge, Boaz embarked on a crusade to convince the council head that the village's real touristic potential lay on the lip of the crater. He petitioned for moving the lodge out there, to entice tourists with the panoramic vista, and perhaps even convert the simple hostel-like accommodation into a luxury hotel. It took a few years, but the council head finally came around to the idea. However, it wasn't Boaz that managed to convince him but Mandy Bialika, a well-off businessman with money to burn, who recognized the potential while traveling through the area with his wife. By dint of charisma and humor, he was able to finagle a special construction permit to build his dream house on the tip of the Cliff in exchange for bequeathing the property to the council upon his and his wife's demise. As long as he was alive, the villagers showed some measure of tolerance to the ostentatious eyesore that gobbled up the view from the Cliff, and the funds he donated toward the building of a new country club certainly didn't hurt. But two years after the construction on the house had been completed, Mandy died of a heart attack, and with him the affection the Bialikas had been shown. His wife, Hannah, was ideologically cold, an attribute she herself attested to when asked by a waiter why no tip. During her husband's shiva she shooed away neighbors seeking to pay their condolences and, when the seven days of mourning were up, wasted no time before cutting the funding for the country club, consigning it to a permanent pit on the village outskirts. Her communication with the villagers consisted of biweekly visits to the local grocery store and slamming the door on elementary schoolers going house to house for the Israeli Cancer Association. If rumors were to be believed, even when her only son, who lived in Europe, knocked on her door for a surprise visit, he was asked to wait on the stoop until the daily episode of her favorite Argentinian soap was over. As far as the villagers were concerned, more than a lonely old shrew, she was a technical glitch, a thorn in their side, the only thing standing between them and access to the fancy house and unmatched view. And while no one outwardly wished her dead, the question "That old crone's still alive?" had become something of a catchphrase on the Cliff.

Eli was also interested in Mrs. Bialika's well-being—or lack thereof. The council head had promised that after her passing, part of her mansion would be converted into a new tourism center under his father's management. Eli knew it was a rare opportunity for his father to bump up his salary and boost his career, perhaps even while cutting back on his work hours—instead of a modest lodge, overseeing a prestigious tourist site, a place that didn't require twenty-four-hour personal care and greeting travelers checking in at three a.m.

Eli glanced at the computer screen again. Twelve minutes had passed from the moment they hit send and Hannah Bialika's reply.

"Too bad we didn't put money on it," Naomi said with a smile.

May the good Lord bless you for your kindness, dear Madam!

It is by no means self-evident that you would make room in your heart for the story of a battle-weary general. I am writing you from the San Blas Islands, off the coast of Panama. I have a spacious summer abode here, which, over time, has become my only home. I am sure you are asking yourself—how did a man like me find himself on a small island on the edge of the Pacific? How did the roaring gales of life sweep me ashore here? I admit that I too have contemplated this question. And yet to explain the answer, I must first tell you the story of how I became a general of the third army division of the Peruvian military, a tale so long it could take up an entire memoir.

Therefore, before I relay my story, I would like to repay you for opening your heart on the other side of the world. As I wrote, during my far-flung travels I was blessed to acquire a fortune so large that even my great-grandchildren's great-grandchildren would not be able to squander it. However, I have found that money is essentially evil and corrupting in the hands of the likes of myself. While searching far and wide for a compassionate, charitable soul to pass on my riches to, fate led me to you. It is indeed a substantial sum— approximately nine million dollars, I believe (I stopped keeping track years ago). I would like to hand over my fortune to you, with merely one small request: that you donate a million of it to a charity of your choosing. In addition, since, as you can imagine, pirates don't possess an international bank account, I must ask that you open a local account for the petty sum of five dollars (see link below). Complete your credit card details and the money will be transferred forthwith, my noble lady.

Yours always and forever,
General Luciano Rodríguez Ancelotti III

Hannah Bialika didn't immediately reply to Eli and Naomi's second email, but others did; the general's inbox quietly buzzing, nine people from Eli's blast list wrote back. In the evenings, after the last of her long video calls, Naomi went over the messages. Eli admitted defeat, but by then Naomi didn't care about the bet, it was the responses themselves that piqued her interest; why write back to someone you don't know?

"The money, obviously," Eli ruled.

"Yes, but it's more than that. Some of them don't even want the money." Arranging the emails into an Excel sheet, Naomi replied to each. To those who expressed their interest in the general and his fortune she sent instructions for transferring a large sum of money so that the general could in turn transfer his secret funds via special courier. From the curious but hesitant she asked for only a few dollars, and from the peeved not a penny—only sent back an email with another chapter of the general's autobiography. She labored for hours on it. Eli couldn't understand what compelled her, which was in line with a lot of things he couldn't understand about his sister.

Summer was at its zenith, coinciding with the annual rush of European tourists to the lodge. Eli arrived early to his shifts and stayed on late. Walking back home one evening, his father told him it was good to have another hand on deck, "because that Icelander is pretty useless," which was his awkward way of saying "I'm happy you're here."

"Who knows, maybe we're just the last in a long line of lodges he's hustled," Eli joked, mainly because he didn't know how to talk to his father.

"We can send the new volunteer to investigate," Boaz said, then told him that one of the other new volunteers was a writer for an international travel website. "She said she wants to do a piece on the lodge."

"Great! Which volunteer? What website?"

He could see the cogs in his father's brain turning. "That girl . . . the Spanish one. I can't remember her name. Or the website's."

This news gave Eli pause. He wondered whether the intended "piece" was in reality a ploy to glean more information about McMurphy. "To be honest, it's a little exhilarating, imagining my name in the newspaper . . ." Boaz said, and Eli was hit by a slight pang of jealousy at his father's ability to show his true self, to state openly and honestly what he felt.

8

Dear General,
    It is a generous offer, but I too have lived a fortunate life and do not want for money. However, I live in a remote village and am in need of help with a few minor repairs around the house. I'm an old woman and couldn't possibly do it myself. Tell me, perhaps your Israeli friend could send someone over to my house? Needless to say, they would be well compensated.

Best,
Hannah

Naomi was sure Bialika was on to them, that the old woman realized there was no general and her request was a bid to prove it. To show it was all a bluff.

"Okay, so we just don't answer," Eli said, but Naomi had other plans. "How could we pass up a chance to get into that house, and through the front door no less?"

Precious about their privacy, the Bialikas allowed precious few visitors through their gates. The lucky ones would later tell of a gargantuan, stunning spectacle, grander than any other house designed by the Swiss architect. Some would claim it was three stories tall while others swore four; one would recall the faucets being twenty-four karat gold plated, and that visitors exited through a metal detector to check for pilfered faucet handles or renegade doorknobs.

"I'm not going over there," Eli said, but Naomi laughed. "Who asked you to? I'm going," she said, already drafting a reply.

I could arrange for someone to be at your house in a few days. What's your address?

The General

Hannah Bialika's reply arrived later that evening:

> *7 Inbal Street, The Cliff. I'll leave the gate open. He can come by Tuesday evening.*
>
> *Best,*
> *Hannah*

9.

Eli and Boaz waited for the Spanish volunteer behind the front desk, father in a crisply pressed white shirt, son in a black tee.

"Sorry I'm late," she said when she finally appeared, under a mop of messy hair.

"No problem," Boaz said, to which she smiled, a smile that had annoyed Eli since their first meeting at the counter. They went into Boaz's office, where five large topographic maps hung next to a filing cabinet crowded with binders. The pile of papers usually strewn across his desk had been stuffed into the drawers. At Boaz's offer of coffee, she asked if he had an espresso machine.

"I meant regular black, from the kitchenette," he said with embarrassment.

She smiled. "Then water would be great."

Boaz returned with a glass of water filled to the brim, spilling some on himself as he crossed the office. She placed her phone on the table and asked if it would be okay to record the conversation.

"More than okay," Boaz said, and whipped a small notepad out of his pocket and flipped it open, revealing blue bullet points. "I thought about starting with a brief historical overview," he said, "just so you have the general background." Offering to lend her any photo she might need for the story, he removed a small album from the drawer. For ten minutes he showed her pictures of houses in the village and told her about Morgenstein, pausing to admit that in all the excitement, he had forgotten to ask her name. Eli grimaced at his father's need to confess his every weakness.

"Tamara, but my Jewish mother insists on calling me Tamar."

Eli felt she was trying to build a rapport. It didn't work on him, but it sure did on his father. When Boaz asked with genuine interest about her ancestors, she explained they had been expelled from Toledo to

Saloniki, and that her grandparents had arrived in Madrid after the Holocaust, "like salmon crossing the ocean back to the river where they were born."

This need to chronicle the entire evolution of Jewish migration in his dad's small office left Eli exhausted. Boaz then recounted the history of the lodge, and then brought up his yearly tourism plan, which he had printed out for her.

Tamara glanced at the wall clock. "I'm not sure we have time. How many places will we be visiting today?"

"Places?" Eli asked.

"Places for the article. I didn't explain yesterday how it works?" The question was met by a puzzled look.

She handed him her phone and showed him her travel blog, in which she presented a different village around the world every week and told its story via five "must-see" sites.

"Good, the more places the better." Boaz beamed with a wider-than-usual smile and passed the phone to Eli, who proceeded to skim the website. Each "must-see" site was described in two sentences.

"More than two lines scares our readers away," she explained apologetically.

Boaz nodded. "Then Eli, why don't you take her to see the board-walk? I've still got lots to do." He wrapped things up and threw the wall clock a glance of his own.

Tamara said they were still missing a few more tourist attractions.

"I'm sure Eli can think of something," Boaz replied while stuffing his notepad back into his pocket and the photo album into the drawer.

Outside, Tamara grew pensive. "You know it's always there, that chasm, between someone's lived life and a reporter summing it up in just a few words," she reflected to Eli. Eli realized his annoyance hadn't gone unnoticed, which was arguably even more annoying.

"Let's start with the restaurant," Eli offered with a sigh. To call the room they had walked into a restaurant was more than a stretch. Food and beverage orders that required minimal to no preparation—such as bread with labneh or stuffed grape leaves from a can—were placed at the counter by the entrance, by whichever volunteer happened to be staffing it. A few groups of travelers sat at the small tables, with one group plopped on the big floor pillows in the corner, sharing a hookah. "What's that buzzing?" Tamara asked. Eli explained it was from the AC's engines in the storage room. She snapped a few photos of the restaurant, ordered an orange juice, and told the volunteer to put it on Eli's tab.

They sat at the table overlooking the crater, his gaze wandering with unveiled boredom along the thin crack running the length of the wooden ceiling.

"Would you move here?" Eli asked.

"Hell no," she blurted, but quickly qualified, "I mean, don't get me wrong, it's really pretty here, but I wouldn't want to live so far from the center."

That word irked him to no end. Who got to decide where the center was? And that he was the one living on the outskirts? As if the dreams of city people were better than everybody else's.

"What can't you do here?"

"Buy milk at one in the morning," she said with a grin, and when her answer failed to impress him, added, "It just feels a bit limiting, that's all. If you want to become a movie star or a chef, you can't really do that out here. Am I wrong?"

She wasn't the first to tell him the Cliff was basically the boondocks. His sister had said it years ago, before getting out. Two years after they had moved to the Cliff, she enrolled in a boarding school for stellar students in Jerusalem, saying she wouldn't live on the sidelines watching the rest of the world pass her by. As an adolescent, Eli wished he would someday match his sister in determination and resolve. He even hitchhiked north one day without a destination in mind, before freaking out, getting off at the first gas station and calling his dad to come pick him up. His high school homeroom teacher used to go on and on about how normal it was to rebel, how it was a natural, inseparable part of becoming an adult, which always left him to wonder how abnormal it was *not* to rebel. To feel perfectly content with where you lived. To not feel the need to challenge anything, but on the contrary: to hope everything stayed the same.

They left the lodge and hit the boardwalk along the lip of the crater, where he took her to his favorite lookout point thinking she could take a few nice pictures.

"Whose castle is that?" she asked, staring at the hulking mansion made of light desert stone surrounded by a tall and thick wooden wall. Eli told her about the Bialikas, and for a moment he considered confiding in her about the private invitation he had received; instead, he waited silently while she took photos of the house from several angles. "How much is that place worth?" she asked, but Eli blatantly ignored the question. For the life of him he couldn't understand how she could find a house, fancy though it may be, more impressive than a panoramic view of an expansive crater.

"Did you know this is the world's largest erosion crater? That's a crater created from a natural geological landmass and not a meteor impact or volcanic eruption."

"Wow, impressive. How many of these are out there?" she wondered, her camera snapping away. Actually, he had no idea. How many times had his father told him it was the largest erosion crater? More than he cared to remember. And yet he had never asked himself how many others there were. He took his phone out and checked. According to Wikipedia, there were only a few dozen erosion cirques (apparently their official name) in the world.

Nearing the end of the tour, Tamara expressed interest in taking some photos of a "typical house in the village." She said travelers were often drawn to interesting architecture, and that the whole business with Morgenstein could make a good anecdote—a choice of words he found irritating. "Write that he's a big name in Switzerland," he said, and proposed photographing his family's house.

When they reached his street, he pointed out the house and said he needed to pop in for a moment to use the bathroom. The street was empty when he got back, and the gate to the backyard open. In the middle of the lawn, his mother stood reading the instructions on a canister of liquid nitrogen through yellow safety goggles. Tamara stood beside her, mesmerized by the inventions scattered across the grass. Sarai didn't seem to acknowledge her or her son's presence.

"She's a robotics teacher, she invents things in her spare time," he quickly explained, thinking Tamara wouldn't be able to decipher his mother's behavior without his mediation. But she seemed to be doing just fine, and was clearly impressed by what she saw. Weaving her way between the gadgets on the grass, she paused next to a small blender. She pressed the on button and jazz took to the air.

"A maker!" Tamara exclaimed with a thrilled clap, looking directly at his mother.

Sarai looked up from the canister at Tamara, narrowed her eyes and asked, "Meaning?"

Tamara explained that the definition applied to inventors who build technological devices, "people who test the human capacity for invention." And Eli saw that in one sentence she had managed to crack his mother's hard shell of indifference, for which Sarai awarded her a smile.

"You should know I'm a fan. It's so exciting to actually meet you in person. The things you've built—it's art."

Eli was used to his mother inspiring awe, but it was usually suffused with fear or doubt. There was nothing but adoration in Tamara's eyes.

"Yup, she's special," he said in a hushed voice, not knowing why he was averse to his mother hearing. After explaining to Sarai that she was writing a piece about the Cliff, Tamara whipped out her phone and started taking photos of her. "I don't know how I didn't connect the dots," Tamara said, snapping photos of Sarai from different angles. "That invention I saw online, I can't stop thinking about it."

Eli considered the possibility that she was right, perhaps his mother's inventions could make for an intriguing hook for the article. "But if you're going to post these pictures," he said to Tamara, "an explanation about the inventions should accompany each one, don't you think?"

"Just the opposite! That's exactly what worked so well in the video—in the first moment you're not sure what's going on, but when you see the bottle, suddenly it's all clear."

"Maybe," he replied. Tamara kneeled to get a low angle, channeling her focus into her camera. "Wait, which video are you talking about?" "The video of your mom that went viral on Twitter!"

"What video is she talking about?" Eli asked his mother in Hebrew, but Sarai said she had no idea. Tamara handed him her phone. "See for yourself. It's up to thirty-eight thousand likes!"

He hesitantly hit play.

"What the fuck?!" That was the first thing he heard, the audible shock of a young man trying to steady his camera. That and the faint sound of an engine. The man must have been standing on a small mound, angling his camera downward. "You gotta see this, it's unbelievable," he said to his imagined viewers. Eli brought the phone closer to his face to get a better look at the woman in the burgundy bathrobe standing inside the crater. He tensed, every muscle in his body clenching as the camera zoomed in on her. She was holding an old red vacuum cleaner, its bag half full, a chunky cord snaking behind her along the sandy desert soil.

His mother took a step closer, looking over his shoulder at the screen with a blank expression.

"Wait, you've never seen this?" Tamara asked, incredulous.

Eli didn't answer. The video was posted on July 9th, a day before she was found; the first footage of his mother from the time of her disappearance.

As the video continued Eli saw his mother vacuuming up the desert, the famous martini glass resting on the sand behind her. A thin plume of dust rose from the bag, billowing into the air, and the camera slowly panned upward to reveal a small, dense cloud suspended over her head. More plumes started spiraling up from small holes poked into the bag, gradually making the cloud denser, grayer, bigger.

"Turning sand into a cloud," Tamara marveled. "It's just incredible what you did there, Mrs. Lilienblum."

Unable to tear her eyes from the screen, his mother clasped her hands behind her back and smiled proudly, like a little girl pleased with her drawing. In the video, Eli saw her hold her hand up to the cloud and wait, until raindrops started to land on her palm, one by one. As countless spots of mud formed on the sand around her, Sarai picked up the bottle of water resting by the vacuum cleaner, unscrewed the cap, returned it to the ground, and took a few steps back. The thought that while pulling a disappearing act on her family she was already becoming an internet sensation was more than Eli's brain could handle. The disparity between the real and virtual world was too much for him. Tens, maybe hundreds of thousands of viewers were acquainting themselves with his mother while her own family had no clue where she was.

"What's wrong with you?!" he snapped at her. "Do you have any idea what we went through looking for you? How worried Dad was?"

"I didn't know I was being filmed," she whispered, which only drove him further up the wall.

"Do you care about anything other than yourself?"

She didn't answer, and he didn't know what to do with her silence. What to make of it. He had never felt more distant from his mother, and it was then that he knew that despite everything she had told him throughout his life, and no matter how much he loved her, they weren't made from the same stuff. "You're really not going to tell us anything, huh?"

Registering his anger, Tamara gently eased her phone from his hand. "Look at the comments," she said, scrolling down.

"Not interested." But she started to read.

"A Yohana Bombach wrote that she wants that machine at home, three exclamation points, and someone named Sandra wrote, 'Who is that genius?' Ricardo called it a 'fucking masterpiece,' and John Chan says, 'She's the 21st century Leonardo da Vinci.' Sasha Gurevich wrote, 'Where is this?' And in a comment below, Yoko4726 replied, 'Israel,' to which an Alexandra Gurevich replied, 'Unbelievable what the Jewish brain can do,' five exclamation points."

"Da Vinci? Someone really wrote that?" Sarai arched her eyebrows. Tamara showed her the screen and Sarai read through the entire thread. Eli sent a grateful look Tamara's way, and she looked back at him with the same kind eyes she had set on his mother. As Sarai pored over the comments, every so often a little smile crept over her face; and despite his anger, it still made Eli happy to see his mother happy. It also made him realize the futility of carrying on with their lives as if she had never disappeared.

10

Later that day, after Naomi finished watching the video, she sent a message to the user who uploaded it on Twitter, asking if he had spoken with the woman he filmed. Eli was embarrassed that he hadn't thought about doing that himself. The man's reply arrived immediately, admitting that he hadn't approached her—sad emoji— because he had recognized the video's viral potential while filming it and worried she might ask him to delete it.

"It's insane that we know exactly where she was and when, but not why," Eli said, and his sister sighed. "I wouldn't be surprised if she didn't plan it, if she just sort of found herself there and ran with it. She's such a scatterbrain."

"If that's the case, why not just say so? Why refuse to answer the question? Why the silence?"

Naomi shrugged. "Because that's our mother."

Eli wanted to go over the video again but Naomi said she didn't have time. She had a bunch of back-to-back meetings with company reps from the New York office and would be lucky to clock out at midnight.

"Wait, aren't you supposed to go over there?"

"Zoom meetings," she said with an annoying smirk.

"To Hannah Bialika's. It's Tuesday. That's what you agreed on, isn't it?"

"Fuck," she said, and her face was tight with exhaustion.

"Maybe . . . I could go," he offered hesitantly, in quest of a good story he could later share with Tamara. His sister lifted her fingers off the keyboard. "You mean instead of me? Actually, if you're up for it, that would be very nice of you."

The street lights leading down the trail to Hannah Bialika's house weren't working. In near darkness, he groped along the stone wall and through the gate, stepping onto the front lawn to the faint sound of burbling water. A pebbled path led him to an open terrace surrounded by sycamores—trees entirely foreign to the desert landscape. Guided by the feeble light of an outdoor lamp, he crossed the terrace up to a slightly ajar glass door, gently pushed it open, and entered the house. Thrumming with excitement, he thought this must be how explorers felt, then caught himself—how vain for a person to believe he could "discover" a place where people had already been living.

Eli entered the house. The first thing he noticed was the gleaming chessboard-tiled floor. It was his first time seeing one; all the other houses in the village had wooden floors per Morgenstein's design; that there could be any other kind of floor had never crossed his mind. The space was enormous, furnished sparsely with a piano with a pipe resting on the lid, an abstract painting of colored squares on the wall, and an old gramophone in the corner of the room. That was it. Nothing more. The eggshell-colored walls reminded him of the beach. At the other end of the spacious living room, a spiral staircase led to a lower floor. As he made his way down it, the basement came gradually into view. It appeared endless.

"Are you coming down?"

Soft, velvety almost—not at all how he had imagined Hannah Bialika's voice.

"Yes," he called out, then softly rehearsed his lines: *My cousin is friends with the general. A naval officer. No, I've never personally met the general. He asked me to do him a favor, so here I am.*

The staircase opened into a bright, expansive kitchen centered around a long wooden dining table, a strong yellow spotlight illuminating a solitary glass of water on its polished surface. Hannah Bialika sat just outside the circle of light wearing a blank expression and thick black wool coat, large earrings studded with black gemstones, and her hair dyed a golden yellow—not a strand out of place. There was a calculator and a stack of papers on the table in front of her. She motioned Eli to take a seat, narrowing her eyes at him. He wasn't sure whether she was hard of seeing or was just studying him closely.

"Are you from around here?"

He nodded, and she leaned forward expectantly. "The Lilienblums," he added.

She waved a dismissive hand. "I can barely remember my own last name," she said, and gestured at a pitcher of water on the table. "Pour yourself a glass," she ordered, and he quickly obeyed, filling the glass and taking a gulp. It was refreshing. Cold.

He waited for her to speak, but she remained steadfast in her silence.

"What's the calculator for?" he finally asked, small talk never having been his strong suit.

"I've been an accountant for the past fifty years," she replied. "I find counting soothing."

"I'm not very good with numbers."

"That's a shame."

Silence again.

"The general asked me to come by . . . I mean, my cousin, who's friends with the general. He's the one who asked me . . ."

"The general is a very dear friend," she said with a pleased smile. "So you're a handyman?"

"I know my way around a screwdriver. What exactly do you need?"

Steadying herself against a cane, she rose slowly and shuffled out of the kitchen. Eli followed her down a long corridor crowded with paintings, including a watercolor of a watermelon and another of a smiling profile. There was also an oil painting of a couple locked in an embrace, the woman of small stature and the man a hulking thing. At the end of the corridor, Hannah Bialika was standing inside a large open elevator tiled with gleaming white marble, waiting for him. Once he entered, she pressed 1 and the door closed. He thought they were already on the bottom floor, but the elevator rode down, opening seconds later onto an enormous bedroom lit dimly by a light that switched off every few moments and then back on again. A giant window with wooden shutters commanded the entire eastern wall. He had never seen such an enormous bedroom in his life.

Hannah paced slowly across the room, stopping in the middle.

"You see that?" She pointed up at a blinking neon bulb. "It's been acting up like that for a week now, very dangerous."

She took a new light bulb from the drawer, handed it to Eli, and sat down on the edge of the bed.

"Do you have a ladder?" he asked.

"I do, but I honestly couldn't tell you where."

Eli cast about the room and spotted a small desk in the corner, next to a slender yellow armchair. He dragged the desk and pressed it up against the bed. Hannah brought him an old newspaper to spread out on the desk.

"Turn off the light, please," he said.

It took her time to heave herself up. She flipped down the switch, leaving them in near darkness. Straining on his tiptoes, Eli replaced the bulb, then hopped off the desk and turned the switch back on.

"Ah, wonderful," she marveled. "Even brighter than before." She turned the light on and off a few times, like a child mesmerized by the magic called electricity.

"Good, I'm glad," Eli said. "Is there anything else I can do for you?"

She fiddled with the light one more time, then pointed to a wardrobe. "Since we've seen how high you can climb, would you mind bringing down a comforter and a few other things from the top shelf?"

That's what she dragged him here for? For a moment he was angry at the general, as if he were a real person who had wasted his time. He thought a rich woman like her was probably used to having people do her bidding. But on second thought, if she needed him there, that must mean she had no one else. He looked around again and realized that the sheer size of the place posed a big, endless problem for a woman her age. He dragged the desk to the closet and hopped back on.

"A little more to your right," she guided him. He took down the puffy blanket as well as a sheet and two towels. He hopped down and plopped it all on the desk. "You're very sweet," she thanked him. "You live in a Morgenstein house, I assume?"

"That's correct."

"Much more convenient. At first the council wanted us to build and live in one of those too."

"So what happened?"

Hannah smiled.

"Mandy happened. My husband was a very persuasive man. He understood people, unlike me." She walked over to the desk and picked up the blanket. He wanted to help her, was worried her frail hand would buckle under the weight. "Don't worry, most of the time I get along perfectly well on my own."

Eli watched her painstakingly move from the closet to the bed, where she lowered first the blanket and then herself, inch by inch, onto the edge of the mattress, taking a few deep breaths.

"When did he pass away?" he asked, despite knowing the answer.

"Two years ago, from a heart attack." She paused. "You know, I stopped dreaming after that. Before I met him, I didn't even know what that was."

"You mean he made you realize your dream of becoming an accountant?"

"You're funny." She chuckled. "I knew I wanted to be an accountant from the day I learned how to count. I meant that until I met Mandy, I never dreamed while I slept."

"What do you mean, you didn't dream?"

"Exactly what it sounds like. I would fall asleep at night and wake up in the morning. Nothing happened in between."

He wondered why she chose to share with him something so personal. Was she toying with him?

"But you knew you were supposed to, right? I mean, you knew that everyone else was dreaming at night."

"I thought it was like the tooth fairy." She grinned, smoothing the blanket. "A story grown-ups tell kids."

She told him that after learning about Jacob's ladder and the angels at school, the teacher asked each student to share a dream they had with the class, and she was sure they were being asked to make up a story.

She didn't understand why hers was the only story that made sense, that had a beginning, middle, and end. "My first night with Mandy was also the first time I dreamed. Imagine that, a twenty-year-old girl having her very first dream. It was about blue snow in Jerusalem."

She told him she had woken up in the middle of the night screaming, thought she had gone off the deep end. "It took Mandy forever just to understand what was going on."

She got up and shuffled to the other side of the bed; only then did Eli notice the small gap between the mattresses. It wasn't a double bed, but two single beds. She reached for the cup of tea resting on the nightstand.

"And you've been dreaming every night since?" His sister would never believe him when he told her about the old lady.

"Only when Mandy slept beside me. When he was on a business trip—zilch."

She told him the story of how they met. He was a young teacher at the time, and she a student. After being courted for two months, she finally relented and agreed to go out with him, fearing that marrying a teacher would condemn her to a life of poverty. "Back then, even Mandy couldn't fathom the level of success he would achieve." She sighed.

Eli took out his phone, searching for an elegant way to end the conversation. "Wow, all this talk about dreams is making me sleepy." He faux-yawned.

"Then you should start taking midday naps! You know, our most interesting dreams happen in the afternoon, something about the body clock going haywire." She turned on the bedside lamp. "After that first dream, I wouldn't leave Mandy's sight for one second. I went everywhere with him, and every chance I had I convinced him to take a nap with me. Crazy, right? Young couples, at least at first, only want to have fun, travel, be out and about, stay awake! And all I wanted to do was dream."

"And he went along with it?"

"What choice did he have?" She laughed. "He loved me a great deal, so what was he going to do, leave me just because I was a little wacky?"

"That's nice," Eli said, and yawned for real this time. "I still have a long walk home ahead of me, so I think it might be time I—"

"Yes, yes, of course," she said, nodding emphatically. "I can completely lose track of time. Remind me how much I owe you?"

He got up and said he didn't know, he assumed she had settled it with the general. She picked up the book on her nightstand—a biography of Menachem Begin. When she opened the cover, he was surprised to see it was hollowed-out. Taking a couple two-hundred-shekel bills out of the carved-out square, she said, "Here, you've been very sweet," handed him the money, and sighed. Eli told himself to just walk away, but when he accepted the bills from her hand, she sighed again.

"Is everything okay?" he asked, stuffing the money in his pocket.

"It's just that ever since Mandy died, I haven't been dreaming, you see?"

"I do, it must be hard."

"You know, I suddenly have an idea . . . maybe . . . you could stay?"

"Where?"

"We'll push the beds apart. You on one side, me on the other. Only for tonight. It might help me dream." She held the blanket in one hand and her tea in the other. Her hands were slightly shaking. The proposition was so outlandish, the only thing he could think was—the old lady is completely crazy.

"I think it's better not to, I really do have to head back," he insisted.

"I know this all sounds very strange," she said and fell silent, as if considering her next words carefully, "but imagine not being able to dream. Can you? It's soul-crushing."

"I have to go," he said with the most determined yet gentle tone he could find, and took two steps back. She got up.

"Wait, hold on a moment, for heaven's sake!" she cried out, and the cup of tea slipped from her hand. The lukewarm liquid spilled all over the blanket, spraying Eli's pants.

"Oh, dear! I'm so sorry," she said. "Look at me, falling apart."

"It's okay, it's not hot," he said, and seized the opportunity to change course. "Is there a towel in the bathroom? I'll dry my pants and be off." She nodded.

The bathroom was extravagant. The bathtub was giant, the sink see-through and the faucet gold. He wiped his pants with a plush white towel neatly folded by the sink, took out his phone, and texted his sister. *Listen, she's insane. I'm talking BATSHIT.*

As he exited the bathroom, he saw that the bedroom light was off. "I'm going, Mrs. Bialika," he called out, barely discerning her face in the thin shaft of light.

She lay in bed under the blanket, staring forlornly at the ceiling. "Take the elevator up to the third floor," she instructed. "I'd appreciate it if you would shut the gate behind you when you leave." After a few labored breaths, she added, "Thank you for keeping a lonely old woman company."

Halfway to the door he turned around and saw that the light from the bathroom was in her eyes. He went back and, just before switching off the light, asked, "Would you like me to stay for a few minutes, until you fall asleep?"

"No no, there's no need. You're very sweet."

"I can spare a few minutes, it's no problem at all."

After a moment's silence, she said, "If it's not a terrible inconvenience, then yes, I would like that very much."

He turned off the bathroom light, sat down in the yellow armchair in the corner, and texted Naomi again:

I'll be back in an hour. Everything is okay.

Staring into the darkness at Mrs. Bialika's silhouette, he watched the slow rise and fall of her belly, the calming effect of his presence. Fixing his eyes on the ceiling, he let his mind wander to the general, trying to envision him—did he have a beard and a peg leg? Or maybe he was averse to pirate clichés and walked around with glasses and a Hawaiian shirt. It was to these thoughts that Eli fell asleep.

11

When he woke up, Hannah's bed was empty and the room awash with bright desert daylight. It took him a moment to orient himself; rising from the armchair, he walked over to the enormous panoramic window, where the crater was splayed out in all its glory. Almost bumping his nose against the glass, he saw the ridge line looming above him, and only then did he realize the room itself was carved into the crater, the rock polished and repurposed as one of the house's walls. Merely a fraction of the house was visible from the outside—the bulk of it had been excavated deep into the rock. The crater appeared different from this angle, more primal. The window, visible only from a bird's-eye view, was hidden from all travelers. He recalled his father telling him that the most extraordinary wonders of nature are something money couldn't buy. And now Eli was looking around and thinking, boy, was he wrong.

He stood at the window a few more moments before taking the elevator up to the kitchen, where he found Mrs. Bialika at the table in the exact same position as the previous night. Spread out before her were a hard-boiled egg, two slices of bread, and a dish of butter. Although he hadn't been expecting breakfast, he couldn't help but feel disappointed by the meager fare.

"The egg is cold," she said, more as a statement than an apology.

Eli sat down and spread a thin layer of butter on a piece of bread. He wasn't hungry, but felt it was the polite thing to do.

"Did you dream?"

She smiled. "I did, thank you. And it doesn't work with just anyone, I'll have you know."

"You mean you've tried this before?"

"A few times. But it was the best with you. Except for Mandy, of course."

She was all spiffed up again in fancy clothes, and her hair sprayed perfectly into place.

"How many people spent the night here?"

"I honestly don't remember. The more interesting question is, when are you coming back?"

"I don't think I can. But I'm sure the general can arrange for someone else to come."

"I'm sure he can, but with you I already know it works, and if it ain't broke . . ."

"It was a one-time thing because you asked. I don't—"

"Five hundred shekels a night," she interjected.

"It's not about money."

"It's always about money. I'll give you a key. I'll be asleep by the time you get here, all you have to do is sleep. You can leave in the morning whenever you want."

There was not a hint of the fragile woman he had encountered the night before; he now found himself negotiating with a shrewd businesswoman who knew exactly what she wanted, and he couldn't help but wonder whether the lightbulb and the top-shelf business was nothing more than a ruse to get him to stay.

"A thousand shekels a night."

"A thousand?"

"Cash, per visit. We'll start with twice a week. Next Sunday works for you?"

"Sunday," he mumbled, which she took as confirmation. She handed him a key. "I'll leave the gate open. Come by after nine, I'll be asleep by then," she said, and handed him an open envelope with money.

"I don't know . . ."

"Then I suggest you think it over on your way out. She's been waiting for you for at least the past thirty minutes."

"Who?"

"If you don't know, don't expect me to."

Eli checked his phone. It was off, the battery must have died some-time during the night. He turned to leave, and when he opened the door, Hannah called out, "See you next week!"

Outside, he saw Naomi across the terrace, ogling the house.

"You moron!" she shouted, and gave him a shove. "I almost called the police. What were you thinking? Disappearing for an entire night without giving me a heads-up? Inspired by Mom, were you? What did you even do in there for so long?"

"Listen," he said, and started laughing. "It was even weirder than you think."

124
DAYS
TILL
RAIN

1

On one of the many Lilienblum family trips up north, Eli and Naomi invented a game called World's Worst Superhero. Whoever came up with the most useless superpower was the winner of the game, which provided hours of fun and spawned figures such as Handkerchief Man, who always came prepared with a handkerchief should the need arise, and Bathroom Huntress, who could locate the public bathroom in even the most labyrinthine of malls. When they grew up, Eli often told his sister that her ability to provide a rational explanation for even the weirdest phenomena, like lightning striking the same person three times or fish raining in the sky in Sri Lanka, was a top contender for the title of Most Useless Superpower. Nothing was too abnormal or logic-defying for Naomi. Which is why he wasn't surprised that she had an explanation for why Hannah Bialika could only dream when there was someone else in the room. "Basic psychology," she said. "The fact that she can't remember her dreams doesn't mean she isn't having them," she explained as they neared their house. "The only thing that proves is people's puerile need to find causality where there is none. A mystery is merely something science hasn't figured out yet—"

A sharp cry interrupted their conversation, and two kids bolted out of their yard, soaked from head to toe, faces flushed with fear.

"Hey, are you okay?" Naomi called out, but the two kept running until they turned a corner into an alley and disappeared. Entering the yard, Eli and Naomi found their mother in a red-and-white-striped dress and purple socks, standing by the gate next to a big puddle. An old, deflated soccer ball was resting by the motion-activated water fountain she had built for the cat. Eli picked up the ball.

"They should have been more careful, the fountain's mechanism is extremely delicate," their mother murmured.

"How were they supposed to know they had to be careful?" Naomi barked. "They couldn't have known they were stepping on a cat's water fountain."

"They didn't need to know, they just needed to not step on it."

Taking out a monkey wrench from her toolbox, Sarai crouched by the puddle to attend to the dripping pipe, the mud splattering the hem of her dress.

"Has it ever occurred to you that you're not the only person in the world? That other people exist too?" Naomi asked while stamping past her into the house.

Eli stayed in the yard with his mom, picked up the old rake leaning against the wall, and carved out a channel to redirect water from the puddle to a small pit in the ground, where it slowly seeped into the soil.

2

At 10:03 A.M. the neighborhood WhatsApp group pinged with a text from an unknown number:

> **I don't want to point any fingers before we have all the facts, but (!) it's absolutely unacceptable that children in our neighborhood should feel unsafe. I expect immediate action to be taken!!**

Realizing the rumors were already spreading through the community, Eli decided to stay home, just in case. And that case came knocking on the door later that afternoon, in the form of the council head and a woman with frizzy black hair standing on his stoop.

"I told you, a spitting image of his father," the council head said to the frizzy-haired lady when Eli opened the door. "Mind if we come in, young man?" he asked, then brushed past Eli with a fatherly pat on his shoulder and the woman in tow.

Taking a seat at the kitchen table, the council head asked for a strong cup of black coffee, and after introducing the woman as the council-appointed social worker responsible for community development, inquired if everything was going well at the lodge.

Eli nodded.

"Well, I'd expect nothing less of your father. Your generation doesn't seem to produce people like him, huh? You youngsters can't seem to stay the course, always want to switch it up."

"Mm-hmm," Eli said. He was too tired to argue. He didn't appreciate being pigeonholed and mass-analyzed with the rest of his generation. He didn't know if this bad habit of adults stemmed from laziness or shallowness, but he couldn't feel less *Gen Z*. He neither lived in a "constant state of confusion" nor "thrived on disruption, change and fast-paced living," as he'd read in some article. Nor was he "tech-savvy." The one time he tried taking a programming e-course, he couldn't install the software.

He served the council head his coffee along with a box of alfajores.

"It's great to see that you've joined your dad at the lodge," the council head said. "We need our youth to stay right here by our side, help us make the desert bloom."

"You know, people have been trying to make the desert bloom for seventy years now. Maybe it's time to start lowering expectations," Naomi said, walking into the kitchen and pouring half a cup of tepid tea down the sink.

"On the contrary, I think you're the example that we're doing a pretty good job," the council head said and smiled. "Watch out, Mark Zuckerberg, Naomi Lilienblum is hot on your heels!"

Although his sister didn't answer, Eli knew the comparison made her feel warm and fuzzy inside. The man was fond of Naomi not only because he appreciated her intellectual prowess, but because she was partly, indirectly, responsible for his winning a second term as council head. A decade earlier, after Naomi won second place in the Junior Science Olympiad and headed off to boarding school, the council head saw an opportunity; centering his campaign around education, he championed improving the standard of the local school so as to prevent talented students like Naomi from seeking education elsewhere. While too late for Naomi, the campaign struck a chord with many of the Cliff's residents, leading not only to his reelection but to the establishing of a new robotics elective—which Sarai taught.

"Is your mother home?" the social worker asked.

"She's busy," Eli and Naomi replied in chorus.

"It'll only take a few moments of her time," she promised.

Drying the cup with a frayed kitchen towel, Naomi nodded to Eli to go fetch their mother. Moments later, Sarai walked into the kitchen with tar-stained hands, extending one first to the council head and then to the social worker, both who shook it reluctantly.

"You've had us all worried," the council head said. "Maybe now you might tell us where you've been?"

"I met McMurphy," she replied casually.

The council head laughed. "Well, you can't say we didn't try."

"The incident this morning, I assume that's why you're here?" Naomi cut to the chase.

The council head and social worker exchanged a tentative look. "We have no doubt there was no malice involved. We know Sarai is always working on something new and exciting, and that's wonderful, honestly, just wonderful," the social worker said. "The sole purpose of this visit is to put on our thinking caps and try, together, to ensure that this inexhaustible burst of creativity doesn't jeopardize the residents of the neighborhood."

"Jeopardize?" Naomi scoffed. "Two kids got wet. I mean, really, they're not made of sugar."

"No one is making any accusations," the council head reassured. "It was never an issue when she worked inside the house, and there's no reason to change that now."

"So you're here because you want to lock her back up in her study? That's what this is about?" Naomi asked.

Letting out a deep sigh, the council head looked Sarai in the eye and said, "Mrs. Lilienblum, what you did in the desert for three days is your own business, but asking people not to voice their concerns after you return without offering any explanation and building a rocket in your backyard, well, that's a pretty tall order."

"A lot of people happen to be very excited about my mother's inventions," Eli ventured with a tremulous voice, hoping no one could notice that deep down he agreed with the man before him.

Sensing where her jittery brother was going, Naomi took over. "That's right. And I think her thousands upon thousands of fans will have no reason to come visit the Cliff if you keep her and her inventions stashed away somewhere."

"Oh, honestly, Naomi, what fans are you talking about?" Sarai muttered, but the council head's brow was already arched in interest.

"What did I miss?" he asked.

Naomi told him about the video. "Oh my, look at that!" the social worker trilled when Eli pressed play. He could tell they didn't really understand what they were seeing, but the council head was the kind of person who could sniff out a good investment without needing all the details. "This is absolutely mind-blowing! I had no idea we have such an internet sensation in our little village!"

A small smile crept over Sarai's face.

"You see—" Eli began, but the council head cut him off. "Of course I see! We have to make this thing public. Maybe we should have a press meeting, celebrate the achievement!" he said, impressing Eli with his resolve.

Later at dinner, Boaz watched the video starring his wife perhaps twenty times. Unlike his kids, he seemed unbothered by the question of why Sarai had disappeared. Marveling at her invention, he repeatedly declared, "Every desert traveler would die to have one of those!" When Eli informed him of the council head's intention to hold a press conference, he smiled contentedly. "It's about time everyone knows how talented my wife is," he said. Sarai attempted to appear nonchalant, but Eli discerned a hint of anticipation hidden in her eyes.

3

As the number of internet views continued to grow exponentially, and with a mention of the upcoming press conference in the council's monthly newsletter, an increasing number of villagers and travelers had begun wandering around the town square. It offered a fine vantage point of the Lilienblum residence, prompting curious glances and smiling selfies from the bystanders against the backdrop of Sarai's gadgets still strewn across the lawn. In the afternoons, clusters of schoolchildren walking home would pass by, stand on their tiptoes, and call out to each other, "That's that Sari woman's house!" People tended to get Eli's mother's name wrong. Sari. Shiri. Sarah. Shiran. He always felt it was another attempt to compartmentalize her, and it drove him crazy. When he was a kid, he had asked her about the meaning of her name, and she told him it was of Brazilian origin. Sarai. He imagined an exotic Portuguese dialect that rolled off the tongues of Rio de Janeiro natives. Pictured the name sailing on fishermen's boats to the coast of Israel and traversing the country until it landed on the ears of his late grandmother, who decided to bestow it on her only child. Sometime later, when he asked her again about the name's meaning, she pointed at the night sky and told him it had dropped out of a black hole at the center of the Milky Way; and on yet another occasion, she claimed it had cruised the Indian Ocean on the backs of whales until washing up onto the shore. Out of all her tales, he had latched onto the one about a small Spanish village whose inhabitants made a living from crafting names, and the Spanish tourist from that village, who, after stumbling into Sarai's parents' store in Haifa one day, paid for groceries with the name in lieu of money. That Sarai was the original name of the biblical Sarah, the wife of Abraham, Eli learned only later in high school. He never asked his mother if she was actually named after this first Jewish matriarch.

Eli realized there was something truly big going on when his sister called him during a shift at the lodge and told him to open the link she had emailed him. The link led to the Twitter page of a man named Ben Gould, who had posted their mother's video alongside the caption, "If in four months this device brings down rain on an entire town, I'll make an offer. No lower than twenty million."

Twenty-three thousand people hearted the tweet, and nearly fifteen hundred shared it.

"That's a shitload of people!" Eli exclaimed. The man in the profile photo had on an astronaut suit and black sunglasses. "Why four months?"

"Who cares," Naomi said, "a tweet from Gould is gold for us." According to his sister, he was one of the most famous people in the tech industry—not much older than her—who sold his first company at twenty-two for a billion dollars.

"And he's interested in Mom's invention? That's amazing!"

"He's interested in lots of things. It doesn't mean he's serious about buying. But it's a great tweet, that's for sure."

Eli read some more about Ben Gould, billionaire extraordinaire, his imagination running wild. He tried picturing what would happen if he really did buy his mother's invention. A moment ago he'd never heard of the man, had been completely oblivious of his existence, and now he was dreaming about the change he could bring to their lives.

The sound of splashing water snapped Eli out of his daydream, only to reveal Tamara standing over a big puddle, holding a wet, empty bucket and a mop. He sprang up, took the mop, and quickly began pushing the water toward the door before it made for the furniture.

"You should have said you don't know how to mop a floor."

"It's true, I don't. But it's like riding a bicycle, at a certain age it's too awkward to learn," she said, trailing him across the wet floor.

"Did you see that Ben Gould shared the video?" he boasted.

"Ben Gould?! Shut your mouth!" she shrieked, before bursting into laughter. "I have no idea who he is. Someone famous?"

"Almost as famous as McMurphy." He grinned.

"I actually have a meeting tomorrow about McMurphy with some woman who lives nearby. She says she's the last person who saw him. If that's true, it could make an interesting article."

"A rare find." Eli nodded. "Only half the people on the Cliff claim they're the last ones to have seen him."

"You want to come with me?" she suddenly asked. "I'll need someone who can tell me when I'm being bullshitted by a villager." He tried to think of something witty to say, but he couldn't think of anything, so instead just answered, "I think I have a knack for that." He grinned again.

4.

He made a beeline from the lodge to Hannah Bialika's house with the mandate to make an old lady dream. The gate and front door were open, as advertised, and a faint glow emanated from the lower-level kitchen. With Hannah nowhere in sight, he walked down the hallway, called the elevator, and perused the pictures on the wall. The one that caught his attention was of her husband, Mandy, before the house was built, standing on the edge of the Cliff with his arms outstretched, the yawning crater below. There were a few photos of them as a couple, and a giant family portrait with their children and grandchildren sitting around a table at a fancy restaurant. They looked happy. The elevator opened onto her darkened bedroom. She had kept her promise by separating the two single beds, one of them cradling her sleeping form with a blanket up to her neck, the other now standing guard at the other end of the room. Wavering between the armchair and the bed, he finally tossed his jacket onto the former while settling for the latter. He stared at the closed shutters, trying to glimpse the outside world through the narrow slits.

"Long day?" Her voice rose from the dark.

"Yup. A ton of work."

"Work means your body and brain are still up for it. It's a good thing."

"Maybe, but also tiring," he said, hoping that would be the end of it.

"Word around the grocery store is that your mother is now famous."

"It's true. They're holding a press conference for her on Thursday."

Hannah asked if they were at least capitalizing on the video's popularity, if they had seen any money from it, and he said they had not. At least his mother hadn't.

"That's just unfair," she protested. "A lot of people can post videos, but how many can create clouds?" She lamented the economic system's failure to reward genuine creativity, favoring instead those who could

translate the creativity of others into money. "Now that I think of it, I
don't know what you do for a living."

"I help around the lodge. My dad runs the place. It's temporary." He
wasn't sure why it was important to him that she know.

"I had no idea it was a family affair. How nice. You know, Mandy
used to work at a hotel, before going into business."

"The lodge isn't quite a hotel, it's more of a hostel . . ."

"It was the King David Hotel. In Jerusalem. Do you know it? He
was a driver there. Hated every moment. If it was up to him, he would
have quit on his first day."

"Who was it up to?"

"Me. I wouldn't let him," she said. Even in the dark, he could tell
she was smiling. "He wanted to be a teacher, Mandy, can you imagine?
He was sure he was going to spend his life in service of the Ministry of
Education, with holiday gift cards and the occasional retreat at some
wretched B&B."

Eli kept quiet, again hoping the conversation would die there.

"I'm sure you're asking yourself how a hotel driver ended up making a name for himself in the business world."

"How?" he asked perfunctorily.

"It all changed after we bought our first factory," she explained.
"This was about a year into Mandy's job at the hotel. I was working as
an accountant at a collection agency, dealing with all kinds of miserable
souls who had fallen into debt and faced bankruptcy. By then Mandy
had become chummy with many of the hotel regulars, rich guests who
enjoyed chitchatting with him, a local *commoner*." Before buying a
business in Israel, they would ask him about its reputation, trusting that
he'd tell the truth. One such guest was a middle-aged mustachioed Jew
named Alejandro, who had made his fortune from real-estate and
tipped thirty percent out of his Zionist convictions. "He and Mandy
became real bosom buddies. Alejandro used to tell him about his
globe-trotting, and in return Mandy offered up stories about our studio
apartment and strict policy of buying vegetables only on Friday, half an
hour before the market closed for the weekend. Alejandro was so appalled

by the thought that a young, working couple living in the Holy Land couldn't afford fresh vegetables, that he offered to help us get started."

"So he bought you a factory?"

"Heavens no," she scoffed. "If the rich simply gave away their money they wouldn't be rich, now, would they? He offered to extend us a loan so we could buy a property or business, something to help us build a better life for ourselves. The only condition was that we pay in one dollar for every four he gave us. Not that he needed our pennies, obviously, but he said that people had to risk their own money to value their investment. Mandy, that schlemiel, didn't know what to do with the loan, but lucky for him he at least had enough sense to consult with me. I grabbed him with both hands and told him, 'Mandy, this is a once-in-a-lifetime opportunity, far better than any mortgage we could take.' I tried to explain the meaning of interest rates, to show him that with the money we'd make off a sound investment we could buy a small house, that he could finally be a full-time teacher, like he had wanted, without worrying about side income."

"And you managed to convince him?"

"Mandy was never a numbers guy, even after he became a wealthy man. But after a long, dragged-out conversation, he finally said that if there was one thing he knew, it was that I was the one with the brains, and if I was sure about it, so was he. And that's how we started shopping around for a good bargain, looking to buy or build a business. The problem was that our savings were barely enough to buy anything, even if we only had to put up a fifth of the total. Mandy kept saying we shouldn't force it, but I wasn't about to throw in the towel." She paused. "It's like a tidal wave, this life. Everything happens so fast, hits so hard. The daily grind drags you down, and you have to fight not to go under. Good grief, the strength one must muster just to get through the day! Pay rent, take care of the bills, deal with leaky roofs in the winter and mosquito bites in the summer. Groceries-kids-dinner-bedtime-morning-alarm. God, even brushing your teeth is a bi-daily chore! And I knew, I just knew I didn't want that life, you know? That's how my parents lived, a couple of German immigrants who thought you had to make do with the tiniest, simplest pleasures and be grateful just to have a roof over your head and food on your plate, because life was endless drudgery, a war of attrition with no clear winners. Even as a kid, I knew they were wrong. I believed I could achieve more, that Mandy could achieve more. And that we deserved more. That's the god's honest truth. Cocky? Maybe, but the truth nonetheless." Between each sentence, she took long, labored breaths. Listening to her, it all became clear—it wasn't about dreaming, or at least that wasn't the only reason she wanted him there. She was a lonely old woman in need of someone to talk to. A pair of ears to take in her words. Another person's breathing to fall asleep to.

She told him that at the collection agency, she would go over the repo accounts, punching in numbers and calculating customer debt. One day she came across the records of a small metal factory located in the industrial area of Petah Tikva. Unlike most of the accounts she handled, the owner of this one wasn't doing great, but wasn't carrying significant debt either, and a lightbulb went on above her head. "After all, we were looking to buy a business, and those poor people needed the money."

"I assume it wasn't exactly legal to use that information."

"Completely illegal, yes, absolutely," she confirmed. "But indulging in legalities was a luxury I couldn't afford."

"And you shared the idea with Mandy?"

"Heavens no! Mandy was far too honest a man. He would never have gone along with it." So she fed him a cockamamie story about a distant cousin who'd heard about a factory looking for buyers. "We hopped on a bus the very next day, or rather a couple of buses, then made our way from the station on foot. It was nearly dark by the time we arrived. We entered through a busted metal gate, sweaty and exhausted, approached the first person we saw and announced that we were interested in buying the factory—although calling that place a factory was a bit of a stretch. It was more like a storage shed with a few workers." The man was visibly nervous, and they soon realized he thought they were goons sent by loan sharks to intimidate him into handing over the business. "Can you imagine? Little old me and scrawny Mandy, mob collectors! He tried kicking us out, yelling that the place wasn't for sale. I was sure that was it, that we'd reached a dead end, but then the most remarkable thing happened—I discovered Mandy's skills of persuasion. I'd never seen anything like it." Mandy told the guy it was no problem at all, they'd leave, but if he could just get a cup of tea before they set off, because it was a long journey home. "There was a softness to his voice that made the man relent, and before we'd even sweetened our tea, he was already pouring his heart out. We ended up staying there for three hours. If it was just me, I wouldn't have gotten him to talk in a million years, but Mandy killed him with kindness."

"What did he do?"

"He was soft, disarming. You have to understand something, Mandy's persuasiveness wasn't despite his nebbishness, but because of it. Mandy was never the fierce businessman people imagined him to be, a tough tycoon looking to strip a company for parts. Quite the opposite. He walked, talked, and looked like a nebbish. A gangly Jew with thin wrists, someone who gave off the feeling that he could be trusted. The man we had been talking to turned out to be the owner himself, and Mandy had gained his trust. He told us his parents had built the place and that he'd been bleeding money for two years after doing business with the wrong people. He talked and talked, spilled his heart out, and you see, when he finished talking, Mandy didn't even have to convince him to sell us the place, the man suggested it himself. Said he was done, had given it his all and had nothing left to give. It was the quickest deal we ever struck. He took the first offer we made, didn't even try to bargain. He only asked that we keep the factory going, explaining that he thought of the place as his parents' legacy. That they'd built it with their own two hands. And Mandy of course agreed right away, because he was just a big old softie."

"So that was your first factory?"

"Oh, no, no it wasn't. I've been rambling, you live long enough you can barely get your own stories straight. When did we buy our first factory? Years later, '66 I think, or maybe '67. It was a cement factory, near Naharia, right next door to the bakery that made the best rugelach in Israel."

"I don't understand, I thought you bought the metal factory."

"We did, of course we did. But two weeks after buying it, we sold it to a real-estate company that tore it down and built a very impressive skyscraper. We made a sixty-percent return, which I can assure you is rare, what you'd call beginner's luck."

"But you promised the owner you'd keep the factory running."

"Mandy made that promise, and he had every intention of honoring it, but the truth is that factory didn't stand a chance. Not even Henry Ford himself could have saved it. The day after we finalized the sale I went over the numbers; there were an awful lot of expenses and very little revenue. But I also discovered that the total square footage of the factory was substantially bigger than we thought, and it sat on pretty pricey land. Worth a lot more than what we paid. The previous owner somehow failed to factor that in. Some people, when life gives them diamonds, still insist on trying to make lemonade. I showed Mandy the numbers and explained it was the only way we would ever profit from the deal. That if we kept the factory running, the business expenses would run us into the ground. Mandy understood what I was saying with his head, but not his heart. He wouldn't renege on his promise, he said a man's word was the most valuable thing in his possession. I told you, Mandy was a big softie, too soft for business, at least in the beginning. That's why he needed me."

"So how did you talk him into it?"

"I didn't," she replied. "I sold the factory behind his back. It was the only time I made a business move without him. I took an ad out in the paper and prayed Mandy wouldn't see it, and sold the factory to the first person who made an offer."

"And how did he react when he found out?"

Hannah was quiet for a moment. "Deep down, Mandy wanted it just as much as I did, if not more. It was convenient for him to pin it all on me. But given the chance for a do-over, he wouldn't have changed a thing, believe me. That deal was the foundation for everything that came after. Alejandro was so impressed with Mandy's instincts that he made him a partner in his investments in Israel. That's when the big money started rolling in."

"But how did Mandy react when you told him?"

"He wouldn't talk to me for three days. When he finally opened his mouth he said he loved me very much, but he'd never forgive me for what I did."

"And what happened afterwards?"

"He really loved, and he really never forgave."

5.

The next morning, he found Hannah waiting for him in the kitchen in the same spot as last time, with the same meager offering of hard-boiled egg, tea, and two slices of stale bread. This time, however, there was an envelope wedged between the plates. He sat down across from her, took a sip of tea, and bit into the bread.

"Put some egg on it," she told him.

The egg was a strange shade of beige. "It's okay, thanks," he demurred.

"Mandy used to eat it like that too, just bread, plain. I never understood it." She picked up her cup. "Did I ever tell you about the time Mandy took me to see blue snow in Jerusalem?"

"In your first dream? Yes, you did."

"Oh my, I must be more senile than I realized." She gave a sad grin. "It was a recurring dream, he had it every few weeks and I enjoyed it tremendously."

"*His* dream?" he asked, but Hannah was too engrossed in her own story to notice.

"You know, a lot of the beautiful dreams floated through my Mandy's head, about big cities, the wild outdoors, but the dream with the blue snow was always my favorite . . ."

"Why do you keep saying they were *his* dream?"

Hannah took a long sip of tea, lowered her cup, and started scratching at a small oil stain on the table. "Because his dreams were my dreams," she said, her fingernail digging into the table. "For sixty years, I dreamed Mandy's dreams. He didn't know, at first. I mean, I didn't either. I was so thrilled by experiencing the act of dreaming, I had no clue the dreams weren't mine. How could I have known? It's not as if couples routinely wake up in the morning and discuss their dreams. Women spend years sleeping by their husbands without even sharing their thoughts."

"Did you dream my dreams too?"

She was quiet.

He tried to recall his dreams, to figure out what she knew, but could only dredge up a few blurry images that didn't snap into a clear picture.

"Why are you telling me this?"

"Because Mandy chose to marry me, with all my craziness, but you didn't. It wouldn't be fair if you didn't know."

"You should have told me before we started dreaming." He scraped his chair back and got up.

"This isn't the first mistake I've ever made, but you're right, absolutely right. A thousand apologies. And now that I've apologized," she said and slid the envelope across the table. "See you next week?"

"No! This . . . it isn't right."

"I can pay more, no problem."

"It isn't about that!" Eli protested, pushed the envelope back and made for the door. "Money doesn't solve everything."

"Take the envelope, kid, I don't do debts." But he flung the door open and shot her an angry look. Struggling to put his insult into words, he murmured, "It's just not right."

"I'll be right here if you change your mind." Hannah pulled the plate with the egg closer and sliced a sliver of egg.

He left. The realization that someone who was essentially a stranger had pilfered his dreams was troubling, but even more troubling was the fact that he couldn't remember them. He had always believed that dreamers were alone, locked inside their own minds, and learning that he was mistaken suddenly made him question all his assumptions about the world. A disturbing idea crossed his mind, that perhaps Hannah wasn't the only one encroaching on his dreams. Maybe there were others out there, all around the world, in countries he'd never heard of, dreaming nightly dreams which he believed belonged only to him.

6

Eli was hoping for a quiet morning, a chance to recover from the old woman's eerie invasion of his dreams, but when he reached the lodge he found Tamara waiting for him at the front desk, sporting round-rimmed sunglasses and a black tank-top. "Yalla, let's go find McMurphy," she exclaimed, her heavily Spanish-accented *yalla* giving him a chuckle.

It took him a few moments to remember that he had accepted her invitation to join her meeting with the alleged last person to see McMurphy. "Let me just grab a coffee and we'll go," he said, but Tamara shook her head and hooked her arm with his in a painfully pleasant touch, saying she didn't want to be late.

Eli gestured northwest and took the lead.

The six shops on Nahal Grupit Street made it the closest thing to a main street within a hundred-mile radius. Number 10 stood on the corner by Paulina's dry cleaners, where they had the lodge's laundry done. The door to the dry cleaners was open, revealing startlingly blue walls and about a dozen laundry machines, some stacked on top of each other, most spinning in a flurry of activity. Eli spotted Paulina's red hair peeking out of the back room. Despite her enduring presence in Eli's life, all he really knew about Paulina was that she was in her forties and had two cats that were more frenemies than friends.

"I'm coming, I'm coming!" Paulina emerged from the back room with a heavy bag of clothes in each hand. "The first six kilos is seventy-two shekels, then it's ten shekels for every additional kilo. Payment's after, cash only, there's an ATM outside around the corner," she said, dumping the bags by one of the machines and disappearing into the back room again. On the counter across the room, a silver-framed photo of Paulina stood between the cash register and a small vase of flowers.

"We're not here for laundry," Tamara called out.

"This is a dry cleaners, hon, laundry is all I can offer," Paulina replied in English when she came back with another bag of clothes. She looked up. "You're Boaz's kid." He nodded.

"We're here about McMurphy," Tamara said. "You said you had some things to tell me?"

"Right, yes. I did say that." She sighed. "Okay. But we'll keep it short, I don't have that much to say anyway. I only met him once. The guy came in to get his laundry done."

"When was this?"

Paulina sighed again. "I can't say exactly, we're talking years ago. But you could see he wasn't from around here. He was quiet, withdrawn, waited maybe an hour until I came out of the back room. A polite European, not like us."

She said that inside his laundry bag, there was a garment of sentimental value that he wanted to make sure wouldn't get ruined in the wash. "I told him I'd throw it in with a load of delicates, and he wouldn't stop thanking me." She claimed that he had told her he would be cycling from the dry cleaners straight to the crater, where he planned to spend the night, get up early, and head farther south. "I mostly remember asking him if he had a tent and warm clothes, and he asked if it got cold there at night."

"Seriously? He didn't know?" Eli asked with a look of surprise.

"Unreal, huh? A kook. I was surprised he'd even made it to the Cliff."

"We get travelers like that in the lodge sometimes, people setting off to hike the desert without taking sunscreen."

"But that's usually from stupidity, with him it was something else," Paulina said. "There was something pure, a certain innocence about him, one of those rare people untainted by time."

"That's some pretty deep insight about someone you only met once, a decade ago," Eli said. He was done wasting time on another McMurphy expert.

"Some things you can tell straight away about someone," Paulina resolved.

"Well, it seems a lot of different people saw a lot of different things in McMurphy's eyes, so it's a little hard to keep track."

A washing machine started to beep. Paulina opened the door, pulled the wet heap out, and plopped it into a purple laundry basket.

"Why are you interested in McMurphy?" Paulina addressed Tamara.

"There are so many things about his story that don't make sense, clothes found all over the place, on the Cliff . . ."

"I didn't ask what makes it an interesting story, I asked why *you're* interested in it."

"I think," she began, her eyes wandering up as if the words she was looking for might be on the ceiling, "that McMurphy wasn't an ordinary person, and I want to try to understand what made him different, what made him live off the grid."

Eli didn't understand what she meant, and Paulina looked equally puzzled. She slammed the machine door shut and disappeared into the back room.

"You practically told her to her face that you don't believe her, why?" Tamara hissed.

"Just a little healthy skepticism. You should try it."

Paulina reemerged from the back room with a pressed green shirt and placed it neatly on the counter next to the framed photo. "I think you're right," she told Tamara. "There was something different about him. He sat quietly on that bench over there with his goofy orange beanie, and out of nowhere suddenly asked me if my mother had died." She gazed at one of the machines with a faraway look and her voice softened. "What a question to ask a stranger. I remember it really irked me, but instead of snapping at him, I asked him how he knew." She tilted her head at the framed photo. "He said that at work, people usually put up photos of their kids, not of their parents. He told me his mother had passed a few months earlier and it made him more sensitive to those things."

Eli took another look at the photo; it was a close-up of a young woman's face, smiling at the camera against the backdrop of a field of buttercups. It wasn't Paulina after all. Her hair was a similar red but much curlier, and her face narrower.

"At the time, the photo had been standing here for a whole year, and he was the first person to ask about it." Another machine beeped, then another. "He told me he had decided to come to Israel because his mother had traveled the country when she was young, and he wanted to see all the places she'd visited, trace her footsteps." Biting her lower lip, Paulina added in Hebrew, "You see, Eli, sometimes it doesn't take much to see into someone's heart."

"I'm sorry for your loss," Tamara said, and Eli noted genuine empathy in her eyes. "I hope it got a bit easier over time."

"It never gets easier with time." Paulina smiled at her. "But in a strange way, I remember I felt better after talking to McMurphy. It's as if he was so intertwined with my pain . . ." she said and hesitated for a moment, "that he absorbed some of it himself."

Paulina offered them the shirt, saying it would be better displayed in the museum collection at the lodge than left to gather dust in her storage room.

Tamara held it up, stretched the fabric and inspected it closely. It was a long-sleeved T-shirt with the words "Christmas 2006, St. John's Church" on the back.

"So what do you think, Paulina?" Tamara asked. "Do you think . . ."

"That he's dead?"

Tamara nodded.

"No," Paulina replied calmly.

"I don't get it, so you think he's alive?" Eli asked. "Survived all these years in the desert—"

"I only know two things, Eli," she cut him off. "The first is that the travelers who don't make it out of the desert are the arrogant and irresponsible kind, and McMurphy was neither. Maybe a bit of a scatterbrain, but not irresponsible."

"And the second thing?"

"That the laws of physics work a little differently here, and that the things that happen here don't happen anywhere else."

On their way back to the lodge, Eli thought about Paulina's description of McMurphy. He realized he knew by heart all the stories about McMurphy's disappearance, but he didn't know much about McMurphy himself.

"Did you know he had lost his mother?" Tamara asked Eli.

"No. And his mother didn't know, either. She was here on the Cliff a year ago, and spoke to my dad on the phone only last month. He did say she sounded a little tired, but dead? Like, six-feet-under dead? That's one long-long-distance phone call—I hope we didn't pick up the charge!"

It took her a moment, but Tamara started laughing. For Eli, people's laughter came with a color. When he heard his mother laugh, for example, he heard yellow. Tamara's laughter was light blue.

"McMurphy's mother visited the Cliff about a year ago." A few weeks shy of his army discharge and still living on the base at the time, he hadn't met her himself, but had gotten the full account from his father. She appeared at the lodge out of nowhere, a woman in her sixties who had no qualms about bunking with twenty-year-old backpackers. It was only on the fourth day of her stay that she revealed her identity to Boaz, confiding that she and her son had fallen out of touch in the years leading up to his disappearance, and that she felt the need to see the place where he had gone missing with her own eyes. "My dad said she wandered around the village like a loon, looking for him in people's backyards. She still contacts him about once a month, asking if there's any new information. So if McMurphy really did talk to Paulina about a dead parent, I'm guessing it was his dad, who really did die a little before his trip to Israel. From my understanding, the whole family situation there was pretty messed up."

"But why would Paulina lie?" Tamara's face scrunched with confusion.

"I don't think she's lying, I think she remembers it the way she wants to. That's the thing about McMurphy, people project their own stories onto him."

"So when your mother says she ran into him, it's some kind of subconscious fantasy?"

"No!" Eli retorted firmly, but then added hesitantly, "Maybe. I don't know. Anyway, I believe the basic details in Paulina's story are true."

"So why didn't you tell her she got the story about his mother wrong?"

"Because it would just upset her, and make her question her own memory."

"Okay, and who said that was bad?"

"People are sensitive, you can't just go confronting them with . . ." He fell quiet. What he wanted to say was that he didn't want to play Jenga with someone else's reality. There were certain rules his mother had taught him, rules he understood perfectly well but lacked the words to explain.

She stroked his arm gently. Eli resisted his natural inclination to recoil from the touch, and instead surrendered to it. "It's okay, you can tell me on the next date," she said, and he smiled.

7

That night, trying to explain to himself why he had not corrected Paulina, Eli was reminded of the tale his mother had told him when he was little, about the wise men of Chelm and the moon. The wise men were so enchanted by the silver light of the moon that they decided to try to capture it. They thought long and hard how to go about it until, one day, the wisest of the wise men hatched a plan. On the night of a full moon, he placed a barrel of water by his front door, watched the moon's reflection in the water, and at just the right moment, threw a towel over the barrel and tied it with a piece of barbed wire. The next morning, upon gathering the townspeople, he proudly announced that he had trapped the moon. The wise men wanted to see, but he refused, explaining that he couldn't risk the moon escaping. To this day Eli wasn't entirely sure he understood the story, but he remembered well what his mother had told him at the time—that everyone believes they have a moon hidden in some barrel, and that even if it's not true, the towel must never be lifted, "because sometimes one's belief that they are in possession of the moon is the only thing they have."

8.

The press conference was held the following afternoon. Sarai agreed to be accompanied by only one family representative, and after a quick chat it was decided that Eli take on the task. When he arrived, he found his mother in a plain purple dress and sneakers that had once been white.

"You look nice," he said, walking up to her. Usually indifferent to flattery, she added a sliver of teeth to her smile that spoke of genuine delight. "Excited?"

"No," she replied. "Why, does it look like I am?"

Like most of the architecture perched on the Cliff, the rec center was a wooden affair. By the entrance, on a fold-out table covered in a disposable cloth the color of Sarai's dress, lay an assortment of refreshments: dry cookies, wafers, water, and grapefruit juice. As they headed for the table, they passed a closed door with a sheet of printer paper taped to it, announcing, "Press Conference."

"They set it up nicely," Eli said tentatively.

"Mm-hm. Pulled out all the stops."

Mother and son laughed, and Eli poured himself a glass of grapefruit juice. He wasn't a fan, but downed a few drops once every few years just to remind himself.

The small meeting room assigned to the press conference had been set up with two wooden tables and about a dozen worn-out chairs carelessly scattered about. In the only occupied one sat a chubby journalist in a striped shirt who kept his gaze glued to his phone screen even as they entered.

Sarai settled into her chair while Eli claimed a spot in the front row. At 4:03, the council head and spokeswoman blustered in, along with another reporter.

"Sarai, darling! So good to see you!" the council head proclaimed, pecked her on the cheek, and looked out at the audience of three. Clearing her throat, the spokeswoman got up and announced, "I'm delighted to open this press conference." After introducing the council head, she gestured at Sarai and trumpeted, "It is my great pleasure to introduce Shiri Lilienblum, the inventor. I'm assuming everyone here has seen the video, but just in case"—she waved a small remote control and pointed it at a projector mounted on the ceiling, but nothing happened. Eli and Sarai exchanged glances.

"Well, I guess we're a little less tech-savvy than our inventor here," the council head muttered. "We'll skip the movie. I'd like to talk about the reason we're all here, in this pearl of the desert we call 'the Cliff.' Everyone in this room knows that when Ben-Gurion spoke about making the desert bloom, it was the Cliff he had in mind. Unfortunately, the state failed to deliver the support they'd promised, and even though we've accomplished extraordinary things here, we could have done more."

The council head spoke about the hi-tech companies crowding the top floors of Tel Aviv high-rises, about kids making 30K a month. "Not one shekel of that booming economy finds its way here." He recounted the ambitious attempt to develop a modern industrial zone fifteen years ago, half a mile from the Cliff, back when they thought the money would be pouring in. A road had been paved and water and power cables installed—they even built a few large hangars—only for the obvious to be discovered: that no hi-tech company would relocate to the desert, hours from Tel Aviv. "The place has been deserted ever since. What can I say, at least the deer seem to enjoy the clover. Chelm." Through his mother's stories, Eli had misunderstood Chelm to be a symbol of creativity, of people who dared to dream big, to think outside the box. It took him years to understand that for everyone other than his mother, Chelm was the original Idiotville, a universal stand-in for *stupid*.

"Like the cactus, the Jewish brain has already proven it can flourish in the most dire of circumstances," the council head pressed ahead, "and Mrs. Lilienblum has really defied the odds. Under different circumstances, in Tel Aviv perhaps, the talented woman to my left could have been a renowned engineer with a promising startup, but she chose to pitch her tent on the Cliff."

Despite his mother's blank expression, Eli felt that something in the council head's words had clicked, that perhaps, unwittingly, the municipal politician had managed to articulate a repressed sentiment—that for Sarai, life on the Cliff came at a price; but in a few cliché-laden sentences, the council head had pointed out another possibility—an alternate reality in which her dreams could be realized.

One of the two reporters raised his hand. "So what are you saying? What's the goal?"

"I want the voices of impressive women like Mrs. Lilienblum to be heard," the council head said, nodding in agreement with himself.

The journalists asked Sarai some questions. Did you expect it to go viral? ("No.") How does it feel to be a star? ("I don't feel like one.") Have you already thought about what you will do with Ben Gould's twenty million dollars? ("Honestly, I didn't even think about it.")

When they were done, the two reporters got up, congratulated Sarai, and walked out.

"You did great," the council head told Sarai, "really terrific."

Slow clapping sounded from across the room.

"Great presentation," a voice familiar to Eli called out. He turned around to see a smiling Hannah Bialika. She carefully rose and walked up to them, the small white purse slung over her shoulder thumping against her black wooden walking stick. Brushing right past him, she stopped directly in front of Sarai, on the opposite side of the table. The room tensed, and Eli got the funny feeling that Hannah Bialika's petite form was exerting a gravitational tug on the attention of those surrounding it.

"Mrs. Bialika, what an honor!" the council head exclaimed.

She smiled at Sarai with an assessing look. "I'll have you know, Mrs. Lilienblum, that as a Bialika Industries board member, I've been privy to more technological innovations than you can imagine." She paused and leaned heavily on the table. The physical strain made Eli wince, and chipped away at his anger toward her. He pulled up a chair and tapped her gently on the shoulder. "Sit."

Grabbing Eli's arm for support, Hannah Bialika slowly sat down and placed the cane on her lap. "Thanks, kiddo." She looked at him as if she had never laid eyes on him before.

"Well, I saw that video that's going around. This invention of yours, dear, the little cloud factory, is extraordinary. Truly extraordinary. Bialika Industries would be happy to invest in your invention, if you're interested."

"That's a wonderful idea!" the council head cried out.

"For what percentage?" Eli asked.

"We'll leave that to the lawyers, I really don't concern myself with those things," Hannah said without looking at him. "The real question is how much money you need. A million? Two?"

"A million shekels?!" the spokeswoman gasped.

"Heavens no!" Hannah replied. "That wouldn't get you more than a few months of rent and payroll, and that's before you even said one word about R&D. I was talking dollars of course."

For everyone other than Hannah Bialika, the idea of a million—or two!—dollar offer casually dropped in the side room of the local rec center existed so far outside the realm of the possible that it rendered them dumbfounded. But the council head bounced back from his shock in a matter of moments. "Mrs. Bialika, your generous offer only serves to prove once again how lucky we are to have you as a member of our little community. If I may, I'll give our head of business development a call right now and set up a meeting for tomorrow, do it by the book."

"If Mandy or I had ever done things by the book, Bialika Industries would never have happened," said Hannah. "And also, you gave such a convincing speech that I'm eager to get going. It's high time there's a talented CEO who'll build a tech company down here. To make the desert bloom!"

"Excuse me, Mrs. Bialika," the spokeswoman said, "do you already have a particular CEO in mind, or are you talking metaphorically?"

"Does she look like a metaphor?" Hannah Bialika lifted her walking stick and waved it at Sarai.

"Ah, yes, of course, and that's a lovely idea," the spokeswoman offered, "it's just that management skills and inventiveness don't necessarily go hand in hand . . ."

"Phooey!" Hannah said and gave a dismissive wave. "All you need is common sense, and this one has it. She'll do very well."

"That's very flattering, Mrs. Bialika, honestly," Sarai said, thrown off by the surprise job offer, "but at this stage my invention is just a prototype. I don't exactly know yet what guarantees I can make . . ."

"No guarantees needed. If it works—good. If it doesn't—no harm no foul," she replied, opened her purse, and pulled out a pair of chunky black-framed glasses, a pen, and a checkbook. "Could someone please check the dollar rate and multiply by two million?"

"No, no, not like this," Eli insisted.

"Why not?" Hannah asked. She flipped open her checkbook and placed it on top of her purse.

"We're not signing any agreement before we understand exactly what we're committing ourselves to here." Eli's voice boomed. "And I'm not even sure two million would cut it."

"Drives a hard bargain, this kid. I could use him in my business department," Hannah remarked, smiling at Sarai. "All right, then we'll draft a proper agreement," she said, her pen still gliding along the check. "But for now, let's not waste any more time."

She capped the pen, tore out the check, leaned forward, and nudged it across the table. "I'm not twisting any arms. The first installment, half a million shekels, comes with no strings. Out of good faith. And a belief that down the road we'll reach an agreement that makes everyone happy."

"And if we don't?" Eli asked leerily.

"Then the money is on the house, as they say. A donation made by Bialika Industries to help develop the South."

She fished out of her purse a small white business card that said *Mandy Bialika, Founder of Bialika Industries* in silver embossed lettering and placed it on the table. "I ran out of mine, but that's our home phone number," she said, pointing to the number at the bottom. "Feel free to deposit the money and start scouting out office space and employees. We can handle the paperwork later, let's not waste time dotting i's and crossing t's." Saying it was time for her nap, she stood up, thanked the room, and started hobbling toward the door.

"How are you getting home?" the council head asked.

"There's a taxi waiting for me outside," she said, then paused.

"Eli, go help her," his mother prodded. He walked up to the old woman, took her arm, and, stooping to her height, guided her slowly across the rec center's empty foyer, whispering, "You're usually steadier on your feet."

"It comes and goes."

"It's not part of the act?"

"Act?"

"Pretending this is the first time we've met."

"Oh, I didn't want to embarrass you. I assumed you hadn't told them about your sleepover at the old kook's."

"So that's what this is about? All this just to try to get me to come back?"

"Oh, please, don't flatter yourself, I wouldn't go to that much trouble even for Charles Aznavour himself."

"Who?"

"Oh, to go through life without knowing who Charles Aznavour is." Hannah sighed. "Anyway, I would never invest in an idea I didn't believe in."

"Two days after I stop dreaming with you? Sounds like too much of a coincidence to me."

"You told me about the press conference, and I was curious to see the video. So I did. As simple as that."

The taxi was waiting for her in the parking lot. Faltering on the uneven cobblestones, she steadied herself against Eli, who in turn tightened his grip around her arm.

"And offering half a million shekels string-free, that's not weird?" he asked and opened the car door for her.

"That's a negotiation tactic," she replied. Carefully lowering herself into the passenger seat, she finally let out a sigh of relief. After the driver helped buckle her in, she took her walking stick from Eli, closed the door, and rolled down the window. "And besides," she grinned, "I told you, I don't do debts."

122
DAYS
TILL
RAIN

1

After asking him a third time to let her see, Naomi finally had to pry the check out of Boaz's hand. "She actually filled in that amount on the spot?" she asked. "I know people say she's nutty, but damn, that's wild!"

"They also bought the lot on the Cliff on their first visit," Boaz reminded her. "People used to say about Mandy that he could sniff out a good deal miles before anyone else. I guess she's the same."

"What do you think we should do?" Eli asked Naomi, placing a tray of baked potatoes on the table. His mother stabbed her fork into the tanned skin of one of them, feigning indifference to the conversation; but seeing how methodically she went at it, he could see she was listening. "Doing business with a capricious eighty-year-old doesn't sound like the best idea in the world, but then again . . ." Naomi remarked, her finger gliding smoothly across the dried ink on the check, "if she wants to throw a heap of money at Mom without any commitment on our end, it seems we've got nothing to lose."

Boaz smiled. "We need to grab this with both hands before she has a change of heart."

Sarai plopped a giant spoonful of chopped salad onto her plate with a blank expression.

"Don't tell me you're going to turn her down," Boaz said, resting his hand on her shoulder. She flinched.

"Come on, Boaz, I can barely manage a classroom of thirty kids, so building a startup from scratch?"

"Teaching thirty kids is a lot harder than building a startup," Boaz said, to which Naomi rolled her eyes. "At least give it a chance. You've been saving up for a new plasma cutting machine for a year now. With that check you could buy ten machines tomorrow!"

"I don't need ten," she replied with a note of disdain.

"Well, right now you can't afford one."

She shot him a pointed look. "I wonder whose fault that is."

The debt, like a fundamental physical constant, continued to affect their lives years after it had been paid off, indelibly engraved in the annals of the Lilienblum family history, and manifest in the smallest details—the notebook Boaz always carried around with him to write down every expense; Eli's heroic commitment to never eat out; Sarai's habit of diluting the dish soap. Having already shipped herself off to boarding school in those lean years, Naomi was the only Lilienblum who hadn't developed one or another frugal mannerism. If anything, it was the opposite. She often said she was busting her ass putting in twelve-hour days precisely so she could buy the most expensive tea at the store without giving it a second thought.

Eli and Naomi had seldom spoken about those years of debt, but the few times they had, he couldn't find the right words to articulate the trauma. "It's not like you were starving, or afraid you'd end up on the street," Naomi had rightly put it. And yet. There had been a devastating blow, and it left the three of them bruised. It was then that he had felt language's betrayal, its failure to describe the effect of such experiences, which certainly weren't the worst of human catastrophes but still upended something fundamental within the soul. In those years, Eli was plagued by an insatiable hunger, not for food but for something that to this day he struggled to explain. Solid ground? Air? Shelter? Yes, but not only. He tried to parse the feeling, thought back to moments when that hunger was particularly intense, like when he was fourteen, sitting at his mother's desk to write a school essay and discovering a rejection letter from a factory she had applied to—one in a long line of places where she had sought employment at the time. He remembered the sting of indignation, right above his diaphragm, outraged on his mother's behalf. His parents had experienced, during those taxing times, the brutal, painful awareness that they weren't destined to realize their dreams; eventually, his mother renounced her attempt to complete her engineering degree, and his father gave up his dream of turning the lodge into an international tourist center. Those were years of work, chores, sleep, and repeat. Life's untamed beauty had whittled down to an endless series of tasks. The world faded, and even after things had sorted themselves out, it never regained its former splendor.

"Go for it," Eli urged his surprised mother. "It's not about the money, it's about the opportunity," he stressed. Boaz nodded and added, "Exactly! What's so scary about opportunity?"

"If you think opportunity is what scares me, you must really not know me." Noting the insult stamped on his father's face, Eli marveled how he hadn't developed a thicker skin given the amount of snark he had gotten from his mother over the years. But Boaz often said that was the price of true love—letting your insides hang out.

"Come on, Sarai, it'll be an adventure, I'll help you."

"What do you know about startups?" she replied, exasperated. "Be real."

"Building a startup is not that different from building a hostel."

Naomi snorted. "Let's start with the fact that startups don't communicate via fax machines?"

"I have a phone, you know. And email!"

"That you don't know how to log into because you forgot the password," Eli remarked.

Boaz's brow unknotted. The three looked at him and burst into laughter so contagious Boaz couldn't help but chuckle. "Fine, technology isn't my strong suit. But can we at least agree that there are areas where I can be helpful?"

"I can think of a few," Sarai offered. Boaz's smile widened, and their son was soothed by the thought that amid the chaos that was his parents' relationship, there was love there too.

2.

The next day, a messenger appeared on the Lilienblum's doorstep and handed Naomi an envelope containing a legal document signed by Hannah Bialika, stating that a sum of five hundred fifty thousand dollars had been advanced to Sarai toward the development of a "cloud machine," without any conditions or limitations.

Another wave of rumors circulated through the community, the village abuzz with talk of the part-time teacher turned CEO of a promising hi-tech company, which received an investment of millions of dollars. Sarai didn't commit to spending the money, but she didn't rule it out either, which left just enough room for Boaz to wiggle into. Flipping his little notebook open, he made a list of potential office spaces, fixed a few sandwiches, took a bottle of water out of the fridge, and told Sarai they were going office hunting. He convinced Eli and Naomi to join, saying he could use their sway with their mother.

In their white Mazda they cruised the entire village, driving by an apartment for rent on the boardwalk and a vacant house right at the village entrance, a kindergarten on the verge of foreclosure and an empty floor in the council building. Boaz measured every room they walked into with his yellow measuring tape and jotted down numbers in his little notebook, despite Sarai ruling out every option one by one. When they arrived at two empty shop spaces on Nahal Grupit Street, the owner, a broad-shouldered man sporting a baseball cap with the logo of an American basketball team, greeted them warmly, having caught wind of the new startup. He said he'd love to help, promised to install a new AC unit in each room and offered a small discount in return for stock in the future company—having heard that the guy who painted the first Facebook offices became a millionaire after striking a similar deal. He described the dirt bike he'd splurge on if Ben Gould actually did end up buying the company, but his get-rich-quick dream was quashed when Boaz told him the space was unfortunately too small for their needs.

"That's too bad," the man lamented. "I do have a bigger place but it's a hangar out in the abandoned industrial area, and I doubt you'd be interested."

"What hangar?" Naomi asked.

He explained that fifteen years ago he was one of the suckers who'd bought into the council head's spiel about a thriving new industrial area. Not one to pass up an opportunity, he quickly took out a loan and bought two enormous hangars, vacant until today. "Bought a good few acres of nothing," he said with resignation. "Not even connected to the grid."

Sarai looked south, to where the industrial area lay hidden from view behind dozens of ski chalets. "Can we see it?" she asked.

"There's nothing to see, sweetheart, it's a dump."

"I understand that," Sarai said. "I'd like to see the dump."

It was a short drive, but at a certain point the road made way for a bumpy dirt trail and the white Mazda struggled to pull through, the bottom thumping and thudding along. When Eli got out, he saw six giant hangars standing side by side, some with pockmarked walls and caved-in roofs and others that were mere skeletal frames. Two dead traffic lights heralded the entrance to the compound, and weeds sprouted through the cracked asphalt of a defunct gas station. A small rock hyrax darted between the ruins, bobbing up between shards of glass and piles of plastic. "As you can see, not the best investment I ever made."

"Which one is yours?" Sarai asked, and the man pointed at the two closest ones, built across from each other and slightly less battered than the rest. The one on the left was nearly complete. With the others in tow, Sarai walked into a large space cluttered with dismembered furniture.

"A bit of a mess, huh?" The owner snickered. "I turned it into something of a scrapyard, you could say. Salvage dealers come by every now and then."

Sarai wandered around the junk-strewn place, her gaze traveling across the ceiling with her left eyebrow raised, something Eli had noticed her doing when she was working out in the yard, deep in thought.

"You were right, it's not for us," she told the owner as they walked out.

"Actually, I think that could work," Boaz said. "We'll take the hangars. We'll take them both."

"Whoa, wait a minute, Boaz, wait," Sarai interjected.

"Give me a few days to set the place up, and you'll see it's just what you needed," he asserted with a confidence that Eli noticed appealed to his mother while slightly unsettling the owner.

"I'm the last person to turn down money, but I feel I ought to reiterate that other than bare bones and plumbing, I can't offer much else."

"Don't worry." Boaz patted the man on the back. "We'll take care of the red tape."

"This is dumb as fuck," Naomi muttered under her breath. "No offense, but you're about to rent a junkyard, quite literally."

"You won't be calling it that in a few days." Boaz beamed, and Sarai silently nodded her consent.

"Flipped their lids, those two," she said to Eli, wiping her forehead.

He shrugged. "Don't tell me you're just now realizing that."

3

Boaz took on a one-year lease for both hangars, paid a few volunteers from the lodge to help him declutter the compound and patch up the walls, and made calls to the council and the electric company to power the area. The council head was so excited about the prospect of reviving the industrial zone that he promised to cover most of the repairs and fix the access road.

With everything set in motion, Boaz sent a mass text to all his WhatsApp groups: "Hi-Tech Employment Opportunity!!! Seeking individuals with strong technical skills and hands-on, can-do attitude, competitive salary and perks for the right candidates." He wanted to create a fait accompli before Sarai could change her mind.

Watching these developments with growing alarm, Naomi decided to extend her stay on the Cliff, and while it certainly made Eli happy, he suspected it was probably two parts concern, one part curiosity.

As the sun set on the village, Eli finished reviewing the list of expected hostel guests, and out of boredom found himself exploring the artifacts at the McMurphy Museum. He sought to learn more about McMurphy's life but soon realized that the objects there—mostly clothes and some maps—revealed little about the person he was. The only more personal items were torn pages from his notebook, filled with scribbling of strange abstract shapes, numbers, and faces of people Eli didn't recognize. Many of the faces bore a hint of sadness, prompting Eli to guess that they reflected McMurphy's own state of mind.

"Yes!" Tamara suddenly called out from the front desk, raising a triumphant fist in the air. She sat next to the computer, the T-shirt they had received from Paulina folded on the table next to her. Eli looked at the screen. She had entered "Robert McMurphy + St. John's Church + Dublin" in the search bar and clicked on the third result, which led her to a page with a photo of a man named Robert McMurphy.

"What does it say?"

"That he's a parishioner of the St. John's Church, and likes soccer—a Shelbourne F.C. fan—blueberries and hip-hop," Tamara replied.

"What gave you the idea to add Dublin and his first name?"

"Educated guess. After my first two hundred educated guesses didn't work."

Eli squinted at the screen. "It's a different guy with the same name," he said, but she was adamant. "It's him."

The guy in the photo was clean shaven, sporting a buzz cut, crisp white shirt, and blue tie, and bore absolutely no resemblance to the bearded, scruffy McMurphy captured in the dozens of photos taken in Israel. Eli got up, went to the museum room again, and came back with a photo of McMurphy posing by his bike with the Dead Sea stretching placidly behind him. Holding the picture up to the computer screen, he carefully compared the two images.

"You're right, it's him," he murmured. The same eye color, same eyebrow shape, same slightly larger-than-average jaw. It seemed he was looking at a man who had set out to reinvent himself.

Tamara navigated to the dedicated page for St. John's Church parishioners, learning that it was a Christian missionary organization centered around community involvement. She found an email address at the bottom of the page and sent an urgent request to be contacted regarding a parishioner named Robert McMurphy. "I can't believe you found that," Eli marveled. He assumed that over the years, his father had tried an infinite number of keyword combinations, and none had led him to that particular page. It took Tamara from Spain to crack the precise combination. She turned on some music, a live recording of a song in Spanish performed by a woman with a deep raspy voice and an energetic band. Cranking up the volume, she sprang to her feet and started dancing, sweeping her left hand high above her head and flicking her wrist with a tap and a stomp.

"Are we celebrating the accomplishment?" Eli asked.

"Not everything has to have a reason," she said, and extended her hand with a smile.

Before he could come up with an excuse to avoid dancing, Tamara grabbed his hand and yanked him toward her. Tumbling into her, he threw her off balance but immediately dove in to catch her in an awkward dip, and for a few breathless moments they danced clumsily—or rather, he danced clumsily, stiffly, his hand jammed between them, while she moved with elegance and rhythm. The idea of kissing her flitted through his mind, instantly crystalizing into desire. But before he could hatch a plan, a group of travelers walked in and Tamara broke free.

"Next time think faster," she said with a wink as she pulled away, her body still swaying to the music.

At night, strolling home along the boardwalk, he replayed the moment his hand brushed against her forehead. He wanted to imprint the scene—along with the scent of her hair—on his consciousness. Almost two years had passed since he'd last been that close to a woman's body. He had met his first, and so far only, girlfriend at an environmentalism seminar organized for soldiers serving in the south. They were together for five months, which sounded like a lot considering they only met up once every two weeks when their leaves aligned, and slept together a few times (sometimes he thought it was six, sometimes eight). They mostly met at her parents' house in Be'er Sheva because she told him it was too much of a hassle to get to his village, a fact she later cited as one of the reasons for breaking up with him.

Not far from Hannah Bialika's house, he spotted his mother in a purple sweatshirt peering out at the crater. As a kid, he avoided looking into the bottom of it at night. When he confided in his mother about this, she took him to the boardwalk one night, pulled out a laser pointer, and shone a bright green beam into the crater so he could see where it ended.

He walked up and stood quietly beside her until she turned to look at him, before shifting her gaze back to the crater. "Remember when we used to go to the colored dunes?" she asked.

It had been one of his favorite spots. Nine small mounds scattered at the heart of the crater, each in a different color. "I remember bottling the sand and selling it on the street. Ten shekels a pop. It was the most money I've made to date."

"And remember how angry you got when you found out the sand wasn't originally from there?"

He did. Vividly. It was a Saturday and Naomi, home from boarding school, told him the sand didn't originate in the crater. That it was transported once a month from various locations across the country and put there to dupe unsuspecting kids like him into believing it was a rare natural phenomenon.

"You wouldn't talk to me for three days straight," his mother said. "Your anger really stayed with me, you know? I don't think you realized how angry you were. I told your father I was afraid you would never speak to me again. And when I saw the colored dunes again a while back, it hit me. Suddenly it was completely clear to me that what bothered you wasn't the lie itself, but—"

"Wait, you were at the dunes? When? In your great disappearance act?"

"I just saw the dunes," she repeated. He could tell she'd just tossed him a clue, but he didn't know what to do with it.

4

With construction work on the hangar still underway, Boaz received the council's approval to hold interviews in the modest indoor basketball court at the rec center. "There's no point conducting interviews before you know what positions you're interviewing for," Naomi argued, but Boaz pretended not to hear. He was so happy Sarai had agreed to sit in that even his daughter's very sensible argument wouldn't deter him.

"That's not how hi-tech companies go about doing things," Naomi persisted, and Boaz said that was exactly why it was so important that she be involved in the interviewing process and teach them. He convinced Eli to join as well, citing the need for another young person's perspective.

When Eli, Naomi and Sarai arrived at the basketball court in the morning, Boaz had already set everything up. By the entrance stood a small coffee station, a handwritten "Welcome!" sign, and an applicant list. The basketball court was as small as Eli remembered, with only enough space for a single row of chairs against the wall. A folding table covered in a disposable white tablecloth was placed in the middle of the blue rubber surface, right on the white line. Hannah Bialika was already waiting for them at the table. They all settled around it and Naomi asked, "Can we maybe take two minutes to discuss what this company even needs?"

Sarai rubbed her earlobe. "I honestly have no idea. I've always worked alone."

The door swung open and in walked a woman wearing a tailored blouse, her red hair pulled into a tight ponytail. Eli had to do a double take to realize it was Paulina.

"Just a sec, please," Naomi called out, "we still need to wrap a few things up here."

Boaz shook his head. "People show up for their interviews on time, we shouldn't keep them waiting, it's unprofessional."

"Help yourself to some pretzels dear," Hannah said, while Naomi rolled her eyes. "Now, why don't you tell us a little about yourself?"

In a halting voice, Paulina shared her experience running a dry cleaners for the past fifteen years, describing her interactions with customers and suppliers.

"So, basically, tons of motivation, but no relevant experience or background, am I right?" Naomi said.

"That pretty much sums it up," Paulina confessed.

"And what would you say your edge is over more qualified applicants?" Hannah chimed in.

"I think I'm a very fast learner . . ." Paulina's voice quivered. "To be honest? I'm not sure why you should hire someone like me. But I do know that I really want the job, and that when I see an ark sailing by, I want on it."

"Ark as in Noah's?" Sarai asked.

"I think everyone you're going to interview from around here feels the same, that you've built Noah's Ark," Paulina said, looking Sarai straight in the eye. "You know better than anyone that down here people don't get too many new chances, so when opportunity comes knocking, they grab it with both hands."

Sarai leaned slightly forward.

"We're not building a nonprofit, we're building a startup." Naomi said, "and if we hire people who aren't right for the job, this ark is going to sink before it even leaves the port."

"You're absolutely right," Paulina agreed. "Business is business."

A silence fell on the room, and Paulina nodded with the understanding that the interview was over.

"True, but it happens to be an area relevant to our project," Sarai replied confidently.

"Relevant how?" Naomi burst out.

"Well, there is going to be a lot of technical work involving water," Sarai said, not clear to whom. "All that rain pouring from the clouds—

someone will need to make sure it doesn't ruin the machines. I actually think the technical department could use your services." Sarai smiled toward Paulina. "We haven't even decided yet whether we're going to have a tech department," Naomi seethed.

"Well, I just made that decision, and we are," Sarai said, her eyes shining brightly, and Eli realized she had just identified what truly got her motor running—ushering Paulina, and all the other future employees, through the gates of the promised hi-tech land.

Sarai asked Paulina if she had any questions she would like to ask them.

"Does your company have a name yet?" Paulina asked curiously.

Hannah mentioned she was thinking about "The Cliff Clouds" in Hebrew, but Naomi shot it down, arguing, "It has to be in English, and catchy."

"How about Cloudies?" Eli suggested hesitantly.

"That's an excellent name!" Paulina said, and Hannah nodded. "Yes, it's actually not half bad."

Giving her son an earnest look, Sarai said, "All right, that's settled then," agreeing on a name for her company in a matter of seconds.

They saw a total of twenty candidates that day. To Naomi's chagrin, the interviews consisted primarily of idiosyncratic questions that sprang from Sarai's and Hannah's fevered minds (What did you want to be when you were a kid? Who would you rather have coffee with, Clint Eastwood or Marie Curie?). They interviewed a salesclerk at a stationery shop, three teachers, a doctor, a private detective, a pastry chef, a blacksmith, a puppeteer, a wedding singer, and a multidisciplinary artist. Naomi lost interest after the sixth interview, spending the rest of the day staring into space or answering emails during the candidates' introductions. While he could empathize with his sister's frustration, Eli enjoyed seeing the sparkle in his mother's eye, excited about the prospects this venture held for her future. The only worthy candidate was the last, a business analyst from Microsoft named Sagi, who came all the way from Herzliya for the interview. But Sarai wasn't sure if he was suitable, arguing that letting a business analyst work in the business department is a bit "too obvious."

"You two are mental," Naomi said and screeched her chair back and stood up. "You hired every loon that walked through the door, and when finally, finally, by some miracle, a normal human being drives three hours to be here, you have doubts?! None of you at this table is qualified to determine the employees needed for a hi-tech company."

Hannah smiled at her peacefully. "In principle, you're right," she said. "To say I understand what your mom has in mind? I can't. But I can't say I understood what she was doing when she built her cloud machine either, so I'd rather follow her, than have her conform to how others do things."

"Okay, do whatever you think is best. I'm only here for a few more days, you're the ones who are going to have to deal with the repercussions."

"You can stay for more than a few days," Sarai said. "Be the vice president, or something like that."

"Vice president of what exactly?" Naomi huffed.

"Of whatever you want," she replied, making Eli envious of the invitation his sister had just received.

"And if I want to do things my way?" Naomi asked.

"Then you do you, and I'll do me." Sarai smiled.

"Are you actually considering taking Mom up on her offer?" Eli asked his sister at night from the other side of the wall. "If you're so sure this thing is going to flop, why be part of it?"

"You're smart enough to figure out why," Naomi said.

"I don't know. A more senior position for your CV?"

"You really see me as some heartless, career-obsessed woman, huh?"

"I don't think you lack a heart. It's just smaller than average."

She laughed.

"So, tell me, why?"

"Because if a month from now Hannah Bialika croaks, Mom's left with fifteen employees whose salaries she's responsible for," she said solemnly. "People are about to quit their jobs to join her mad tea party ride."

"I thought you said the problems on the Cliff weren't your problems," he reminded her.

"I have no idea what you're talking about," Naomi said, and Eli then reminded her of the summer break before her senior year of boarding school. She was home for a visit, and he told her about the debts their parents had racked up and about their mother taking a second job as a telemarketer. He knew his parents had been keeping her in the dark so as not to burden her with their problems, but he wanted her to know, wanted his big sister in the same boat as the rest of them. He vividly remembered her distant look when he told her.

"And you're claiming my response was that the problems on the Cliff weren't my concern?" she asked wryly, and he said yes. He knew she was putting on an act. That she remembered.

"Wow, then memory serves you wrong," she said. "Anyway, this time I'm here."

5.

Hours after notifying her boss that due to recent family circumstances she would be compelled to step down from her job, Naomi accepted her mother's appointment as CTO, alongside the promise of managing a team of real engineers.

Naomi's first order of business was to formulate a structured action plan. After a few days of intense negotiations between her and Hannah, the latter agreed to invest four million dollars in exchange for a thirty percent stake in the company. A bow-tied lawyer drove in from Jerusalem to have Sarai sign the paperwork, a task that Sarai delegated to Naomi and Eli, opting to spend her day treasure hunting through the piles of junk in the rented hangars, by the end of which her children had legally been declared the company founders. Despite it being a dull bureaucratic title and no more than a legal formality, Eli was still excited to be the founder of something. Naomi tried to explain that four million dollars was peanuts in terms of hi-tech investments, but Eli didn't know the first thing about hi-tech; he just knew that for him and his parents it was a fantastical sum.

The rumor about Hannah's multimillion-dollar investment spread through the Cliff like wildfire. A day after the contract was signed, several of the villagers approached Boaz asking to get in on the deal, perhaps the most surprising among them being the council's social worker, who knocked on their door armed with a check for ten thousand shekels and a claim of being a longtime admirer of Sarai's "inspiring creativity and genius mind."

Naomi suggested setting up a small fund for the locals who wanted to invest. Even if the accumulated amount would be chump change compared to the money from Bialika Industries, it would still serve as an extra source of funding, and more importantly, an excellent way to foster engagement and garner support from all the Cliff's residents.

As her next priority, Naomi hired an architect and interior designer to transform the old hangars into high-end offices. Sarai thought it was a little excessive and that buying some office equipment and giving the walls a fresh coat of paint would suffice, but Naomi made it clear that the ability to attract top talent hinged on things like the type of wood for the parquet flooring and quality of the coffee. Collaborating with the designer, Naomi opted for an open-plan office layout featuring two glass-walled rooms in the middle of the hangar, one for the team of engineers and another to serve as a conference room. The kitchen would be installed with a dining table in one corner, and the rest of the hangar left open-space with a scattering of round desks, beanbags, and a small recreational area equipped with a ping-pong and a foosball table. As a woman who'd built most of her inventions in the cramped and cluttered confines of her home study, Sarai was all but blind to aesthetic considerations, but a few casual remarks made in passing hinted at an underlying interest in the process ("Just make sure we have a nice espresso machine, and when you buy toilet paper get three-ply, if we're going all out . . ."). Although she would never admit it, not even to herself, Eli knew she was impressed by the excess. They were made from the same stuff, after all.

On the first day of work in Cloudies' history, construction on the office hangar was still in progress. Clad in a long-sleeved purple shirt buttoned to the hilt, the first employee to arrive at the scene paused at the entrance to the neighboring hangar, which was still full of broken furniture and other old junk. Slowly, others began to appear.

Eli took charge, fetching a large jerry can filled with tepid water and a sleeve of paper cups, while Sarai silently observed the newcomers with a curious gaze, eavesdropping on their awkward small talk.

"Shall we begin?" Eli suggested. His mother nodded but did little to advance the matter. Thinking on his feet, he suggested that everyone find a chair amidst the pile of junk. "Should we kick things off with a brief introduction?" A woman named Nava went first, introducing herself as an insurance agent for a company that had recently gone out of business.

"And what line of work would you pursue if money was no object?" Sarai asked.

"QA testing, the role you hired me for," Nava replied.

Sarai laughed, "Oh come on, no one dreams of working in quality assurance. What's your dream?"

"Probably being a baker."

Next to share was Yossi, who had worked as a plumber but dreamed of being a stunt pilot. Then came Paulina, the manager of the dry cleaners, who revealed a surprising desire to be a yachtswoman, and even mentioned her rich experience in reading nautical charts.

When the round was over there was silence, and Yossi, the stunt-pilot-plumber, raised his hand. "Mrs. Lilienblum, could you tell us a little about your invention process? How do you come up with your ideas?"

She told them that in the past, her inventions appeared the same way an itch starts. Out of nowhere. That she suspected everyone had those "itches," and the only difference between her and everyone else was that she couldn't ignore them. "I'm sure you know the feeling," she added.

"Actually, I don't," Yossi replied. "But it's super interesting to hear how a wacky head like yours works."

"I don't think it's *wacky*," Sarai muttered, and Yossi quickly apologized, said he had meant special, as in extraordinary. A tense silence prevailed over the room, until she looked at him and said, "You know what? Why don't you give it a try? What do you say that by tomorrow, you'll come up with a wacky invention of your own?" She smiled and looked around the room. "In fact, I'd love it if you all did that."

Feeling as if his presence there went largely unnoticed, Eli went to the lodge.

He found Tamara up on the roof, wearing a red FC Bayern Munich jersey, hosing the dust off it.

"Bayern? Seriously?"

"Don't tell me you're a fellow fan?" she said, spritzing his feet.

He laughed and said he wasn't allowed to support a German team.

She raised a perplexed eyebrow.

"You know, the Holocaust, the Nazis, all that jazz."

"So you're letting the Nazis dictate which soccer team you support?" She snorted. "Seems like you impose a lot of rules on yourself."

He picked up a mop and helped her steer the water toward the drain. He asked Tamara about her previous travels prior to her arrival in Israel, and she described volcanic mountains in Iceland that transported her to a different realm, cliffs in Scotland where the ocean crashed, and lakes in the foothills of the Pyrenees that looked like they were carved out of the sky. He didn't know where the Pyrenees were but didn't want to ask; he wanted her to think that he was as worldly as her, even though he'd only been abroad once. To Turkey. To an all-inclusive hotel with mediocre food that gave him indigestion. When he told her he preferred traveling within Israel, she nodded and said that for many years she thought you had to travel to the farthest corners of the Earth to truly get away, until one day, during a trip in Spain, she accidentally boarded the wrong bus and let it carry her to a small coastal town on the Atlantic where she spent three days in a hostel nestled inside a charming lighthouse striped white and blue, run by a sweet elderly couple who danced salsa with the guests every evening.

"It was just a thirty-minute drive from the beach I meant to visit, but it was there, out of all places, that I felt I'd reached a place outside space and time. I spent three days holed up on the top floor of the lighthouse just staring out at the ocean waves, and saw the most beautiful sunsets I've ever seen. A three-day break from the oppressive weight of reality," she said, and paused. "You should join me there someday. You'll fall in love."

He smiled. He didn't tell her he could picture only her and the lighthouse. Everything else was black.

6.

The following afternoon, the employees formed a messy line and waited for Sarai, each with their own invention. "I'd love to hear what you've come up with," Sarai said, but no one volunteered to go first.

Watching them, Eli was surprised to realize they were afraid of her.

Finally, Yoel, the security-guard-food-writer, walked over to a five-foot pile of interconnected pipes. In the center of the metal spaghetti ball were three main pipes, each featuring a small round hole. Yoel pointed at the stickers glued under each hole and recited: "Lemon, cherry, and grapefruit." Holding a bottle of mineral water, he explained, "You choose the flavor you want, and get the juice of your choice. At least that's the idea."

It struck Eli as a stale imitation of one of his mother's inventions. With a blank expression, Sarai accepted the bottle and walked up to the metal structure. Leaning slightly forward, her head cocked to the side, she scanned the pipes' intricate pathways. Yoel handed her a paper cup. "Name your flavor."

"Lemon."

He placed the cup under one of the pipes, took the bottle back from Sarai, and poured its contents into the hole. In seconds, the sound of sloshing water reverberating through the otherwise silent hangar, until finally lemonade with tiny bits of fruit came splashing out of the middle pipe onto the floor.

"Oh no, oh no!" he cried, apologizing profusely while looking for something to mop up the mess.

Sarai placed a hand on his shoulder. "You built a machine that turns water into lemonade and you're worried over that?" She gave him a warm look. "And you did all this in a day and a half? Unbelievable!"

Most people would focus on the flaws, but Eli knew that his mother truly didn't care about them, that her mind went instead to the possibilities, on the things that *could* be. To each of the twelve inventions presented to her, she managed to find something kind to say.

"Tomorrow we hunker down on the cloud machine, but I'm asking that each one of you keep working on your personal projects. Set aside at least one day a week for them, even two if you feel the need."

"This is outside of regular work hours, correct?" Naomi asked, leaning against the hangar wall with her arms folded. Eli hadn't noticed her come in.

"Goodness, no!" Sarai replied. "Why would anyone want to spend their free time on a project for work?"

Naomi didn't answer.

When they left the hangar Sarai was visibly excited. "Terrific inventions, huh?"

"Absolutely," her daughter replied, agitated. "If the idea was building a summer camp for adults. People left stable jobs for this adventure. The very least you can do is take their time seriously."

"I thought the whole idea behind startups is innovation, outside-the-box thinking. Was I wrong?" Eli continued to side with his mother.

Naomi sighed. "People left stable jobs for this adventure. The very least you both can do is take their time seriously," she said, and stomped off, leaving Eli and his mother standing next to each other in awkward silence.

7.

Two weeks had passed since the company launch, and construction work on the first hangar, intended to house the offices, was nearing completion. The other one, christened the "invention hangar" by the employees, remained in disrepair and disarray.

The first task Sarai assigned the employees of the R&D department was to build a larger prototype of the cloud machine. Confessing that the original cloud machine from the video was no more—but refusing to elaborate—she presented them with a new one, fashioned out of the old yellow vacuum cleaner she had tinkered with on the first day of work, the small plastic funnel attached to the top. Eli thought his mother would tell them about the construction process, but in lieu of explaining, she silently pulled out an extension cord and dragged the vacuum cleaner out to the hangar, cupped a small mound of sand on the ground, and switched on the device, which started to produce a loud noise. Having worked up the courage, Paulina was the first to step forward, grabbing the vacuum cleaner and driving it back and forth across the soft sand. A plume of white cloud emerged from the funnel, coiling up into the air and amassing over their heads. One after the other, the employees took turns with the yellow appliance, witnessing the miracle of turning sand into cloud. Watching in awe what they had created with their own hands—but without understanding how they had done it—they waited eagerly for the first droplets to appear, but unlike in the video, the cloud grew bigger while failing to release any rain. The workers noticed that the machine worked slightly differently when changing the type of sand; coarser kinds produced more impressive clouds, while gravelly sand proved less effective. This rudimentary discovery led to the establishing of a new subdivision, Sand and Research, that would determine the ideal sand type for cloud formation. Meanwhile, the business department ran a comprehensive market analysis (which mostly included extensive Googling), emerging with the conclusions that their technology was "highly innovative," and set the company's initial valuation at seventeen million dollars. (How the number was calculated didn't interest the employees as much as the number itself.)

It seemed as though the question on everyone's mind was whether Ben Gould would pay even more than he had promised. Most of them knew little to nothing about Gould and his work, but as time passed, his name had taken center stage in their discussions. They talked about his entrepreneurial adventures, about rumors involving an affair with a Hollywood starlet, his strange obsession with learning Yiddish, and paused meetings midway to read his latest tweets. With their words and hopes they spun Gould's image into a Rothschild-like tech deity, a philanthropist with an affinity for the Holy Land. They saw themselves as spirited pioneers and were understanding of the many growing pains, like the weeklong delay in putting in an office bathroom, or the fact that about a third of the first-month paychecks didn't reach their destination because the head of accounting had been a baker.

Additional investments by the company included establishing a restaurant where employees could use their prepaid lunch cards, renting a third hangar to build a movie theater, and allocating a travel budget for an innovations conference in Denmark. But despite Naomi's willingness to support many subjects that surprised Eli, there were certain unexpected investments she vehemently opposed—the chimney topping the list.

Eli encountered the towering ninety-foot concrete chimney one afternoon on his way from a shift at the lodge to the hangar compound. As he drew closer to the cylindrical giant, he wondered how his mother had managed to pull this one off.

A row of trucks stood at the compound's entrance carrying giant reinforced concrete pipes that were being stacked one by one. "One of the employees mentioned that his cousin works for the electric company and they'd just replaced a chimney," Naomi said wearily, leaning against the wall of the hangar, cup of coffee in hand.

Eli approached his mother, who was guiding a large crane with the same gestures as someone trying to straighten a picture on the wall. "Why exactly do we need a chimney?"

She looked at him and smiled. "I'm sure that with time we'll find out," she reassured, and unexpectedly, uncharacteristically, asked him to take her picture, posing with a proud yet slightly self-conscious smile. "By the way, it's a shame you're late, they're waiting for you."

"Who?" His eyebrows arched.

"Your employees," she said, and saw his face scrunch with confusion. "Oh no, no one told you we appointed you as head of the user experience department?" He wasn't even sure what user experience was. "We'll talk afterwards, right now they're waiting," she said, and pointed at the office hangar.

Awaiting him in the clear glass box in the middle of the hangar were three familiar faces whom Eli had met on the company's first day of work—Rivka the history-teacher-South-Pole-explorer, Yoel the security-guard-food-writer, and Paulina the dry-cleaners-manager-yachtswoman.

"Welcome, boss," Yoel said kindly.

"I'm no boss," Eli retorted, physically flinching at the word.

"You're not Sarai's son?" Rivka asked, lowering her glasses and squinting at him.

"He is," Paulina confirmed.

"Well, then you're the head of the department," Rivka said, smiling. "Too late to back out!"

They worked for two hours, although Eli would find it difficult to define their activities as work. The first half of the meeting was dedicated to discussing the associations that the word 'cloud' evoked for each of them. (Paulina mostly thought of "white," while Yoel mentioned more abstract concepts like "freedom" and "expansion"). In the second part of the meeting, they focused on the question of what would be the perfect texture for a cloud, something that could persuade people to pay for a service they are used to getting for free. Eli gently hinted that he wasn't sure this was the most productive use of their time, but his words were largely dismissed as the three employees continued to float ideas about how to make the cloud encounter a "more memorable experience," capping off the meeting with a round of compliments for the excellent work they had done that day.

Evening fell and the office cleared out. Eli made coffee for himself and Naomi. He found her in the aquarium. Handing her the coffee, he asked what she was working on.

"I'm trying to get the Airport Authority to issue an approval to set up a chimney," she said despairingly. "We have to buy aviation obstruction lights, but I can't seem to find the regulation requirements anywhere."

"I'm guessing you didn't have to deal with these kinds of things at your old job," he said, and she laughed, saying, "For now I'm mostly dealing with Mom's miscellany of whims and dreams, and dreams are not a business plan."

"But isn't that sort of how Steve Jobs founded Apple? I heard the stories."

"Nothing has done more damage to the hi-tech industry than *Steve Jobs stories*." Naomi sighed, and said that once every few years a Cinderella story comes along, and a young entrepreneur appearing out of nowhere takes the tech world by storm, making everyone else believe they stand a chance too.

"And what's wrong with that?"

"It's bogus. These people hardly ever come 'out of nowhere.' There's a reason these stories invariably happen in Silicon Valley or London, and not some village in Albania or shithole desert town."

"But look at you—you 'came out of nowhere' and made it."

"Because I left. If I'd stayed here and hoped things would work themselves out, I'd be just like them."

He knew that by *them* she meant *you*. "And yet these people here got a very generous investment from Hannah Bialika and are going about building a hi-tech company, so maybe they have some idea what they're doing," he said.

"You realize that the check she gave Mom, for half a million shekels, only covers one month's worth of rent and salaries?"

"One month?!"

"Hm. Twenty-eight days."

"Okay, but she promised to advance more payments."

"That's still being negotiated, the how and when. In the meantime, someone has to cover the cost of the chimney and the construction work."

"Who?"

"Who else would be willing to take out a two-million-shekel loan for our mom?"

"You took out a two-million-shekel loan?!"

"Are you deranged?"

"Dad?"

"Dad."

"Okay, but it's just temporary, Hannah will pay him back in no time," he tried to reassure himself.

"Nope. He and Hannah agreed to work out the profit distribution later on. He actually believes there are going to be profits."

"And does Mom know?"

"God no. And neither do you. Dad made me swear I wouldn't tell."

His mind was reeling with thoughts about his father. About the unimaginable risk he'd taken and the disaster he might bring down on them, dragging them right back into the pit. But there was one thought that kept bobbing up above the rest. "He really believes in her, huh?"

"You are really your father's son," she said snarkily, but he took it as a compliment. "I'm a little less optimistic than you. I think we need to have some rainy-day insurance."

"Sounds wise, what did you have in mind?"

With a hint of hesitation, she tilted the screen toward him and he noticed she was in incognito mode. Naomi typed in the name of a website.

"I've opened a bank account, and this is the plan," she said. He didn't remember when he'd ever heard her sound less than sure of herself. The amount, seven hundred and forty-three dollars, appeared in small digits in the middle of the screen.

"Your bat mitzvah savings? That's your big plan?" he said facetiously, but not a muscle moved in her face.

"I kept up the *general's correspondences*," she said, and it took him a moment to recall what general.

"Wait, and people actually sent you money?"

"Eleven," she replied, and started hurling numbers at him. "The average amount paid is sixty-six dollars and thirty cents. Most users are over fifty-six, and female—"

"You think I care about the numbers? This is fraud," he cut her off.

"I see it differently," she said off-handedly, as if they were talking about a TV show rather than a criminal act. "It's a social tech service."

Eli burst into an exaggerated laughter.

"You can laugh all you want, but these people sending money are desperate for human connection. To feel close to someone, to experience an unexpected adventure and escape life's monotony. These emails alleviate their loneliness. If you think selling people some kitchen appliance they don't need is a more ethical act, you're wrong." Once again she wielded her greatest weapon—breaking down an inconvenient reality into a series of logical explanations. He knew she was wrong, but couldn't explain why. He took another look at the number on the screen. Seven hundred and thirty dollars. "To break the law for that? It's nowhere near the amount we need."

"With a little work, it could be." She explained that through fairly simple algorithms she could create an autoresponder that could potentially generate a substantial amount of money. "Look, if it's important to you, we can make sure the maximum transfer amount doesn't exceed three hundred dollars, which is money that could add up but also won't make anyone lose their home."

"If it's important to me? What's wrong with you? It's illegal and immoral, and you know it."

"And plunging our parents back into debt, that's moral? Making them work until they're eighty years old to repay the loan Dad took out, that's the moral thing to do?" Her voice cracked. She seemed genuinely upset, and it dawned on him that perhaps the years of debt, when she was far away at boarding school, affected her more than he'd realized.

"Then let's make sure the startup is a success," he replied.

She considered him for a drawn-out moment, then snapped the laptop shut. "I'm not going to do anything serious with the general's emails thing only because I'm afraid you're stupid enough to go to the police with it," she said and got up. "But if everything falls apart, don't say you had nothing to do with it."

8

After the holidays blew over Naomi managed to recruit five qualified engineers to join the company, luring them all the way from
Tel Aviv with a generous signing bonus.

From the sidelines, Boaz, with something akin to childlike wonder,
observed the startup starting to come together. He had no place in the
company that was slowly taking shape. Every evening after dinner, as the
family ferried themselves to the living room and words like "ecosystem"
and "networking" started flying over his head, his body slightly tensed,
like a man ill at ease in his own home. At first he tried to delicately
deflect the conversation and steer it toward topics such as the Nubian
ibex mating season or the new hiking trail that had opened in the
southern part of the crater, but eventually he abandoned his attempts
and withdrew into himself. "What can I say, big things are happening
in the world right now and I won't be a part of them," he told Eli one
evening as they were doing the dishes, and Eli knew he was right,
despite not being sure their startup would become one of those big
things. Paulina had told him that their department was "not so much
research and sand as lost and found," a place where things lost their
original meaning and new meanings were found; where objects were
dismantled and stripped of their familiar uses to be reborn in new,
exciting ways. Sand was transformed into fuel for clouds, an old chimney to a cloud pipeline, a cook into a climate engineer. These reshuffles
created a distinctly unique and fascinating picture, no one doubted
that, but Eli feared that the picture was pretty only from a distance, and
that a closer look would immediately reveal the sloppy brushstrokes,
like embarrassing payroll mix-ups or entire workdays squandered on
heated debates as to who should be awarded employee of the month.
Sarai was disinclined to deal with such trivialities, but the truth was,
she didn't particularly enjoy the more crucial aspects of her job either;

working at a startup meant committing to the same invention for the long haul, which went against her restless nature of bouncing from one invention to another in a matter of days. Eli had often asked his mother why she so rarely finished most of the inventions she started, but surprisingly enough it was his father who replied, explaining that for Sarai, the completion was always the most disappointing part, because it forced her to accept everything the invention wouldn't be.

Sarai had asked all Cloudies employees to take a *creative day*—a day in which they were encouraged to do whatever they felt like as long as it was completely unrelated to their daily office work. Whereas his sister shook her head in dismay, Eli jumped at the opportunity and decided to spend his creative day with Tamara at the lodge. While the prospect of an entire day alone with her was spine-tingling, as evening approached he began to feel a tinge of regret for missing the weekly UX team meeting, and thought that perhaps his mother actually understood a thing or two about management. The thought capsized the following morning when he showed up for work and found a camel at the entrance to the hangar.

9

Tethered to the bike rack alongside a few bikes and an electric scooter, the camel stood tall and well-groomed, munching from a large basket of prickly weeds and drinking water from a metal bowl. The employees who entered the hangar seemed oblivious to his presence, as if he'd always been there. Eli ogled the camel from up close, but the animal displayed utter indifference to the encounter.

Paulina emerged from the hangar with a heavy-duty staple gun and several large, white, cloud-shaped cardboard cutouts. Eli asked her about the camel.

"Never mind about him right now, help me hang these," she said while positioning the cutouts on the exterior wall of the hangar. "They'll be here any minute."

They turned out to be a delegation of international businesspeople invited by the Ministry of Science and Technology to tour Israeli factories, and were making their way to the desert at that very moment. They had planned to view a few factories on the northern border but, due to an unforeseen security alert, were diverted southward.

The employees giddily grouped at the entrance, watching the cavalcade of black SUVs slithering toward the compound. Eli and Paulina, in the process of hanging the last cloud when they saw the approaching vehicles kicking up dust, quickly abandoned the lopsided cutout to join their colleagues. Standing by the door with her ever-present cup of coffee was Naomi, who walked up to him.

"Guess how much that camel cost."

"A thousand shekels? Two thousand?"

"Seven." She paused for a sip and added, "And an extra three thousand for transportation. And five hundred shekels for his food."

"What on earth?"

Naomi shrugged.

The vehicles pulled into the makeshift sandy parking lot, and a group of businesspeople in suits and jackets—an aberration in the torrid desert—climbed out. They regarded the large chimney and hangars with sober expressions that lit up once they caught sight of the camel. With cautious excitement, they inched toward the animal and whipped out their phones to take his photo against the cardboard clouds. A few feet away, Sarai was waiting for the group in a white lab coat over blue jeans and what seemed to Eli—he had to really squint to be sure—a touch of makeup. Before she had the chance to introduce herself, a woman in a navy pantsuit asked her if she was the famous entrepreneur from the video.

Sarai nodded, and the group gathered around her. One of them pointed at the camel and asked if it was an employee's ride to work.

Sarai smiled. "No, no, Alex is our family camel," she said, gesturing at Eli and Naomi by way of introduction. "We used to ride him quite often, but now he's retired."

"There's no way they're buying that," Naomi whispered to Eli, trying to stifle a laugh, but Eli could see how they hung on her every word as she spun a tale about the day Alex ran away from their backyard and after a frantic three-day search was finally spotted in a junkyard snacking on the remains of an old car. She said that in Hebrew there were seventeen different words for camel, and luckily the visitors didn't ask her to list them. He realized the delegates hadn't traveled to Israel to deepen their knowledge of the desert or the country as a whole, but rather to confirm their conviction that life in their faraway homelands was more comfortable and all around better. And that was a feeling his mother knew how to inspire.

Inside the hangar, the visitors were greeted with a modest-to-sad spread of cookies, filter coffee, and the most basic of teabags. There was no sign of the extravagant espresso machine or the elegant cuisine prepared by professional chefs.

Walking into the hangar, Eli was surprised to discover that the heaps of junk had disappeared without a trace. The hangar now appeared spotless, with eight gleaming white tables arranged neatly in the center. The employees standing by the tables were clad in white coats—identical to Sarai's—all holding test tubes of odd shapes and sizes.

"What's in the vials?" asked an older gentleman leaning against his walking stick.

"Cloud compounds."

"They're chemists?"

Sarai pointed at two of the employees. "She's a pharmacist and he's a plumber."

"So what exactly qualifies them to manufacture clouds?" the older businessman asked.

"Nothing, which is precisely why they were chosen."

Yossi the plumber demonstrated to the guests how the yellow vacuum cleaner coughed out a white cloud that floated up to the hangar ceiling before dissipating—a spectacle the visitors giddily documented with their phones.

"And what about the rain?"

His mother was about to answer but Eli beat her to the punch, explaining that "we're just updating versions," a response the visitors seemed to take at face value, even as a few didn't hide their disappointment. "But how does sand even turn into a cloud?" a woman asked, and Yossi confessed that he didn't know.

"Then how do we know it's not some hoax?"

Yossi shifted his gaze to Sarai. "Maybe you can tell us?"

"He's kidding. As you might expect, that's proprietary knowledge," Eli hurriedly interjected. "It's unique, state-of-the-art, completely innovative technology that my mother developed and that's currently in the process of being patented."

The conversation steered toward intellectual property, and Eli knew that had his mother been given the opportunity, she would have come clean, would have admitted that she was equally baffled.

Stepping into the other hangar, Eli discovered that what had only a short while ago been a ramshackle structure was now a state-of-the-art, spotless movie theater with rows upon rows of wide, cushy chairs and a massive screen. Sarai pointed at two make-your-own-popcorn machines in the corner and said she'd built them herself. Inviting the guests to give them a try. When a visitor jokingly suggested watching a movie, "if we're already here," Sarai asked Paulina to switch on the projector.

"Just press that button over there," she said. Paulina did as she was told, and a moment later the screen came to life with the slightly blurry image of two little children and a young woman in a green field.

"That's that movie by the Czech director, isn't it?" one of the visitors whispered, to which another replied confidently, "Yes, it is."

Paulina tinkered with the lens until the picture snapped into focus, and Eli immediately recognized the people on the screen as his mother along with his and his sister's younger selves. His whole body clenched with dread as he imagined the strangers next to him watching a Lilienblum home movie, which had somehow found its way onto the big screen. From his mother's blank expression in the darkened theater, he couldn't tell if it was a glitch, or if she had planted the footage there. Roaring winds sounded from the speakers as the businesspeople stared spellbound at the screen, some of them settling into seats in the back rows.

"Are you sure this is a good idea?" he heard his father's voice in the film, coming from behind the camera. His mother looked up, holding a box of matches. She was beautiful. Young. Smiling.

"Let's find out," she said.

The camera slightly shook as his father called him and his sister over, and they ran past the camera, taking cover behind him. Sarai held a ballpoint pen up to the camera and told Boaz to zoom in.

"Eli asked me if it was possible to make a homemade rocket, so we decided to find out," she said proudly. "We emptied the pen of ink and filled it with incendiary powder we scraped from matchsticks, and—" She placed the pen on a small wooden stand, pulled a long string that she had tied to the pen, and lit the match, burning the string's fuse. As she stepped outside the frame, the flame started traveling slowly toward the pen.

"Everyone, duck!" her voice resonated from the speakers.

The entire theater tensed as the camera swerved; a split second later a loud pop, like a Champagne cork going off, echoed through the room. The lens followed the pen as it shot up into the air, reaching peak point before disappearing beyond the horizon. The guests gasped, oohing and aahing—there was even a single clap. The movie came to a halt and the lights came back on. "I think this is a good place to end our tour," his mother said, looking slightly embarrassed, either from showing the home video or from the collective enthusiasm. Eli couldn't tell.

"Wait. I'd like to say a few words," the older businessman said to Sarai and the rest of the group, taking a step forward and leaning on his walking stick. "I've been in the business world for forty years, Mrs. Lilienblum, and I've never seen a company run like this. With completely arbitrary departments that seem no more than suggestions, and employees without the slightest relevant qualification or experience," he said sternly. "If we're being honest with ourselves, what we've seen here today is mostly chaos." He fell silent, and Eli cast an anxious glance at his mother. "But our world was born out of chaos, and after visiting here today, I'm beginning to understand why. To create something new, you must first tear down the old, and that is something, Mrs. Lilienblum, you seem to know how to do better than any of us."

Many in the audience nodded as the scattered impressions of what they'd seen that day suddenly aligned into something comprehensible. Eli saw his mother's pursed smile slacken and her whole body exhale, giving it more space to inhabit.

The members of the delegation approached Sarai to shake her hand before filing out of the hanger, each to their own car.

A young man in a suit, about Naomi's age, walked up to Sarai and introduced himself as the representative of several businessmen who invested in interesting startups in Israel. He said he'd love to explore the possibility of a professional collaboration, and Sarai promised to pass on his details to their business department.

Eli doubted it would go anywhere, not only because the business department wouldn't know what to do with such a thing, but because he knew his mother, and she wasn't one for collaborations. And while this bothered him at first, now it seemed to make sense. He realized that if they had a shot at making it, it wasn't despite his mother's chaotic and irresponsible way of doing things, but thanks to it.

A few days later, Naomi was contacted by a representative from the Ministry of Science and Technology, who said the visit to Cloudies had been an extraordinary experience and they would be delighted for Sarai to participate in the annual Jewish Hi-Tech Conference in Tel Aviv. She added that her mother's "bold creativity" was exactly the spirit they wanted to present to the world. When Naomi replied that they would have to think about it, the representative admitted that they'd actually already spoken to Sarai and she had accepted their invitation, requesting only that Naomi be updated.

61
DAYS
TILL
RAIN

1

The rare artifact arrived at the museum on an autumnal afternoon. Two Israeli hikers said they'd found it that morning on a large rock with a trail mark on it, right next to the overnight camping site where they'd slept.

After finishing a series of back-to-back meetings at the office, Eli went to the lodge to examine the object. He recognized the black work boot—foreign to the Israeli desert—from a few photos in their possession. It was McMurphy's. Inside the boot the hikers found a drawing, which Boaz now showed to Eli: a yellow square Post-it with a pen sketch of a young woman's face, and his initials, RM, in the bottom left corner. The woman's long hair fell over her eyes, and her features were soft and delicate.

"I think she mattered to him, the woman he sketched," Tamara said, studying the image over Eli's shoulder. He thought it a presumptuous statement to make, and yet, when he looked at the sketch himself, he felt that there was a measure of truth in her words.

"Hey, maybe you could bring your parents' car and we'll go see if there's anything else lying around there, at the bottom of the crater?" she suggested. Eli wasn't sure he wanted to spend the night in the crater, but he was very sure he wanted to spend it with her.

They arrived at the overnight camping site, which stood on a small hill at the side of the crater, as the sun was about to set and the temperature started to drop. A solitary car, gray and abandoned, was parked at the far end of the site. Tamara started walking toward the rock with the painted trail mark the hikers had described, and Eli followed. She was wearing her coat with the pink, gold, and white triangles, while he remained coatless and cold. Seeing him hugging himself, she reached into her backpack and fished out her white scarf. "I've already learned that Israelis are ill-equipped to handle any weather below fifty-nine degrees Celsius."

The rock sat at the exit to the camping site, large and impossible to miss, with a clear and prominent trail mark—a horizontal blue stripe between two white ones. Tamara canvassed the area like a pro, leaving no stone unturned, going at it with gusto. She reminded him of his father when his mother had gone missing. Eli advanced a little farther into the desert, recalling an article that claimed there wasn't a single patch of land in Israel where you couldn't find evidence of human interference—some road or power line was always bound to be nearby. When he told his mother about the article, she said it made her feel trapped. But he found it comforting, the idea that wherever you went, you would never be completely alone.

Darkness descended and they walked back to the car, opened the trunk, and took out a tent and some sleeping bags from the lodge's storage shed. Eli set up the tent while Tamara stacked the logs they'd brought with them and lit a small bonfire. Sitting side by side by the fire, he told her about the time he went on a trip with the local scouts. He was very young, and when the counselor asked him to fetch some twigs to build a fire, he didn't know that twigs were just small branches, and was too embarrassed to ask. For half an hour he searched high and low, without knowing for what, and eventually returned to the group with every type of flower he could find, hoping that one of them was a twig. The counselor and kids couldn't stop laughing.

He chuckled, but Tamara stared silently at the fire. "Sounds lonely," she said, and slid her hand into his front shirt pocket. With her free hand, she reached into her own pocket, took out a creased, folded note, and gave it to him. Opening it, he saw it was an address scribbled in English: 7 Fine Street, Tel Aviv, ground floor.

"It's the address of the church McMurphy must have visited on his trip," she said. "That's where he got the shirt Paulina gave us. I sent an email to the parish office and they wrote back. When you go to Tel Aviv for the conference, pass by the church," she requested, and he felt oddly envious of the inexhaustible interest she took in McMurphy.

"Hey, what did you want to be growing up?" she asked him, and he told her his mother always said that was the dumbest question you could ask a kid. "It's like telling them—in the end, out of the infinite possibilities—you'll only be one thing, so you better start getting used to the idea."

"That's a great answer," she said, smiling. "But what do you want to be? Let's say the startup blows up, and each one of you walks away with ten million dollars, then what?"

For a moment he let his imagination run wild, getting lost in a reverie about a big exit. Making millions. He told her that if that happened, it wouldn't be the wealth itself that would make him happy so much as the idea of financial security. He tried picturing a life free of financial stress and compared it to imagining a world void of gravity or air. A fanciful existence. "Seems like that's what you're always looking for, constant certainty," Tamara said, and when she noticed his brow furrowing, added, "That wasn't meant as an insult, Eli, it's human."

"So what do you want to be when you grow up?" he asked, hoping to shift the focus away from his defects.

She said that traveling around the world made her realize there were a lot of people whose voices weren't heard, and that she could be their megaphone. Maybe a serious journalist, or a politician.

"And how exactly does being in this godforsaken part of the Israeli desert bring you closer to that goal?"

"It doesn't." She surprised him, admitting it was by strange circumstances that she'd found herself in the Holy Land.

"What circumstances?" he asked, but she wouldn't say.

A sudden gust of wind sent sparks from the bonfire flying into the air, falling like rain onto the tips of their shoes. She dug her hand deeper into his pocket and leaned into him. Her kiss was soft and startling, his body remained stiff and he didn't know what to do with his hands.

She leaned back with her head tilted and gave him a searching look.

"You don't have a body," she said.

He didn't understand.

"Desire is a corporeal experience," she explained, stroking the scarf around his neck. "You move through the world as if you're bodiless."

She took a cigarette out of her pocket, lit it, and exhaled a cloud of smoke before asking if it bothered him. He said it didn't.

She laughed and stubbed out the cigarette. "Who do you think you're fooling? It obviously bothers you. But you're always like this, self-sacrificing, especially with your family. Devoting your every waking hour to their dreams instead of taking a moment to find out if you have a role to play in them."

"What does my family have to do with anything?"

She glided a warm hand across his stubble, melting away any traces of budding anger, then silently rested her head on his shoulder. He closed his eyes, and she put her hands under his shirt to keep them warm. Her hands were freezing, and yet, he hoped they would stay there for good.

A few wayward strands of her hair brushed up against his nose, tickling. He smiled.

She shook him awake before the crack of dawn. The fire had died out and the cold hit him hard. "Get up, get up already," she chided. "He's here."

"Who?" he asked. Without answering, she got up slowly and stealthily, to gaze out at the far end of the site. Darkness surrounded them. He heard noises, heavy footsteps in the distance. "See?" she asked.

It took his eyes a few moments to adjust, but when he saw it, his heart started to race. The figure was advancing toward the marked rock where the boot had been found, a few dozen feet away. It walked with a stoop, its feet illuminated by a flashlight's feeble beam. When it reached the rock, it started circling it slowly. As Eli strained to focus his gaze, the tiny beam began to dance in an eerie glow. For a split second the light shifted upward to reveal an orange beanie and blue scarf. All those years, he'd dismissed the stories of tourists encountering a mysterious figure that appeared in front of them out of nowhere, smack in the middle of the desert, and now there it was, in front of Eli. He recognized McMurphy's hesitant and anxious body language, having heard so much about it. Could it be?

A second light lit up the darkness, this time right next to him. Tamara had inadvertently touched the screen of her phone. "Turn it off," Eli whispered, but the figure must have detected them, as it started to draw away deeper into the crater.

"Hey! Wait!" Eli cried out in English and began running after the figure, who in the meantime had switched off his flashlight. "Hey!" he called out again. Tamara hurried after Eli, who was focused on his steps, afraid of tripping in the dark. When he passed the pile of rocks, the figure disappeared.

"He probably went there," Tamara said, pointing to the wadi at the foot of the hill, and started down the slight slope. He rushed behind, trying to keep up with her. He couldn't match her nimbleness as she weaved between the stones and rocks. Though difficult to admit even to himself, he was relieved to have been spared a confrontation with the figure.

"We lost him," he said. Ignoring him, Tamara kept wandering around the wadi, searching, with Eli lagging silently behind.

They returned to the tent at dawn, the desert chill seeping into his bones. Before he could decide if and how to sidle up against her, Tamara was already slithering into her sleeping bag.

He followed suit, slipping into his own bag. The care label claimed it was suitable for temperatures down to twenty-eight degrees Fahrenheit, but that turned out to be a lie. McMurphy drifted further and further out of his mind, until all that was left in it was the cold, and the distance between him and Tamara.

They woke up with the first light, side by side and silent. As the sun rose in the sky and warmed the landscape, they wriggled out of their sleeping bags and Tamara started walking toward the signpost rock.

"Look," she called out, picking up a key with a yellow cover from the ground. She handed it to him with a satisfied grin. "I bet you wanted to kill me when I insisted on going into the wadi, huh?" She laughed, and the distance he imagined between them dissipated like a cloud. Eli took the dust-coated key and inspected it; it bore no signs that betrayed where it had come from, yet confirmed the presence of the person they had seen the night before. "You think it belongs to McMurphy?"

"I have no idea. But I know he was looking for it."

The whole ride back, Tamara held the key in one hand and Eli's hand in the other—leaving him with only one hand to steer with and little desire to mention the safety issues it posed. Halfway back, next to an unmarked dirt trail, she told him to take a right. When he asked why, she told him to trust her. He navigated the car along the narrow footpath, small stones crunching under the wheels. They drove silently for five, maybe six minutes until she said, "Pull over there."

The "there" she was pointing to seemed entirely arbitrary to Eli, seeing that nothing marked the spot, not a tree, not even a rock. Tamara rolled down the window and jutted her chin forward. "That's where they found her."

"Who?"

"Your mother." She told him that on the day they first met, she went down to the crater with a few hikers to try to shed some light on what had happened; their hope was that the person who had been discovered was McMurphy. Eli pulled the handbrake, switched off the engine, and got out of the car. Walking toward the spot Tamara had indicated, he couldn't understand how she had recognized it. There was nothing there but a scattering of stones and a ravine hiding between the bushes. He squared his shoulders and took in the landscape.

"Okay, don't go all Debbie Downer on me, it's just the spot where they found her, not the Memorial to the Murdered Jews of Europe," she said, and he burst into a liberating laugh. He told her he'd already begun to feel like the world's worst son, standing in front of the spot where his mother was found and not feeling anything in particular.

"Sounds like she would have reacted the same way."

He started wandering around, trying to picture his mother in her bathrobe roaming the exact same place. He cast another glance at the bushes, and something red caught his eye. Was he imagining things? He couldn't believe he was seeing what he was seeing.

Nestled innocently behind the thorny branches was the red vacuum cleaner from the video, the very one Sarai had used to bring down the rain. Unpacking the equipment in the lodge's storage room, Eli asked how it was possible that no one before him had noticed the red vacuum cleaner there. Tamara suggested that the rescuer might have been so shocked by the sight of a woman in a burgundy bathrobe and martini glass that he'd missed it. Or that maybe something in the terrain had changed since she was found. Or maybe a goat had dragged it out of its hiding place. Pondering the possibilities, Eli recalled his father telling him that there was nothing more alive than the desert. He stashed the vacuum cleaner in the back of the closet and decided not to tell anyone about it just yet, fearing overzealous fans might try to steal the famous appliance featured in the video. He examined it from every angle, but couldn't find anything special about it. Nothing that could explain why that particular machine yielded rain when all the others they had experimented with at Cloudies had failed so miserably.

As they returned the supplies, they came across Morgenstein's blueprints on one of the shelves. Tamara was intrigued, and Eli unrolled the sheet onto the floor. It was a design of a house on the Cliff, he didn't know whose. Poring over it together, he showed her two narrow Morgenstein alcoves connecting the rooms, and a door in the bathroom that led nowhere. A few short notes in a language he didn't recognize were scribbled along the margins, together with a large X in the corner of the page and three words in English—*Do Not Use!* Breaking the promise he had made to his father, Eli told Tamara about Morgenstein, the architect who was never an architect. "That explains a lot," she said with a smile, sweeping her gaze across the other items on the storage room shelves. "What's that?" She reached toward something resembling a can opener taped to a black pen.

"No no no!" he called out, and she quickly withdrew her hand, as if from a smoldering coal.

"Relax, it's just a pen," she scolded.

"It's not. It's a laser pointer. The gadget is supposed to be a can opener with a laser cutter."

"I gather it doesn't work if it ended up here."

"On the contrary, it works *too* well." He told her the can opener was so impressive that his father asked Sarai to make him another one as a birthday present. "But when he inaugurated it by opening a can of corn, he also cleaved the table and scorched the floor with the laser beam." Tamara laughed that light blue laugh of hers.

They had almost finished organizing the storage room when a thick, dense cloud began to gather over the lodge.

2

Eli and Tamara didn't know about the cloud-stabilizing experiment scheduled for that morning, but even if they had known, they probably wouldn't have paid it much attention. The experiments had become an everyday event for the employees of the R&D department, who persisted in their search to find the exact chemical composition of a rain-producing cloud. Among the frustrated employees, a stubborn rumor had begun to circulate that maybe the droplets in the video weren't real, and that even the great Sarai Lilienblum didn't know how to turn sand into rain. But then, one morning, Yossi the plumber added a little baking soda and green dish soap to the sand, and the cloud ballooned. Sarai declared it the progress they'd been waiting for and decided to inaugurate the big chimney, hoping the experiment would finally yield the much-anticipated rain. However, as he was writing down the recipe, Yossi inadvertently tacked on two extra zeros to the baking soda, and not a single employee thought to second-guess the numbers. (The pharmacist overseeing the experiment suppressed her suspicions, not wanting to miss out on the complimentary taco truck.)

The cloud invaded every house, spilling into the lodge's compound. Tamara and Eli were alone in the storage shed of the nearby restaurant when a delicate, cumulus layer swept into the room, slowly covering every inch. Eli thought it was just an especially misty morning, and it was only when the village's alert system sounded that he realized something wasn't right.

Tamara left the storage shed and opened the lodge's front door to see what was going on; within moments, a thick cloud invaded the room, forming a dense white screen.

Virtually blind, Eli called out her name, fumbled his way forward, reached out, and pulled her close. Even when she was in his arms, he still couldn't see her face. He took his phone out of his pocket and called Naomi.

"Don't bug me, I'm working on it!" his sister shouted at him and hung up.

"Well, this is no fun," Tamara said.

The alarm ceased, and an announcement blared throughout the village informing of a cloud leak from the factory. The residents were instructed to stay where they were even if they knew their way around, with a polite reminder that they lived on the edge of a crater. Apologizing for the temporary inconvenience, the announcer assured them the best and brightest minds were working to resolve the issue.

"He expects us to just stand here?" Eli huffed, mostly on Tamara's behalf. He was used to the village's mishaps and malfunctions.

"I have no idea what they're expecting." Tamara broke free of his embrace and started for the restaurant door, where she bumped into a table and let out a miserable groan. Eli felt his way to her, the sound of the industrial ACs outside rumbling through the silence.

He heard coins rolling across the floor. "Leave it, just go see that my note hasn't fallen somewhere," Tamara said.

"What note?"

"With the church's address. McMurphy's church."

"McMurphy's what you're thinking about right now?" He took her hand.

"Why, are you jealous?"

"No. I just don't get the obsession."

She pulled her hand away, and he regretted the word choice. She lay down on the floor and he joined her, their shoulders touching.

"Do you know the story about Jim Carrey's dad?" She told him she once saw a video of Jim Carrey giving a speech at some hippie college graduation, where he described to the graduates that his dad had always dreamed of being a comedian, but chose to work as an insurance agent because it was a secure job. His father spent his whole life miserable, only to get fired in the end, because he was never actually any good at his secure job. "And that was the moment Jim Carrey realized that if

you could get fired from a supposedly secure job, you might as well do
something with your life that you want to do."

"And what does that have to do with your interest in McMurphy?"

"Trust me that by the end of the story you'll understand," she said,
and launched into a second one about her parents—"both economists,
total squares, the nerdiest, sweetest couple you'll ever meet. They
worked their whole lives at big corporations with steady salaries only to
realize at fortysomething that they might have missed out. So just like
that, halfway through life, they quit their safe jobs and opened a small
restaurant on a Greek island. We flew to Santorini, the three of us with
one-way tickets, and rented a house with an attached restaurant on one
of the most beautiful streets of the islands. After enrolling me in an
American school, they bought a restaurant, which was for sale. Within
two months the place was booked five days a week, starting with lunch,
and those two workaholics found themselves lounging on beach chairs
at eleven in the morning, each with a glass of ouzo."

"So Jim Carrey was right."

"For about a year. Until the fucking banks in the US collapsed in
the 2008 financial crisis and took all of Greece down with them. They
were planning on going back to their old corporate jobs, but one of the
companies had gone bankrupt and the other laid off half its employees.
And what my parents' story taught me is something Jim Carrey apparently hadn't learned yet—that sometimes you can do everything right
and still be left with nothing. Because when a tsunami crashes into you,
it doesn't matter what a great swimmer you are." She sighed, and Eli
felt her breath suffusing the cloud.

She told him her parents had managed to get back on their feet
and find lesser but decent enough jobs. They still believed in the old
world order, but she couldn't. She didn't complete her last year of
architecture studies and couldn't seem to hold down a job for long, said
she couldn't see the point of building something that would eventually
fall apart. So she started writing freelance pieces for the tourist magazine and traveling the world. "And when I heard in Tel Aviv about an
Irish traveler who'd disappeared, but not without a trace, I decided then

and there to come to the crater and try to retrace his footsteps. And I've been here ever since."

"So how did McMurphy manage to keep you in one spot?" he asked, secretly wishing she'd confess that he was the reason, not the Irishman.

"Because I thought maybe he had found another way to live. Managed to find his way out of reality, and I wanted to understand how."

"And did you?"

"No." She sighed again. Her leg brushed up against his and the cloud enveloped them both. "But I'm starting to think the question isn't how to step outside the boundaries, but to learn to be free within them."

As night fell, the white turned black. The movement of the world halted inside the cloud. The street outside the restaurant was empty. His father called to make sure he was okay. And he was. He was with her.

At a certain point he groped his way to the fridge and returned with a bottle of water, a bunch of bananas, and a few apples. She told him she had to pee but was holding it in because she wasn't sure she'd be able to find her way back. Then she hummed a song by a band he wasn't familiar with. She said it was called Patrick Watson. It sounded like the name of a singer and not a band, a thought he kept to himself. Several hours of silence ensued, of clothes taken off and tossed, of a body exploring another on wooden floorboards. He marveled how even in the blinding cloud, she moved as if she could see. They both existed through touch alone, all their other senses melting inside the whiteness, along with any trace of self-consciousness. Eli had never felt comfortable inside his lanky frame, always feeling like a stranger in his own skin. But now, the shackles and anchors dissolved inside the cloud, leaving only their two intertwined selves.

He wasn't sure who fell asleep first, but in the morning, he woke up before her. The cloud had turned pale and dim. The floor was still completely white, but he could already make out everything above it—the restaurant itself, the tables, the kitchen, Tamara's freckled face. He regretted that the cloud had dispersed, wishing he could still be enveloped inside it with her.

Careful not to wake her, he got up slowly and walked over to the window. A herd of goats sauntered by the lodge, ambling nonchalantly amid the small clusters of clouds. The world unfurled back into its regular dimensions. He returned and lay back down next to her, listening to her breathing and thinking to himself that in such moments of happiness, he felt as if the whole world shrank to the size of the room he was in. He closed his eyes and tried to fall back asleep, but the grunting ACs made it impossible. When he finally gave up and opened his eyes, he saw the Icelandic traveler emerging from the hidden room.

3.

For a long, awkward moment, the Icelander stood in the corner of the restaurant.

"What are you doing here?"

"I was here the whole time," the Icelander said.

Tamara opened her eyes and sat up.

"The whole night?"

"Yes . . . I was over there," he said, pointing at the hidden room at the end of the kitchen.

Tamara got up, made a beeline for the hidden room and flicked the light on. The floor was still cloudy. "Why'd you even go in there?" she asked. "And what's that noise?"

Eli followed her into the tiny room. "It's the noise from the air conditioners."

"No," she insisted, "there's something else in there."

She was right. A faint yet steady hum was coming from behind the small door at the end of the hidden room. Eli knew it was locked, since no one had ever tried to open it. Until now. He gave it a try, but it wouldn't budge.

"What's in there?" Eli asked.

The Icelander was quiet. Tamara ran her hand along the door, then paused, took Eli's hand, and guided it to the middle of the door. "Feel that? There's a small groove there," she said, and gave the door a good push. Inch by inch, it split open into two separate parts that folded inward, revealing a long, narrow, windowless space.

It turned out to be an expansive Morgenstein alcove—thirty feet long and six feet wide, maybe slightly larger, with a succession of small wooden tables. New computer screens were perched on each table and two large TVs mounted on the wall, one displaying the world map with dozens of virtual pins marking different locations, and on the other, a table of steadily rising numbers. A red coffee maker stood on a small table in the corner of the room, the kind that also grinds the beans. Eli didn't know what he was seeing. A shared workspace for travelers? A secret office?

Tamara sat down at one of the tables, jiggled the mouse, and watched the screen light up. From behind her, Eli looked over her shoulder at an open inbox with an email message that had yet to be sent. Eli didn't recognize the language. His eyes swept over the words until they came to rest on the last six: General Luciano Rodríguez Ancelotti the Third.

And he immediately knew who was behind it. Knew there was only one other person in the world who was there the day the general was born.

A curtain was drawn over the glass wall of Naomi's office as she sat on the windowsill smoking a cigarette and talking on the phone with a representative from the Ministry of Environmental Protection. "No," she said. "No. I'm telling you with absolute certainty that the leaked cloud contained no toxic substances. You can send as many inspectors as you'd like, but the emissions from driving from Tel Aviv to the desert would cause more environmental harm than a cloud made of sand and dish soap."

She hung up and blew a smoke ring out the window.

"What the fuck, Naomi?" he said, shaking with anger.

"Don't overreact—my first cigarette in two years after a local climate crisis is completely reasonable," she replied calmly.

"Jeopardizing everything for a dumb email scam? Seriously? Building a secret sweatshop behind the restaurant to make a few more bucks a month? What's gotten into you?"

"Oh, you're talking about that," she said in a tone either weary or disappointed, Eli couldn't quite tell. She took another drag before stubbing out the cigarette on the windowsill, then locked the door and sat down at her computer. "I thought you'd pick up on it faster." She paused for a moment, then added, "And it's not a sweatshop, it's fucking hi-tech."

"Does Dad know about it?"

"God no," she said menacingly, "and we're both going to make sure it stays that way."

"How much could you possibly be making from it? A thousand bucks? Two thousand? I thought—"

"Six hundred thousand shekels. Eight hundred thousand by the end of the month. And besides, you're not asking the right question."

"Which is?" he asked, just as the numbers started to sink in.

"What our family would lose if I stopped."

Naomi clicked on a list of folders and opened one—an Excel spreadsheet. She tilted the screen in his direction. "See for yourself."

There were two columns, income in green, expenses in red. He leaned forward and squinted at the numbers, but they failed to enlighten him; he just saw a lot of red and very little green. On the bottom row of the left corner he read, "Remaining account balance—156,000 NIS."

Eli tried to reconcile the expenses, but despite his best efforts, it just didn't add up. "There's no way we've already spent almost all of it! How much could that stupid chimney have cost?" He leaned in closer to the screen as if a clue might jump out of it, clarifying everything.

"Wait, are you kidding?" he muttered with a chuckle. "You didn't include Hannah's four million dollars."

"I recorded everything that's in the account," she said, and he didn't understand. "Remember there were a few employees who didn't get their paychecks after the first month?" She admitted that initially, she too thought it was only a technical glitch. It was only after the complaints had piled up that she decided to look into the matter of the misplaced checks. It didn't take her more than a few minutes to realize that the payroll blunder was the least of their problems. "The real problem was that we were about to run out of money." She discovered that they'd spent most of the funds on office setup and the chimney their mother had insisted on buying. The company account had dwindled to four hundred thousand shekels, when salaries and rent alone added up to half a million a month, and that was before factoring in the happy hour budget, pub, and potential business trips abroad. She spent an entire evening playing with the numbers, seeing how she could trim the fat, but no matter what angle she came at it from, every scenario led to debt within a month.

"And no one in accounting noticed? I mean, there's only so much a person can overlook, even at Cloudies."

"They actually did notice. And they even took it to Mom more than once," Noami said, picked up a cigarette and, deciding not to light it, put it back down. "The first time they mentioned it, she said she didn't want to be bothered with petty concerns. The second time, she told them there was nothing to worry about because any day now Hannah Bialika's money would be coming in and sorting things out."

"So we need to tell Hannah that she has to transfer the rest of the money now? That's all?"

"That's what I thought." She told him she went over to Hannah's house the very next day, hoping to go about it discreetly, and that Hannah was friendly and welcoming, the exact opposite of all the stories she'd heard about her. "And then, just as I take a sip of the orange juice she all but shoved at me, that bitch tells me she isn't transferring the rest of the money. That we need to find a way to get by on what we have."

"Oh, come on, I'm sure she was kidding," Eli said. "It's not like she can just back out of her commitment now."

Reaching under the desk, Naomi opened a drawer and took out a many-paged, single-spaced, eight-point document. She rifled through the stack, plucked out a page, and directed Eli's attention toward a paragraph at the bottom—clause 12.4. The paragraph ended in obfuscating legalese. Eli stared at it dumbly until his sister translated that it meant the transfer of the funds was contingent upon the approval of legal and business councils appointed by the investor. "She made sure to bury the clause in a pile of paperwork, and now she's claiming her advisors concluded that it wasn't a wise investment. You get it? She basically talked us into circling the globe, but didn't bother mentioning that she had only filled the tank a quarter of the way. All Cloudies has now, other than her initial investment, is the money the residents put in and the loan Dad took out. And that's the money we're currently burning through."

Eli gawked at the page. When he said he didn't understand why Hannah would pull out after giving them an advance, Naomi lifted the curtain an inch and peeked outside, making sure no one was within earshot. Standing on the other side of the window were a few employees from R&D trying to attach a bicycle pedal to the cloud machine while munching on sushi and burritos. "Simple. She's a sharp businesswoman who realized this company is a complete joke and decided to cut her losses."

"No, no," Eli muttered, "I don't think that's it."

"Then ask her on your next date," she said dismissively. "The only thing I care about right now is making sure this company doesn't crash and burn, and the emails are the closest thing we have to a parachute." Naomi told him she had been doing it from the moment she became aware of the company's finances. She had stumbled upon the Morgenstein alcove behind the hidden room in the lodge's restaurant on one of her visits home from boarding school; it was where she'd smoked her first cigarette. When she realized the only way to make the venture profitable was to blast the emails across huge numbers of addresses, she decided to transform the alcove into a secret workspace. She bought servers in Gibraltar, hired a screenwriter she knew to craft the content, and developed an algorithm capable of sending the emails and generating automated answers for approximately eighty percent of the scenarios. She said that while only four percent of the recipients responded, four percent still translated into a hundred thousand replies, a few thousand of which turned into paying customers. They informed the customers that the general only accepted cryptocurrency, which was also how she paid the people working on the venture. She explained to Eli that it was the best way to fly under the legal and tax authorities' radars while simultaneously capitalizing on the surging value of the coins, giving them a little more breathing space.

In the beginning she hired a few travelers to review the automated translations and edit any mistakes. Then she realized that some element of human involvement was needed after all, a smiley here, a few words there, that the combination of smart algorithms and human touch was "what sets us apart." She assured him that they never exceeded a three-hundred-dollar limit from any individual user, just like she'd promised him when they'd first talked about it. "It's an amount that won't ruin anyone's family, but could possibly save ours."

"And your employees sleep well at night?"

"The travelers I recruited aren't apprised of the business plan. They think it's just for research purposes, that they're training an algorithm for a secret cyber security startup that is trying to catch these scam emails."

"They aren't suspicious?"

"I had them sign NDAs that stipulate a million-dollar penalty if they blab for the worst case scenario, but for all they know, it's all just simulations, they are sure there are no real people on the other side."

At that moment, there was nothing he didn't find irritating about his sister. Her self-satisfied grin, the satisfaction she derived from finally applying the tech skills she had struggled to put to use at their mother's company. He knew it was pointless to try and convince her to stop what she was doing by using ethical or legal arguments. Eli wasn't even sure anymore whether he was morally opposed to the idea or merely jealous of yet another of his sister's successes. "If anyone finds out this project is tied to the company or lodge's money, you'll be bringing Mom and Dad down with you," he warned.

"If you have another way to make sure our parents don't go into millions of dollars in debt that they will never be able to pay back, I'm all ears," she said. He didn't know what to say.

"When I have to choose between my family and breaking some rules, the answer is very clear to me," she said. "I really hope it's the same for you."

Propping her feet up on the table, Naomi assured her brother that their parents were completely in the dark about the scheme, and that the emails couldn't be traced back to the company because the two simply weren't linked. The venture was covering its own costs, which is how things went when you let her handle things. "It's the oxygen we need to make Ben Gould's deadline, but it's just a parachute, not a rescue plane."

"And if Ben Gould doesn't buy the company?"

Grinning, she threw her hands up. "Then we really are screwed."

His phone pinged with a question mark followed by a heart from Tamara. Eli considered his sister, baffled by her ability to think so clearly amid total chaos. She drove him batty, and yet she was the only person he wanted to share the crisis with.

"Can I help somehow?"

Surprised, she looked at him searchingly, trying to figure out if he was being serious or cynical. "If you really mean it, you're welcome to join me tomorrow in a meeting that might improve things."

4

They traveled north the following day. After a forty-minute drive, they arrived at the nearest town, perched at the edge of the wilderness encompassing the Cliff. Eli spent the entire ride thinking about the mystery man he and Tamara had seen in the desert, and about the many enchanted hours they'd spent together in the cloud. In both cases, the specifics of the memories were gradually fading, but that otherworldly feeling—somehow both comforting and creepy—remained.

They pulled into the parking lot of a rundown strip mall nestled between an old police station and grim-looking café. Naomi told him they were about to meet the representative of a VC that had shown interest in investing in Cloudies, and Eli hated him in advance; a man who had come all the way to the desert to bite off a chunk of his mother's idea. His sister said the man was bringing along two reps from a company that developed cooling systems, and Eli hated them too. He imagined them waiting at the dingy café, dying to get back to Tel Aviv and to their almond-soy lattes, texting their friends camel emojis and saying they couldn't believe the shitholes people lived in.

"I don't understand why we even need them."

"Because it's not just that we need money, it's the simple fact that even if we get it, we wouldn't know what to do with it," she said. "Even with another hundred million dollars invested in the company, there's a good chance we still wouldn't have a cloud machine. We have yet to produce a single drop of rain, and our head of R&D is a plumber."

"But you saw that colossal cloud they whipped up," he said.

"And we didn't see a single raindrop out of it. Even the employees are starting to question Mom's abilities, wondering whether she even knows how to make rain, or if that viral video from the desert was staged, or if she might have filled that vacuum cleaner with water or something."

"Oh, come on, they're just a bunch of jealous morons," Eli snarled, unable to stomach the notion of people second-guessing his mother.

Gathered around a wobbly table, the three investors sat waiting. Conspicuous in his white sateen shirt, the VC rep was instantly recognizable to Eli; it was the same young man who had approached his mother during the delegation's visit and proposed a business collaboration. The two others, a man and woman in their sixties, blended oddly into the landscape. The man wore a wrinkled button-down and his glasses dangled from a blue string around his neck, below a long white beard. The woman, similarly bespectacled, her glasses perched halfway down her nose, sported a simple T-shirt and hiking sandals.

The VC rep introduced the pair as chemists working for a company that developed cooling technology, Alice a retired professor and Albert a senior chemist, who said he was proud to invest in such brilliant minds. "We're nearly as passionate about cooling as your mother is about clouds," he added with a chuckle. He then asked if Sarai would be joining them, and Naomi replied that unfortunately she couldn't make it. Without trying to hide her disappointment, Alice said she was a huge fan of their mother's. "I became aware of her work when the video came out and I must say, that woman leaves me speechless." Alice's kind eyes made it very hard for Eli to hate her, no matter how hard he tried. He noticed the small note placed beside her on the table: "Demonstrate appreciation, present our technical system (clearly and concisely), end with genuine proposal for a partnership (!!!)."

Albert did the heavy lifting for Alice. With animated hand gestures, he explained that the cooling technology they had been working on for the past few years was aimed at streamlining the cooling process, rendering it faster and more energy-efficient. He picked up a napkin and sketched shapes of molecules and names of chemicals Eli had never heard of. His mind wandering, he wondered if Alice and Albert were just business partners or also a couple. He was almost certain they were a couple. They had similar speech patterns, probably the product of years of cohabitation. Maybe they had once been a couple, but no longer were? Or perhaps what he was picking up on was a mutual attraction never acted upon? Maybe they met only after marrying others, and now they were forced to sit next to each other in a professional setting while their hearts still burned with desire?

"And what does cooling have to do with our company?" Naomi asked.

"We heard you're experiencing a few technical problems with producing precipitation," Albert said. Eli glanced at his sister, whose reluctance to meet his eye revealed that she was the one who'd told them. Pointing at the drawings on his napkin again, Albert explained that theoretically, cold temperature wasn't a prerequisite for precipitation, but it was quite possible that in this specific case, their cooling systems could contribute to denser clouds. "At this point it's just an assumption, but it may very well be the missing component, what you need to turn your clouds into rain clouds."

"And to make us all rich." The VC rep chuckled and gave Eli a slap on his back. Eli bristled. He loathed the man.

"We're looking for a real, honest partnership. Technological, business, and ethical, of course. It's important to us that the product we develop is ecologically sustainable—"

"What are you expecting in return?" Naomi cut him off.

The rep said he wasn't sure it was the proper forum to discuss the matter, and suggested these important questions be directed to the lawyers who'd be sending them the detailed proposal. "If such a partnership interests you, of course," he added.

"A partnership is fifty percent," Naomi said.

"Maybe we really should deal with that later on," Eli suggested, to which Albert and Alice quickly expressed their agreement, appearing as confrontation-averse as Eli.

The VC rep nodded. "We just want to make sure we have all the tools we need to succeed, Naomi, that's all."

"Is that what you tell every company, or just those run by fifty-year-old women from the sticks?" Her tone was amused, but Eli could tell that deep down she was seething.

"If we had even a shadow of a doubt about your mother's abilities," the rep said, "we wouldn't have asked for a meeting. Our stipulation of taking part of the company's decision-making process is an industry standard."

"And if we say no?" Naomi leaned back in her chair.

The VC rep smiled. "Then we'll wish you good luck with Ben Gould's visit."

When Alice glanced at Naomi with concern, Albert rested a gentle hand on his business partner's knee.

Definitely a couple, Eli thought, pleased.

As they turned onto the highway, Eli stared out the window at the two big signs, one pointing toward Tel Aviv, the other toward the crater.

"I know you think that everyone in the tech industry is an asshole."

"What?"

"That the only thing people in hi-tech care about are the perks in their contracts, and that their orange juice is squeezed right in front of them."

"Okay, let's say that's what I think. And . . . ?"

"And you're right." She surprised him. "They're a bunch of jerks."

She confessed that when she started out in the industry, she was just like him, all but blinded by rage. She viewed her coworkers as a bunch of spoiled brats who complained about the lack of variety in the cafeteria salad dressings, while most people in the country could barely make ends meet. They actually believed that making three times the average income must mean that as human beings they were worth at least three times more than the rest of the population. She told him their condescension reared its head subtly, never explicitly, such as when they spoke about their kids' teachers, who "weren't exactly accelerated math types," or the office cleaning lady, who "got such a crazy holiday gift card she can probably afford to get her own cleaning lady!" Eli was waiting for a "but," or any kind of qualifier, but it never came. She said she lived in constant fear that one of her colleagues would find out she was an outlier. "That's why for years I did everything I could to not be Naomi Lilienblum from the Cliff."

"But being from the Cliff isn't something to be embarrassed of," he said.

A slight smile crept across his sister's face. She told him about her first day at boarding school, and he was surprised by her sudden candidness. When the teacher asked her to introduce herself, she bravely shared with her classmates that she hailed from the Cliff, the place she'd only moments ago done everything within her power to escape, but which was the only anchor she had. Her classmates nodded as if they'd heard of it, and eyed her with almost envious looks, much to her satisfaction. "Because I knew the Cliff made them see me, and not through me." Her first year in boarding school wasn't easy, but the Cliff shielded her somehow. And then, during her second year, a young, handsome geography teacher joined the faculty, the type to spawn many a schoolgirl crush, and at the start of their first class, he asked the students to share a sentence about their hometown. "And I said the Cliff was the only village in the whole country whose houses were built entirely from wood. And do you know what he said, Eli?" she asked, briefly meeting his gaze in the mirror. "That he wasn't sure what I said was true; and then he asked if the Cliff was that kibbutz up north, by the Sea of Galilee."

It was at that moment that she realized the Cliff was the center of the universe only for those who called it home. "That story about everyone being captivated by the Cliff, in awe of the rare geological phenomenon we live on, that story was meant for us, the people who live there," she snorted, tightening her hands on the wheel so that her knuckles turned white. "You spend your whole life thinking you're in the center, just to find out that you're not even on the map."

"I'm just blown away to hear you defending the Cliff. Ever since we moved here all you cared about was getting out."

"I don't know what to say. That VC guy really got to me. Reminded me of how the world tries to bring people like our mom to their knees." She was trying to articulate feelings that floated free-form around her head, but couldn't get them straight. She said that after the incident with the geography teacher she was determined to never look back. She realized the place she came from was indeed an anchor, but instead of steadying her, it hemmed her in. She felt that the only solution was to sever all ties with the place. According to the parents of a boy she was in love with at the time, hi-tech was the next big thing, so she decided to do everything within her power to hitch her wagon to it. At the boarding school she looked around, trying to identify kids she thought were tech-bound, those who had the right background, the right interests, the right parents—those you could just tell were poised for success. She studied them closely, and then reinvented herself in their image. Blended into them. Laughed at their jokes. Committed quotes from their favorite shows to memory, listened for hours on end to the music they liked.

"But my overwhelming desire to be just like them didn't for one moment contradict the fact that I wanted to burn down the world they'd built."

"Burn down?" Eli was confused. His sister was the poster girl for the new world, the perfect immigrant. Wanting to burn it down was completely contradictory to the very actions she had taken to get there.

"Burn down," she repeated. "To the ground." She told him that when she landed her first job as a junior programmer, she decided to take on the role of a spy sent to pass through the valley of darkness into the rich and prosperous land from which most of the population was excluded. A land whose inhabitants affected the lives of billions. She knew that she'd enter this hi-tech world of theirs not to become a member, but rather to study the inner machinations of the system she so deeply despised. She was hoping that if she infiltrated deeply enough— became a CEO of an Apple or a Google—she'd find a way to dismantle it all from the inside, and redistribute the wealth so that everyone had a piece of the pie, even those who remained standing on the outside looking in.

"Come on, Naomi, what game are you playing? Who are you trying to fool?" He told her he didn't buy the whole self-righteous act, reminding her she was the one who had fled at the first chance she got. Left him to handle their frustrated, debt-addled parents by himself.

"You're right. I had an intense loathing not only for the place I wanted to get to, but for the place I had come from." She said she saw how, from being people with big dreams, her parents had turned into people fighting to keep their head above life's choppy waters. The debts they had to repay over the years not only quashed their dreams but also altered something fundamental in their DNA, whittling down their hopes and desires to petty aspirations and fatigue. To fix the leaky roof, to take care of that persistent back pain, to pay the accountant. She saw their father's small lodge and mother's oddball inventions a testament to the fact that they had taught themselves that desire had to be limited, and that only within those limits could one live. "And if I ever wanted to get to the place where I stood a chance to change something in this messed-up system, I had to do everything in my power to make sure that toxic idea about limits wouldn't go to my head."

She lowered a hand from the wheel and reached into her pocket, causing the car to veer off course.

"Hey, what are you doing?!" he shouted. She took out her slim wallet—a card holder, really—and pulled out a note. "Read this," she said, handing it to Eli.

It was a small page from a notebook, with light blue lines, laminated in clear plastic. In the right corner, in her prim handwriting, was the date 15.9.2008, and under that:

From their insult an armor I will build,
Before learning their language better than them,
And donning their clothes better than them,
And charging into their lavish city
A Trojan horse through the front gate
Until they realize who they have let in
Leading a thousand hungry souls
To claim their share

"Hmm. Well, it's definitely subtle," he said.

"Yeah, right?" She laughed. "I guess I won't be poetry's next it girl."

Eli looked at the horse tattoo on his sister's nape with new eyes. Could she be telling the truth? That all these years it wasn't merely a wooden horse, but a Trojan one? He could count the number of candid conversations with his ever-cynical sister on one finger, and now that he wanted to understand more, he didn't know where to begin.

"So, what, it's Workers of the World Unite against Amazon? To each Apple shares according to his needs? That's your solution? Because I'm pretty sure a few people tried that and it didn't turn out so great."

"God no!" she snorted. "Anyone who believes in full economic equality doesn't understand the first thing about economics, and even less about human beings. The criticism is valid, but the solutions people have come up with are completely off." While the system couldn't be fixed, "everything that went down with Mom and Cloudies over the past few months has made me realize that I don't care about all that anymore. All I want is to take care of the people who are important to me. The rest of the world can go to hell."

He believed her. He couldn't discern any coherent ideology behind her hard-boiled critique of the hi-tech world. Not even a desire to upend the natural order. The real answers as to her motivations could be found in the lines hardening her face: anger, confusion, maybe a touch of loneliness too. Suddenly, it all clicked. The choice to put in eighteen-hour workdays as if work was all there was to life, her utter disinterest in dating, and the decision to carry out a thriving email scam stealing from the rich and giving the money to her family. A digital Robin Hood. He knew that she told herself it was all part of a meticulous master plan, but to Eli there was a much simpler explanation for the way his sister navigated the world. There were many things out there that caused her pain, and she was willing to go to great lengths to keep them at bay.

"But something got lost along the way," she admitted, confessing that in her eagerness to fit in, the boundaries between her and her colleagues had gradually blurred over time. When she finally emerged on the other side of the rabbit hole, all her objections to the hi-tech world had virtually vanished. "They suddenly seemed to me like the half-baked thoughts of a silly, naïve girl, an inane idealism that had nothing to do with the real world." There were still the occasional disconnects over the years, like when entire buffets of fresh food were unceremoniously tossed into dumpsters, or a colleague ridiculed an applicant for submitting a CV with spelling mistakes, small, isolated incidents that nevertheless served as reminders: I'm not from here. I'm not them. But the truth is, those incidents became increasingly rare. Her coping mechanisms had grown more sophisticated, to the point that she even started to doubt her own motives. Perhaps all this self-hatred was mere pretense. "A pathetic moral cover that allows me to enjoy everything the good life has to offer without bearing any responsibility."

"Until Mom brought you back to the Cliff," he said.

She nodded. "All these years I thought my only way to get ahead was to accept the hi-tech world's rules and speak its language until our wacky mom came to show everyone, including me, that you could carve your own path in the sand." She fell silent. "That rep's smug face. I wanted to ram his head into the table. I think maybe we should just keep doing this on our own. With no VCs and people bossing us around."

She said she didn't have an exact plan yet, but had the strong feeling it was the right move, and that while he didn't like the email project, it would give them a little wriggle room, allow them to stay afloat without having to wait for someone like Ben Gould to decide whether they were worthy of his money.

"I don't know if we should rule them out entirely," Eli said.

Naomi blinked with surprise.

"That older couple, who like cooling systems as much as Mom likes inventions, they struck me as decent partners."

"People aren't as good as you think they are," she said.

"And not as bad as you imagine them to be. Going with that VC rep, sleazy as he may be, is the responsible thing to do, and even more so giving Mom's dream a real shot, without jeopardizing her, or us. My heart agrees with everything you said, but my head thinks the exact opposite. And in this case, I'm pretty sure my head is right."

"You sound like me," she said, and laughed, but Eli saw the pain in her eyes and knew he had disappointed her. It wasn't the reaction she had been expecting after spilling her heart out. Eli wanted to make it up to her, to reveal a secret of his own in return. "By the way, I didn't get around to telling you, what with the cloud leak and the email business, but two days ago I found the vacuum cleaner, the red one from the video."

Her face tensed and when she turned to look at him, she almost bumped into the car in front of them. "Where?" she asked. He told her that Tamara had shown him where they'd found their mother in her bathrobe and with her martini, but left out the part about their nightly stroll and the daunting silhouette.

"I meant, where is the cloud machine now?"

He told her, hoping for another window into her thoughts, but Naomi remained silent for the rest of the ride.

That evening, he confided in Tamara about the emails and the general, the money Hannah Bialika hadn't transferred, the loans their father had taken, and his sister's heroic efforts to secure more investors for Cloudies.

"It's amazing how you two are trying to keep your parents from going under," Tamara said, running her fingers through his hair, "but I told you, I'm not sure any of it will help when the tsunami hits." She mentioned that the tourism magazine had offered to fly her out to Mexico to cover some music festival, but that she would probably say no. She wanted to continue investigating the McMurphy mystery with him.

Eli tried to listen, but his mind was racing. He saw a tsunami surging toward him and didn't know how to dodge it.

5

T he next day, in the afternoon, someone in the company had taken the initiative to book them a limo to the convention in Tel Aviv. Naomi nearly lost it when she saw the elongated black car idling outside the house, calculating the cost of the ride as four round-trip taxi trips. Eli knew she was right but was also glad it was too late to cancel, knowing that his mother would enjoy the experience. With the company in dire straits, who knew if she'd ever get another opportunity. The driver loaded Eli and Sarai's suitcases into the trunk. After settling into the back seat, Naomi, who had brought only a small backpack, said she hoped the limo wouldn't keel under the weight of their ludicrously large suitcases. "Do you know the story about the wise men of Chelm who rode a horse all the way from town to the big city?" Sarai asked. Naomi shook her head.

"The wise men saw the horse struggling to support their weight during the long journey, and eased the burden by lying flat on his saddle."

"How did that ease the burden?" Naomi asked.

"That way the horse didn't have to carry their shadow," Eli replied with a grin.

She rolled her eyes.

As the limo merged onto the highway, Naomi took a large laptop out of her backpack, placed it on her lap, and said she was working on a presentation for the convention.

"I don't like going over those things in the car," Sarai said, to which Naomi replied that she didn't either but was left with no choice, considering how Sarai had avoided her all week.

The image of a cloud appeared on the screen with the word "Cloudies" in an elegant font above the caption "The World We Want to Live In." She explained it was important to create the impression of a company with an ecological vision, driven by the mission to bring rain, i.e., clean water, to arid areas. "Green tech is a major buzzword and we should definitely leverage that."

Sarai did her best to feign interest, occasionally nodding as her daughter spoke, but her eyes kept wandering around the limo, from the ceiling lights to the sophisticated ventilation system. She stared at the presentation with the same empty gaze she had directed at her children's teachers during parent-teacher conferences—that of a reluctant participant.

Naomi sighed, snapped the laptop shut, and leaned her head against the window. Abstaining from any response, Sarai started fiddling with the buttons of the folding TV.

Eli examined the minibar. After confirming with the driver that it was included in the fare, he poured himself a glass of champagne. He didn't like the taste, but drank it all the same. The sandy landscape gradually gave way to an earthier terrain scattered with rocks, then bushes, sparse forests, orchards, and green fields. His father always said that for a land so small to encompass everything it aspired to be—a desert, sea, forests, plains, and mountains—it had to remain in a constant state of flux.

Two hours later, Tel Aviv's imposing skyline shimmered in the distance. The limo slithered off the highway and crawled along the streets until it came to a halt in front of a five-story building with crescent windows.

"Here we are," the driver announced, and Naomi rushed to retrieve the suitcases from the trunk. Eli and his mother got out and followed one step behind her. The entrance to the hotel stood wide open.

As his sister took her laptop out to continue her presentation and schedule meetings with a few other venture capitals, Eli decided to take a stroll around the hotel. The dim lobby was crowded with small bonsais and a handsome blue velvet sofa occupied by a couple roughly his age. He took a photo of the dwarfed trees and sent it to Tamara, saying it made him want to visit Japan and asking if she'd ever been. "Nope," she replied, and asked if she could call. She'd been going over Morgenstein's blueprints and couldn't find the one for his family's house.

He texted that he was heading into a meeting and would call her later, the mere thought of another conversation about McMurphy grating. He then called his father, who immediately bombarded him with a seemingly endless stream of questions—How long was the drive? How big were the hotel towels? Boaz relished every piece of information his son was willing to impart. Just before hanging up, Eli asked his father if he happened to know the whereabouts of the blueprint he had received from the Swiss embassy for their house, said he wanted to show something to Naomi. His father thought it was in the storage room at the lodge's restaurant, in a pile with all the other blueprints.

Back upstairs, he saw that the door to his mother's room was open, and walked in. She was standing on the balcony with a glass of white wine, gazing out at the sea. Acknowledging his presence, she gestured toward the minibar. He asked if it was complimentary, and she said she certainly hoped so considering she'd already had two. He grabbed a can of ginger ale and joined her.

"Had I known I was raising a kid who'd choose ginger ale over Scotch," she said, "I'd have spiked your chocolate milk."

"I just don't like losing control," he reasoned.

"The problem is thinking you ever had it."

With the last of the sun gone, they looked out at the joggers loping along the well-lit boardwalk.

"I'd have loved to live by the sea," she said quietly.

Eli said he always thought she was ideologically opposed to nature.

"Only to the desert."

"Then why live there?"

"Because for a very long time I thought being an adult meant giving up the things you wanted for the things you needed."

"And today?"

She didn't answer. Tilting her head, her eyes widened as she stared at a couple on an electric scooter zipping across the boardwalk. He asked if she was ready for her presentation tomorrow.

"Do I seem ready?" She took a sip of wine. "Believe me, Elichuk, the most interesting things in life aren't planned."

"I guess you're right," he admitted. "Like with the home video you accidentally screened to dozens of international investors."

Her smile spread slowly. "Yes, well, the 'Czech movie' definitely wasn't planned," she said, confirming his suspicion.

"Did you find out how it got there?"

"It turns out your father had been going to the hangar at night to watch old videos. The VCR at home didn't work." Boaz told her only after the fact that he had forgotten to take out the videotape, and that's what the investors saw on the screen. The image of his father sitting at the empty hanger night after night in his plaid sweater and stained work shoes watching old home videos tugged at his heartstrings.

"These past few months haven't been easy for Dad. He's kind of gotten left out," Eli said.

"What can I say, big dreams come at a big price."

"That's a bit harsh."

"But true."

He didn't understand her coldness. "He's sacrificing so much for you," Eli said.

"Let's not have a competition about who sacrificed more."

"You know you're not the easiest person to live with, right?" The image of his father all alone in front of the big screen was stuck in his head.

"You'd rather have a normal mom, huh?"

"Feels like it would have been easier sometimes," he said, instantly regretting it.

She continued to stand in front of the dark sea, her wine glass limp in her hand. "If you knew the price people have paid for my attempts to conform, I think you would be singing a different tune." She spoke without anger, slowly. Tipsily. "People tend to single out anyone who's even slightly different, anyone who dares to step out of line, without pausing to consider how challenging it can be for some to spend their entire lives within those lines."

"What price?" he asked. Ignoring his question, his mother confided that she'd been thinking quite a lot recently about how everyone is born into the entanglement of life, "and even before taking your first breath, you're already a daughter, and granddaughter, you're part of the knot, tangled up, and with time that knot only tightens. You become a student, a friend, a spouse, a teacher, a neighbor . . . all these roles and definitions only weigh you down. They're not threads, they're two-ton shackles, and there are moments when all I want is to pull a Houdini. To break free, without thinking how it will affect everyone."

"To be the woman in the desert in a burgundy bathrobe, sipping a martini?"

She smiled.

6.

Awakened by his mother's voice, he opened his eyes and was surprised to see her perched at the end of Naomi's bed, reciting: "My name is Sarai Lilienblum, and ever since I can remember, I have aimed for the sky."

The convention's opening session was scheduled for noon, and he decided to take time out of his morning to visit McMurphy's church. He fished Tamara's note with the church's address out of his wallet; the wrinkled paper felt good in his hand. The encounter with the mysterious figure in the crater had motivated him to find it, and like Tamara, he was hoping for a lead.

He hailed a taxi, and as they drove downtown, the buildings grew grayer and the sidewalks darker. The driver stopped at a dead-end street and pointed into the distance. Getting out of the taxi, Eli looked up and saw that the buildings were unnumbered. On a bench by a dilapidated structure was a small plaque—"In loving memory of Aviva, who used to sit here and smoke."

A young African couple emerged from a footpath between the buildings, clad in white from head to toe. As Eli approached the footpath, he heard gentle drumbeats and the sound of a choir emanating from one of the buildings. Following the music, he arrived at the rear entrance of an old building, where he discovered a half-open door amidst dumpsters and gas tanks. He crept into the room, which was packed with African immigrants, most in white garb, fervently singing gospels in English. With fluorescent bulbs casting a harsh glow above a grimy, chipped linoleum floor and peeling walls, the room resembled the depressing waiting room of a free clinic rather than how he had imagined a church. The walls were decorated with a few framed photographs of Israeli landscapes, among them photos of the crater; Eli immediately recognized the colorful sandy mounds. Immersed in song, the congregation either sat or stood facing a woman in a yellow dress and matching head cover singing in a loud, lucid voice, while three women and two men accompanied her on tambourines and traditional drums. The worshipers showed no interest in Eli; some were singing, others dancing in place to the beat of the drums. Beside him, an older woman hummed the tune to herself, swaying softly as if the melody flowed through her fragile frame.

When the singing came to a close, he noticed a tall, striking man in a black suit and closely cropped hair standing in the middle of the room. Eli recognized him from the international churches' website Tamara had shown him. The reverend addressed the worshipers in English, announcing a thirty-minute break for refreshments in the courtyard, after which another prayer session would begin. People began filtering out of the room, and Eli tentatively approached the man and introduced himself, saying he came from the Cliff by the large crater down south.

"Wow, a long way from home." The reverend smiled, pointing at the framed photo of the crater.

Eli said he was looking for someone named Robert McMurphy. He took out his phone and showed the reverend a photo of McMurphy standing next to his bike against the backdrop of the crater. The reverend peered at the screen and Eli zoomed in on the Irish traveler. A shadow crossed the reverend's face.

The reverend gestured toward two chairs. "Let's have a seat," he suggested, then asked Eli for another look at the photo. "What is your connection to him?" he asked, and Eli recounted the entire story about the Irish traveler who'd gone missing in the desert.

"Ah, yes," the reverend said. "I'm familiar with the story. His dear mother visited our church not long ago. She told us about the museum you built in his honor in the desert, said it was a beautiful place." He recalled the woman was utterly devastated, after searching for years for information about her son, trying to understand what he had experienced on his visit to Israel. The reverend admitted that something about the woman had left a deep impression on him, to the extent that he sometimes still prayed for her and her son, hoping the benevolent Lord would reunite them, or, at the very least, grant her some peace.

Eli had only a vague image of the petite, weary woman who had visited the Cliff a year ago. He hadn't met her in person, being in the army at the time, but saw a photo of her with his parents. None of the three was smiling.

"And did you meet the son, McMurphy himself?" Eli asked.

"Yes, I met Robert," the reverend replied, and it dawned on Eli that until now, he hadn't heard anyone refer to the traveler by his first name. "It was years ago, but I remember him walking in here and patiently waiting through the service to approach me. He said he had a question he wanted to ask. People often come to me with questions about Jesus, life, the Holy Land, but the scruffy young traveler came all the way to the church to ask me where he could find a Chinese restaurant nearby." The reverend laughed. "But I've been doing this long enough to know that when someone asks a reverend for a restaurant recommendation, it means he needs to talk."

"And did he talk?" Eli asked.

"Honesty, not that much. Somehow, we mainly talked about me." The reverend said that back then, his daughter was fighting cancer. Till this day he doesn't understand how he found himself opening up like that to a foreign traveler he had just met. But he did. "I still remember clearly the empathy in his eyes. It was as if . . ."

"He embedded some of your pain in himself," said Eli.

"Yes." The reverend nodded in surprise. Like Paulina, he admitted there was something about meeting Robert that helped him deal with his pain, and Eli knew it was more than a coincidence. "But sometimes I think that he took not only my pain but also my daughter's, because a few weeks later, she started to recover."

The reverend went on to tell about McMurphy's mother. "They hadn't been in touch, she and her son, for many years. She didn't say why. Her journey to Israel was an attempt to see with her own eyes the place where her only son had gone missing, a son she had already lost years before." The reverend's face contorted with pain, and it suddenly seemed to Eli so strange, the ability to feel another's suffering.

"Apparently when she visited your museum, she found a journal belonging to Robert, in which he wrote about owing money to a reverend in Tel Aviv for eggrolls. She insisted on giving me a fifty-shekel bill and refused to leave the church until I accepted it."

Eli asked if McMurphy had mentioned any plans to visit the desert or any other destination, but the reverend apologized and said he honestly couldn't remember. "I'm sorry I don't have more information to share," he said, linking his fingers together. "So many people, so many stories. It's difficult to make room for them all, you understand?"

Eli felt as he had on that night in the crater when he caught a glimpse of McMurphy's shadow. It seemed that the traveler had managed to do two things at once—leave a strong emotional trace with those who encountered him, and yet vanish from within their own memory. Sensing Eli's disappointment, the reverend asked to take another look at McMurphy's photo. Eli took out his phone again. His lock screen wallpaper was a photo of Sarai standing next to the chimney.

"You met her too?"

"No."

"Then why do you have a photo of her?" The reverend pointed.

"Ah, no, that's *my* mom." Eli chuckled.

"I don't know whose mother that is, but that's the woman who was here."

Eli's foot started to bounce up and down. Silently, Eli and the reverend locked eyes, before Eli shifted his gaze to the scattered chairs. Two kids ran in and the reverend waved them out. Eli continued to survey the room, and in a moment of clarity, he realized the photos on the wall were arranged from north to south: the mountains of the Galilee, the Jezreel Valley, Tel Aviv's shoreline, the buildings of Jerusalem, the Dead Sea, the crater, the Red Sea. His attention was drawn to an aerial shot of the crater bisected by the long road, with the colorful mounds of sand on one side and a spacious flat plain on the other.

Eli sprang from his seat and walked up to the photo, his nose almost touching the glass. He realized the clue had been staring at him from the moment he stepped into the church. When his mother talked about the colored dunes, she didn't think about the real ones, but about the picture standing in front of him.

He turned to the visibly perplexed reverend. "You said she was here a year ago?"

"No, it wasn't that long ago," the reverend said, his eyes narrowing as his mind did the math. "Three months, give or take. I believe it was July."

Eli asked if the woman had an Irish accent and the reverend shook his head, confirming Eli's suspicion—his deranged mother had visited the church on one of the three days in which she'd gone missing. But why?

"From the look on your face, I can tell there's something important I've missed," the reverend said.

"You're not the only one," Eli replied.

Leaving the church, he saw a text from his father: "I think your mom took the blueprints a few days after she came back. Ask her where she put them."

And right then he knew, just knew: there could only be so many coincidences.

7.

The hotel hosting the convention was even grander than the one the Lilienblums were staying in. It was an enormous thing, with a giant outdoor pool overlooking the boardwalk and an expansive lobby crowded with elegantly attired men and women. A scattering of food stations offered lavish displays of sushi and salads, as well as several other culinary wonders that left Eli scratching his head in confusion.

Dressed in a crisp white blouse, Naomi stood by one of the stations chatting with an older man in a suit. As Eli approached, he overheard the man complaining about the catering. "People pour half a mil into planning a convention, and you have to eat standing like some animal," he said, and announced he was going back for another salmon tortilla. Eli was sure his sister was going to tell him off for being late, but she just swept her gaze across the room in search of bigwigs.

"Where's Mom?" he asked.

"Waiting inside, getting ready for the opening panel."

"Panel? Wasn't she supposed to give a talk?"

"It turns out she's both a panelist and a speaker," she replied, pointing at a screen displaying the convention itinerary, which opened with a discussion on "Jewish Entrepreneurship" featuring industry leaders, followed by a brief talk on "Cutting-Edge Innovation in Rural Israel" by Mrs. Sarai Lilienblum. Casually, Naomi reached out and plucked the stem of a champagne glass off a waiter's tray. "A panel of four industry leaders and one ill-prepared mother, what could possibly go wrong?"

"Listen, I visited a church this morning—"

"Indeed, nothing left to do but pray," she cut him off, downed her glass in one gulp, and insinuated herself into a nearby group. "Sorry, I heard you talking about green tech and just had to join in."

When the announcer's voice sounded through the lobby inviting everyone into the auditorium, he followed the flow of suits and took a seat in the back row. Onstage, his mother occupied the rightmost leather armchair in an elegant green evening dress and black heels, a departure from her usual style. Beside her, four men in button-downs were chatting. He stared at her, wondering why she would want to impersonate McMurphy's mother.

The moderator, a grinning young blond guy in a suit, spoke in heavily Hebrew accented English. He shared how his first sales pitch was at his bar mitzvah, when the rabbi asked why he thought he deserved such an extravagant celebration, and he replied that he was hoping it was an initial investment that would one day pay off—"or as we say in the hi-tech industry, seed money." The audience laughed. Eli didn't get it. The moderator moved on to the subject of the "Jewish brain," from King Solomon to Einstein, discussing how entrepreneurship was ingrained in the culture's DNA. Finally, he introduced the panelists, delivering elaborate introductions off cue cards. He introduced Sarai as a pioneer in the field of green innovation, noting that she had even managed to pique Ben Gould's curiosity about her "exciting, remarkable startup, led by an equally exciting and remarkable woman."

His mother nodded.

"So, let's kick off our discussion with a fun one!" Grinning, the moderator directed his first question toward the CEO of a large cyber company. "Tell us, how do you see the link between Judaism and entrepreneurship?"

"Well, I think we can all agree that Abraham was the original startup founder," the CEO replied, expounding that Abraham had embarked on his journey to Canaan without a single investor backing him, and without any explicit promise of gain.

"Sarai, isn't that the original name of the Matriarch Sarah?"

The moderator's question hung in the air for a moment before Sarai realized it was directed at her. Eli's heart started pounding. Asking the moderator to repeat the question, she then replied that yes, he was correct. After a brief, expectant pause, it became apparent that she wasn't going to elaborate. It was one of those moments in which Eli felt he was experiencing the world through his mother's apprehension. Responding to the moderator's comment that her startup was reminiscent of Moses striking water from the rock, Sarai hesitated briefly before saying, "Yes, I suppose you could say that," only to pivot a moment later. "You know, actually, no. I don't see the connection."

"To the story of Moses?"

"Between Judaism and entrepreneurship."

There was some sniggering from the audience. The moderator said it was an interesting statement, and one of the panelists remarked, "Well then, there goes the convention!"

Laughing, the moderator asked Sarai to clarify. Stammering, she admitted that she was no expert, but she simply didn't see the connection. The way she saw it, Judaism was more about spirituality than material matters, a way of life filled with learning for the sake of learning.

"Actually, I can relate," the CEO of the cyber startup chimed in, describing how his father, who had grown up in a Haredi household, used to find himself debating Talmud for hours on end, on subjects that bore little to no connection to the real world.

"I can think of quite a few office meetings that fit that description," the moderator chuckled, smoothly segueing to the next question.

From there, the panel carried on without many hitches. Sarai fielded a few more questions, her answers gradually becoming longer, and while certainly uninspired—having failed to live up to the romanticized image of a tech entrepreneur she had acquired—most of her statements were reasonable enough not to raise eyebrows.

For the final question, the panelists were asked for their advice for budding entrepreneurs, and Sarai was encouraged to direct hers to young women in particular.

"My advice would be the same for all entrepreneurs," she replied, launching into a tale about broken vessels, a story Eli instantly recognized from his childhood, albeit hazily.

"As a child, nothing interested me more than the origin of creation. Wanting to know how the world was created literally kept me up at night. I spent my days at the local library, devouring the science section—physics, astronomy, geology, biology, chemistry, you name it. But each book offered only a partial theory, so I shifted gears and moved on to mythology and folktales, hoping to find some ancient wisdom. The sheer number of narratives astounded me. One myth was a love story between the sea and the sky, while another told of a lonely goddess whose tears turned into planets."

Eli sensed that she was losing her listeners, but, undeterred, his mother closed her eyes and continued.

"Of all the stories, my favorite was a Kabbalistic tale that described the creation of the world through broken vessels. According to the story, before the world came into existence, there was infinite light. The light was poured into many vessels, but it was so strong that the vessels shattered, scattering holy sparks throughout the universe and creating the world we know today. The reason I loved that story is that unlike the others, it not only describes how the world was created, but also how we're supposed to exist in it. Simple, straightforward instructions—all we need to do is bring a little order into the chaos, gather the shards, and the rest will sort itself out. There was something reassuring just knowing that all we have to do is strive to live a normal, stable life—family, work, children, friends. To reassemble everything nicely, shard by shard. But when I shared the myth with my son, who was little at the time, he said I'd gotten it all wrong. He explained that by piecing together the shards, you weren't recreating the world, you were actually returning to the state of being before the world as we know it came into existence. He suggested the takeaway should be the opposite: everything in this world, no matter how beautiful, was constructed from shards—intrinsically imperfect. Even the most exquisite flower, or gorgeous city. So if there's one piece of advice I'd give entrepreneurs, it's don't try to put the shards back together. Resist the urge to try to rebuild the world someone else has built for you. Instead, make it your mission to gather the vessels' shards and sparks of light and build new things. And not beautiful, pristine, whole things, but fractured, unconventional, crazy things. Because the way to build the world isn't through replication, but creation."

"Smart mother, smart kid," the moderator said, to emphatic nods from the audience.

During the break, a small crowd gathered outside the auditorium, waiting for Sarai. One of them expressed how moved he was by her story, while another wondered what became of the coffee machine she had mentioned once creating. Clocking Eli in the corner, she waited patiently for her newfound admirers to have their moment with her before finally making her way over to her son.

"How did I do?" she asked with a nervous smile.

"You rocked it," he replied. "The best panelist by far."

She rested a loving hand on his shoulder. "Where were you this morning?" she asked, her gaze gravitating toward the dessert stands.

"Downtown, at a migrant workers' church. Interesting place."

His mother headed straight to a stand with an impressive display of macaroons and took two. He decided to let it go for the time being.

Naomi materialized at their side. "Ben Gould and Bill Gates called, they're in a bidding war over Cloudies." She patted their mother's shoulder. "I'm kidding, but you were amazing. Next thing, we're going to find out you're secretly enjoying this. Come on, your talk starts in five minutes. Show them one more time what a genius my mom is."

"No problem, let me just make a quick stop in the ladies' room first."

Eli took his seat in the back row just as the moderator returned to the stage.

"Give it up once again for one of this year's most exciting entrepreneurs, Sarai Lilienblum!" the moderator called out to a round of frenzied applause, then stepped aside to welcome the anticipated speaker. The clapping slowly died down.

Silence lingered.

The moderator approached the microphone again. "Sarai, the stage is yours!" he announced with feigned excitement, and Eli knew—she wasn't coming. Before he could think up a plan B, Naomi was already making her way to the stage.

"Hello everyone, my name is Naomi Lilienblum, and I'm Sarai's daughter," she said in flawless English, adjusting the microphone to her height. "As I'm sure you can imagine, the cloud business—like the weather itself—is rife with unexpected twists and turns." Smiling apologetically, she explained that the CEO had to tend to a pressing matter, but that she would do her best to fill in. Naomi asked to turn on the projector and dim the lights. Once again, Eli felt how good it was to play on the same team as his sister. A slightly blurry image appeared on the screen—two children and a young woman standing in a lush field, wind whipping around them. It was the home movie of his mother shooting a pen into the sky. This time he didn't look at the screen but at the audience reaction, and saw how, within moments, they became spellbound by his mother's ability to set the world in motion. The video ended with a close-up of Eli and Naomi's ecstatic smiles as the pen disappeared over the horizon. Solitary claps echoed through the auditorium, and soon swelled to thunderous applause.

"As you can see, my mother has always reached for the stars," Naomi grinned, and regaled the audience with a story about the small village in the middle of nowhere, known as the Cliff. She described the unbearable desert heat—as if they slept under the stars and not in a two-story air-conditioned house—and how, over the years, her mother had worked tirelessly trying to solve the puzzle of providing water to even the most arid regions of the desert. If he hadn't known the truth, Eli would have believed her—that's how convincing his sister was.

"And I'm sure you're eager to witness the miracle with your own eyes," Naomi told the audience.

Preceded by the sound of squeaking wheels, Paulina and Sagi emerged from the corner of the stage. Eli had no prior knowledge of their involvement in the plan, but as the day progressed, he became increasingly aware of how little he knew. Paulina rolled the old red vacuum cleaner onto the stage, the cord trailing freely behind. It was the same vacuum cleaner Eli had found in the crater and told his sister about on their way back from the meeting. Sagi was carrying an aquarium filled with sand, which he carefully placed at the front of the stage. Opening the aquarium lid, Naomi announced, "Today, in a first-ever live demonstration, we're going to show you how sand turns into rain-producing clouds."

Eli couldn't believe his ears. From her phone, Naomi's home screen appeared on the large screen behind her, revealing a small icon of a cloud among various apps for restaurants and flight deals. Naomi pressed a button on her phone, and the large screen filled with soothing pastel colors. Having never seen that screen page before, Eli's grandiose *Head of UX* title had instantly lost all meaning.

Within moments, three icons materialized in the middle of the screen: a sun, clouds, and rain. Naomi clicked on the rain icon, prompting an enthusiastic round of applause from the audience. As a bright red light lit up the base of the vacuum cleaner, Naomi placed it on top of the aquarium and it started sucking up the sand. In a matter of seconds, a small plume of cloud rose from the appliance, gradually thickening as it ascended toward the auditorium ceiling. A minute later, the cloud reached its full volume.

"A third of the world's population lives in the desert. An estimated eight hundred million people lack access to running water," Naomi said, and asked the audience to imagine the vast impact their device could create. The photo of a young African boy standing with a bucket in the middle of the desert appeared on the screen. "Very soon, when we complete development, photos like this one here will be a thing of the past."

When she was interrupted by another round of applause, Eli grasped—despite his limited experience in all industry matters—that she wasn't selling a product, but a self-image.

"The future is already here, you just have to choose it." A split second after she concluded her presentation, the first raindrop landed on stage, swiftly followed by a multitude of others. The cloud hung exactly over Naomi's head, almost as if it had been tailored to the stage's dimensions, the rain falling in a perfect, symmetrical circle. Picking up, the rain spilled off stage, wetting the feet of the delighted front-row audience as they erupted in ecstatic cheers.

A few minutes later the rain subsided, the cloud dispersed, and Eli scanned the faces in the audience, rows upon rows of instant admirers not only of the groundbreaking invention, but also of his sister. In the right aisle, he spotted his mother, beaming with pride.

While other speakers followed, it was Naomi's presentation that had everybody buzzing during intermission. People couldn't stop talking about how unsurprising it was that the brilliant Gould had recognized her talent. Eli overheard some attendees refer to his sister as a "young Jobs." As expected, he located his mother by the sandwich stand, debating between egg salad and feta.

"Why didn't you go onstage?"

"It worked out for the best," she replied, reaching for the feta.

"You always get sick of feta after one bite. Take the egg salad."

She did as he suggested. "I might have been a little thrown off learning about your visit to the church," she said, but fell silent when Naomi walked up. "Naomishka, you were absolutely fantastic," she switched gears. "A cut above the rest."

Naomi's lips curved into an uncharacteristically bashful smile.

Eli was dumbfounded. His mother's reaction to his visit to the church, the rain in the auditorium . . . he felt as if reality itself was accelerating.

"You really threw us for a loop there, Mom, but I think we're good now." Naomi pointed at the man standing behind her—the smarmy VC rep from the dingy strip mall café.

"He couldn't wait to meet you," Naomi added in what Eli felt were carefully chosen words. "He knows a lot about technology and has helped countless companies."

"I want you to know, Mrs. Lilienblum, I have a particular interest in disruptive tech, and what you've created meets the criteria and then some."

"Disruptive?" Sarai asked, confused.

"That's not a negative term," Sagi quickly clarified, explaining that the venture capitalist was referring to technologies that shake up the market. He reassured her that it was perhaps the biggest compliment a tech company could get. The rep nodded.

"I think that with the help of our funding and industry connections, your technology could change the world," the rep said.

"You represent a venture capital?" Sarai asked.

"One of the largest in the country, ma'am. We provide our partners with much more than a—"

But Sarai already had her back to him, gently nudging people out of her way to the tapas stand at the end of the hall.

"Oh god, I'm so sorry," Naomi stammered, explaining that these had been long, tiring days, and that her mother was "new to the tech world."

"I get that she wants to do things her own way, and I even admire it," the rep said with a sympathetic smile, "but I'd be remiss not to say that I've been in this industry long enough to know that no one can climb Everest without a little help." He took his leave from Naomi with a friendly handshake.

"Do you understand that there are literally hundreds of CEOs who would kill for an offer from that VC?" Naomi took her frustration out on her brother.

"You weren't exactly thrilled about the idea of working with them either," Eli replied.

"The difference is that I know when to face the music, and she never will."

With Naomi in the front seat, the taxi taking the three back to the Cliff carefully navigated the dark desert roads. Eli's phone pinged with a text from Tamara; she missed him but was so tired she could barely keep her eyes open, and promised they would meet tomorrow. His skin tingled with the thought of seeing her.

"I can't believe they still haven't installed street lights around here. Lousy country," the driver grumbled, but none of the Lilienblums responded.

Neither did they respond to Boaz, who eagerly awaited them at the front door with a slew of questions as he helped haul in their suitcases. Sarai bounded upstairs before Eli could talk to her about the church, and Naomi retreated to her room. Eli had questions of his own, and he decided it was high time he got answers, at least to some of them. He grabbed his father's black coat and set off to Hannah Bialika's house.

8

He found Hannah lounging on her recliner with her feet up, watching TV and draped in an oversized red sweater over white sweatpants. Her hair was messy and her face more wrinkled than he'd remembered, but perhaps he was simply used to seeing her with makeup. "It's good to see you," she greeted him, and shifted her gaze back to the TV.

"Why haven't you transferred the money yet?"

She nodded and pointed at the screen. "That's Roberto Benigni, outstanding Italian actor, I adore him."

Eli walked up and blocked the screen. "Why haven't you transferred the money?"

Hannah looked at him and sighed. "Look, honey, I'd love to explain everything, but once I do, you won't come back, and I need a few more dreams, you understand?"

"You owe me an explanation."

Hannah gently held his hand. "Let me give you some free advice—once you understand that no one owes anyone anything in this life, everything becomes a lot easier," she said. "Three dreams, and I'll tell you everything."

"One dream."

"Two."

"One."

"Fine. Tonight we dream, tomorrow I'll explain."

He shook his head. "First you explain, then we dream."

"And how will I know you'll stay?"

"Do you have a choice?"

"Well well well, look at you." She laughed. "I remember it was the same with Mandy, as if he just woke up savvy one day." She motioned toward the chair opposite her, turned down the volume, but kept her eyes on the screen. "Do you remember I told you how Mandy never forgave me for selling the factory behind his back?"

"Nor should he have."

"I see you came with a chip on your shoulder," she said, considering him. She reached for the glass of orange juice at the foot of her armchair and took a small sip. "I remember that on one of our first visits to the Cliff, when this house here was just an idea, he asked the architect how long the house could last, and the architect answered that *last* was a tricky word. He explained that the foundations could remain intact for centuries, but the interior would crumble at some point." She said that to this day, she believed the architect was describing what he saw in the two of them. "Our relationship—a marriage spanning over five decades—appeared to be built on solid foundations, but between us, everything had already begun to rot," Hannah said. "All those romantic Hollywood movies that try to sell us the idea of love as a journey to Timbuktu. The road is long and hard but the moment you get there it all magically works out. It's all picture-perfect. But that's the image, not the reality of love. In real life, it's like running in your underwear up the second highest mountain of the Himalayas on the coldest day of the year. You always have to keep moving, stay alert."

"Not everything is a battle."

"Not everything, but love is. For by wise counsel thou shalt make thy love. By trickery and schemes."

"I meant that not everything in love is a war." Eli's voice hiked up, and he didn't understand why he was getting upset.

"What isn't?"

"Kids, for instance. Do you battle over kids?" he asked defiantly.

"Of course!" she cried out.

Eli closed his eyes.

"Actually, I don't really know." She was slightly hesitant. "We didn't have kids."

Eli was surprised, said he was sure the pictures near the elevator were of her children, but she said they were her nephews, whom they had only seen once every few years.

Hannah said that even in hindsight she couldn't pinpoint the exact moment when their relationship had gone bust. Was it the sale of the factory? The countless years working together? The child they never had? She'd heard there were certain diseases that lay dormant in the brain for thirty years before the first symptom surfaces. And maybe it was the same with love. "Imagine that. Fading for thirty years without even knowing."

"When did you tell him you were dreaming his dreams?" he asked, weary of her stories.

"When I had no choice." At some point Mandy started to experience burnout and said it was time to slow down. "But I was sure he was wrong. I tried to explain that it was never about the money, per se, but the ability it gave us to lead a meaningful life and leave a legacy that would live on decades after we were gone."

"So how did you get him to change his mind?" Eli asked, having spent enough time in her company to know she'd gotten her way.

"One day Mandy had a dream that we didn't have enough in our pension fund to support our retirement, and I realized this was something that scared him. So the next morning I casually mentioned the word *pension* and let it percolate, and a few days later Mandy decided to postpone his retirement. He said he'd continue working for one more year and then retire. It was always supposed to be just one more year. The problem was that I got careless. I found myself blurting out in our conversations details I wasn't supposed to know."

Eventually, Mandy confided that he was scared something was wrong with his head; he couldn't remember telling her certain things, but he must have told her because how else would she know them? When his fears began to consume him, she realized that if she didn't reassure him that there was nothing wrong with him, he really would lose his mind. That's when she decided to come clean, admitting that she was dreaming his dreams, and that was how she knew. "And you know what? That night he slept better than he had in years. He was so relieved to learn he was sane that he wasn't even angry with me," she said. "But the following night he couldn't fall asleep, and on the third night he slept in his study." He said that the thought of her poking around his subconscious was paralyzing, and while he was sure he would eventually get over it, he needed a few days to process everything. "From that point on, over the next thirty years of our life together, we never shared a full night's sleep in the same bed. If it had been up to him, he would never have slept in our bedroom again, but he knew that without dreaming I'd lose my will to live, so we compromised: two nights a week, three hours of shared sleep in the same room. He'd read somewhere that three hours constituted a single sleep cycle, the minimum required for dreaming. He'd set an alarm clock and move to his study as soon as it sounded." Even in his dreams he drew further and further away from her, often dreaming of other women. "Maybe he even enjoyed making me suffer a little." She admitted that there was nothing more painful than discovering the contents of your loved one's subconscious. "Every mistake, regret, perversion was laid bare. There was nothing I didn't know, and very soon I realized there was a reason human beings were created separately."

Eli asked why he didn't just divorce her if it was so bad for him, and she replied that in their generation it wasn't so simple. And what's more, Mandy was profoundly conservative. Given the option, he'd always choose pain over change. For a long time they managed to find a formula that made life bearable, but in the latter years, when his head wasn't what it had once been, he started seeing a demon in the place where she once stood. He told her that everything in life could be bought except time, and accused her of robbing him of his best years in pursuit of her dreams. "And maybe there was a kernel of truth to it, but that kernel blinded him to everything that was good about us." He could only see the negative, and she didn't know how to dispel his hatred. "You know, Mandy once told me what made us humans so strange was that we were nature's most compassionate creatures, but also the cruelest. It was unbelievable how the world could be so full of man's cruelty and compassion at the same time. Mandy embodied that paradox—he was both cruel and compassionate. In our early years, mostly the latter, but later, the cruelty took over."

"So that's why he left the house to the local council and not you? Out of revenge?"

"Not just the house. All of Bialika Industry's stocks, holdings, investments—the whole shebang. He donated it all to charity. And he could." She explained that he insisted on putting everything in his name because of the incident with the factory, that it was his one condition to doing business together. "All those years I was sure he wouldn't dare move one shekel without my approval. So sure, in fact, that I never even considered the idea of transferring the assets into joint ownership. When I started thinking it might be the prudent thing to do, I knew there was no point in raising the matter. He wouldn't listen. This house," she said, waving at the room, "is like a pyramid built for an Egyptian king. Only I'm not the king, I'm the woman forced to lie in his sarcophagus next to his mummy." To this day she wasn't sure if Mandy truly had wanted to live on the Cliff, or simply relished the idea of her being stuck in Nowheresville with no ability to sell the house, trapped in their wealth. He made her live in the biggest house in the world—the least suitable for an eighty-year-old woman. "It's as if he was trying to tell me, you can have all the luxury you've ever dreamed of, with all the misery it brings."

"So he didn't leave you anything?"

"He left a little."

Eli said it didn't make sense, that surely she could argue for at least half of the inheritance. She acknowledged that he might be right, but said Mandy's lawyer was even cheaper and more ruthless than his client, and that if she decided to take legal action, he would drag it out until she had one foot in the grave. There was a time when she considered moving to a small apartment, perhaps in Haifa. But she realized the real problem wasn't that she'd run out of money, but that everyone would find out Mandy had disowned her, cut her off. To lose the image of a rich person meant losing the very last asset she had. "It's hilarious how everyone on the Cliff is waiting for me to croak, certain I'm wiping my ass with dollar bills, pardon my French, when in reality I'm pinching pennies to afford yogurt."

"But you paid me a thousand shekels for every night of dreams!"

"Of course! For dreams I spare no expense!" She threw her hands up impatiently. She told him she'd once heard an economist argue that the poor had a problem with delaying gratification, choosing a fifty-inch plasma TV over a nourishing dinner. "But anyone who has ever fallen on hard times knows that while a healthy meal is nice, it's the fifty-inch plasma that will make you feel like a human being. So yes, I'd spend my last penny on dreams." She closed her eyes. "But then you told me about your mother and that invention of hers, and I'm no hi-tech expert, but it occurred to me that it could be a chance to pull one last rabbit out of the hat. So I set aside the bare minimum to cover my living expenses for another year, and the rest, half a million shekels, I invested in your mom's company."

"You promised us four million dollars."

"If I'd offered less you'd have turned me away and waited for another investor." She had no idea they would burn through her money so fast. "I didn't factor in the parquet floor and Mexican fiesta week."

Sitting across from him, she looked tiny and ancient, and Eli saw in her what she had seen in Mandy: compassion and cruelty. He rose, placed her glass in the sink, helped her up, and walked her to her bedroom. As she lay down in her bed, he settled into the yellow armchair.

She fell asleep in a flash, and he pictured Mandy occupying that bed twice a week, only to wake up in the middle of the night and move to his study. How resentful he must have felt to set an alarm clock just so he wouldn't have to lie next to her for a few more hours. And yet, he still chose to go back twice a week. For her sake. Even if she believed that everything between them had disintegrated, something essential and alive must have remained beneath the ruins.

45
DAYS
TILL
RAIN

li and Naomi were sitting in her office when the call from Ben Gould's secretary came, a week and a half after the convention. It took his sister almost a full minute to believe it wasn't a prank call, and another minute to snap out of the shock. Operating under the assumption that Ben Gould's impending visit to the Cliff in just over six weeks was widely known, the secretary promptly fired off a barrage of administrative questions: the distance between the Cliff and the nearest airport, accommodations for the press; dry, technical questions that failed to reflect the singularity of the event, that one of the world's wealthiest men was about to make his way to their godforsaken desert village just to witness their mother's invention.

"Ben-Gurion must be doing somersaults in his grave!" Eli exclaimed, but his sister soberly explained that with the visit becoming an imminent reality, they had a countdown of of less than two months to make their cloud machine rain down on the entire Cliff—a mission that bordered on the fantastical. And that was even before addressing the budget shortfall, which Naomi only barely, cunningly, managed to hide—casually claiming, for instance, that the prepaid lunch card had stopped working because of a technical glitch, and that the scheduled business trip abroad kept getting delayed for the sole reason that they had yet to find a suitable hotel. While the email scam she ran from the secret room was the only lifeline keeping Cloudies afloat, the money it generated fell far short of what was needed to sustain the company's operations. It was just enough for Naomi to dispense small handouts that allowed her to maintain a facade of wealth and convenience.

"If anyone can make it happen, it's you," he stated confidently. "What, you think we won't be able to produce enough rain?"

"I have my doubts," she said.

"But you already managed it once, at the convention."

"The problem is I have absolutely no idea how we did it."

She explained that her engineers had been diligently working on it for the last two weeks, dismantling their mom's machine down to the tiniest parts and tinkering with them round the clock. They couldn't figure out what in that simple mechanism—vacuum cleaner, funnel, a miscellany of screw and pipes—defied the laws of chemistry and extracted clouds from desert sand. "And the strangest part is that when they reassemble all the pieces, it works, turns sand into clouds just like it did the first time. For all their fancy degrees they can't explain how it works, as if only Mom's magical touch can create such a bizarre-slash-miraculous phenomenon." She told him it only worked with the red vacuum from the video, the one he and Tamara had found. They discovered that with a specific type of sand from the northern part of the crater, Mom's vacuum could generate a small amount of rain, which she demonstrated at the convention. "But to reproduce it in large quantities, like Gould expects? I have no idea how to pull that off."

"But what does Mom say when you ask her how the machine works?"

His sister shrugged in resignation. "That she doesn't know either."

"So we have about six weeks to get it to work?"

"If only schedules meant anything to Mom," she muttered.

"Okay, so we have to talk to her, explain the situation. Maybe bring Albert and Alice on board. I think they can help her."

Naomi sighed. "There are many things I know how to do, Eli. Getting Mom to listen isn't one of them."

He gave a sympathetic nod.

They agreed to give it a try.

Their mother was in the adjacent hangar, standing alone by a wooden table in the corner, slashing open a large cardboard box with a box cutter. She reached in and pulled out a device that looked like a small fan attached to an old cellphone. He knew this new invention interested her more than any startup.

"Mom, we need to talk."

"About what?" she asked indifferently, placed the fan on the table, put on safety goggles with a magnifying glass on the right lens, and took out a small screwdriver from her pocket.

As his mother proceeded to dismantle the device, he told her about the offer they'd received from the venture capital fund, and about her admirers, Alice and Albert, the cooling inventors who wanted to be part of her mission to change the world.

"That's very kind of them, but not interested," Sarai said.

"Oh, for crying out loud, Mom," Eli snapped, departing from the usual gentle tone he took with her. "There's no more money. It's all gone, you understand?" Slowly, he unraveled the whole story, sparing no detail—the strained relationship between Hannah Bialika and her husband, the nonexistent money, Ben Gould's impending visit, the loan their father had taken, and finally, the looming deadline to save the company.

From behind her safety goggles, his mother's gaze remained fixed on the wind gauge, but the manner in which she disassembled the blades suggested that his words had unsettled her. Naomi told her about their meeting with Albert and Alice and their cooling technology—which might just prove to be the last piece of the cloud machine puzzle—and about the money from the VC fund that would give them some much-needed breathing room.

Slowly setting the screwdriver on the table, their mother looked at Naomi. "So you think we should go for it?"

"Absolutely, there's no doubt in my mind."

"And you?" she asked Eli.

"Albert and Alice seem like upright people. They care about the science."

"Let me think about it," she said, and started lining up the wind gauge parts. "Don't worry, I realize you need an answer quickly."

Surprised by their mother's pragmatic response, Naomi quietly left the hangar, as if any sound or gesture might cause Sarai to reconsider.

Eli remained by his mother, watching her work silently with laser focus. He wanted to thank her for being so cooperative, but instead only said, "Can you believe that Hannah? She really screwed us over, huh?"

Without looking up from her work table, she replied, "Don't ask me to be angry at people who are just trying to carve out a space for themselves in the world."

2

A top the ski ramp, Tamara and Eli took in the pink sunset. Since coming back from the convention he had made it their daily ritual, and twice he had even scurried out of a work meeting so as not to miss the sun dipping below the horizon.

Evening after evening he told her about his life. At first about the things he'd discovered at the church, the camel, childhood memories like the pen his mother had shot into the air, and the feeling that his father had been, to some extent, left behind. He admitted he didn't know what he'd do without his sister beside him. Then he started in about God and how he was at once both a believer and nonbeliever, about his fear of death always lurking in the background, and that time as a kid when he was absolutely convinced he had the ability—through sheer concentration—to become invisible. He noticed her attentive expression as she listened to his stories, and vowed to imprint the memory of it on his mind. The story she seemed most intrigued by was the one his mother had shared at the convention, the tale about the broken vessels. Eli said he had only a faint recollection of the event, and while he didn't remember the specifics, he certainly didn't question her interpretation.

"That's weird, because letting things go to pieces goes against your most basic instincts," Tamara said. "You're constantly busy doing the opposite, piecing things together with whatever means necessary—your hands, tongue, ears. Whatever it takes to keep things from falling apart." Placing a gentle hand on his arm, she said it seemed that at some point in his life, he had taken it upon himself to be the glue holding his family together, even when the pieces didn't entirely fit. "You're like those people you told me about, who build a whole city just for day-trippers. The thing is, you insist on staying in the city you've built long after everyone else has left."

"That's not true." He knew it was.

"Then why aren't you asking your mother what she was doing in that church?"

"Haven't gotten a chance yet."

"You know that's not why."

"Okay, why then?"

"Because you never ask tough questions of the people you care about. It's like you don't want to confront them with reality or make them face the hard truths, like finding out there's no moon in their bucket."

He was surprised that she remembered the story about the wise men of Chelm. "So what do you think she was doing at the church?"

"I think the more interesting question is why she told the reverend she was McMurphy's mother," she replied, a question that Eli was troubled by himself. Over the last few days he went through all the artifacts in the McMurphy Museum. He found a drawing of a face that resembled the reverend, but more importantly, he couldn't find any place where McMurphy wrote about owing him money. Either his mother made up the story, or she had the notes that Robert McMurphy wrote. Notes that have never been found.

"Do you think my mom might be connected to McMurphy's disappearance?" The thought had crossed his mind before, but now he finally voiced it. He confided in Tamara that on the day they found their mother, he and Naomi had tried to activate the universal AC she'd built, which led to the room filling up with sand whose source they couldn't locate. "And after you asked me about the blueprints for our house, I asked my dad about it."

"And what did he say?"

"That my mom took it," he said, lowering his voice.

She put her hand on his knee. "So you're thinking that wherever she's hiding the sand, she might also be hiding . . ."

"No, I don't think she's hiding McMurphy." He laughed. "But maybe something has to do with him. Maybe. I'm not sure."

The following day, while at the office with Naomi and Sarai, Eli announced that he was going home for lunch.

Tamara was waiting for him at his front door. He led her into his mother's white study, empty save for some sand scattered on the floor, and from there into his parents' bedroom, where Eli poked around, careful not to leave a trace of intrusion. Tamara, meanwhile, moved about freely, opening dressers and drawers, feeling very much at home and making Eli feel uneasy. Still, he didn't stop her.

"Everything is so ordinary it's almost too boring to look at," she remarked. It was true. The only unique aspect of their family life was his mother's inventions, and with those gone, the house seemed sad.

She wanted to canvass the other rooms, but Eli was reluctant to stay longer than a typical lunch at home would take.

"What are you so afraid of?" she asked in frustration, and then conceded, "Fine, we'll pick this up tomorrow around lunchtime."

For the first few days he casually offered excuses for his brief midday departures to any Cloudies employee who would listen, until he realized no one cared where he was, least of all Naomi and Sarai. Together with Tamara, he meticulously combed through the bathroom, laundry room, living room, balcony, cabinets, under the beds, and above the AC units. He remembered how his father had once scoured these very spaces in search of his mother, and now experienced a profound empathy bordering on the physical. Even the heavy furniture was moved from its original positions, yielding not a clue. Strangely, this only bolstered Eli's suspicion that his mother might indeed be connected to McMurphy's disappearance.

3.

Lying awake at night, he thought Tamara might be right about him being terrified of leaving the Cliff. He knew it wasn't only a deep connection that tied him to the place, but also the fear that overtook him whenever he imagined the uncertainty of life elsewhere. When Tamara had described the thrill of being in that unmapped lighthouse, he had felt nothing but anxiety at the thought of visiting such a place, where no one would be able to find him if he was in need of help. Through the wall, he overheard Naomi on the phone shouting at one of her engineers. "Uriel, for goodness' sake, patch the garbage bag you tore with gum if you have to, got it? You're not taking out a single part from that vacuum cleaner," she barked.

"That idiot," Naomi said to Eli through the wall. "Yesterday he needed me to show him how to put the batteries in the vacuum. God knows how that man graduated from the Technion."

"Maybe the Technion's admissions committee needs Mom to come show them how to interview," Eli said, earning a chuckle from Naomi. He closed his eyes, trying to doze, but something hadn't sounded right. "Wait, what batteries? The vacuum cleaner has a cord."

"No, no, it's battery-powered; I have no idea how Mom did it. The cord is there just for appearances. It doesn't serve any real purpose."

It didn't make sense. His mother never added parts to a device just for the fun of it. It went against her very nature. And then it dawned on him. The clue had been staring him in the face since the day they brought her home from the hospital, and practically screaming at him in her video from the desert. All along, his mother had been pointing to one spot.

God, how could he have missed it?

The entire night he alternated between sleep and wakefulness, but around five in the morning, he found himself fully alert. He dressed silently, tiptoed downstairs, closed the door gently, and headed to Cloudies, where he found the red vacuum cleaner standing upright in the engineers' area, its electric cord neatly coiled around a table leg. He picked it up and carried it home.

Around seven, when his sister woke up, he told her he had a headache and would join her at the office later. He felt bad for the poor engineer whose table he had taken the vacuum cleaner from, knowing the famed machine's absence would soon be noticed. When he heard his parents and Naomi leave the house, he called Tamara. It was only in her presence that he could test the limits of his courage.

Tamara finally showed up. With the vacuum cleaner, they entered Sarai's empty white study. He pointed at the thin layer of sand on the floor. "I don't understand how I didn't pick up on it from the beginning," he said, and gestured at the wall in front of him. He carefully unspooled the cord and approached the triangular outlet in the middle of the wall. "The vacuum cleaner actually works on batteries."

"So the cord and outlet are what, ornamental? I don't get it."

"No, they have another use. In her head it was never a power outlet."

"So what is it?" Tamara was visibly confused.

"A key," Eli replied, connecting the cord to the outlet.

Nothing happened.

"Maybe you have to turn it," Tamara suggested.

The plug-key turned easily, and the lock clicked open. A small fissure emerged in the wall, just above Eli's head.

"Feel it," Tamara said, pressing against the wooden panels. At Eli's gentle touch, the crack extended itself, slowly slithering along the wall. Similar to the restaurant's hidden room, the wall gradually parted in the middle, folding outward on both sides to reveal a rusty steel door with a small, gleaming lock.

"Do you have the key we found?" he asked with a tremulous voice. Nodding, she rummaged through her bag for her wallet and produced the key. Eli's body tensed as she inserted it in the lock. It wouldn't budge. She gave it a few more attempts before stepping aside and letting Eli try. It wasn't the right key. "She must have switched locks."

Tamara bent down and traced her finger along the lock. "You mentioned a can opener earlier? The one your mother invented?" Eli ran to the kitchen and came back with his mother's laser can opener.

"Fingers crossed," he mumbled. Aiming the laser pointer at the lock, he placed a hesitant finger on the button.

"Yalla," she urged him with a Spanish inflection. "Press it."

He pressed the button and a small purple beam made contact with the lock; within moments, it began to melt the metal as if it were ice cream on a hot summer day. The metal sizzled and oozed until it separated into two pieces, the upper part of the lock remaining suspended on the latch and the lower part falling to the floor. With a smile, Eli touched the door, which opened as soundlessly as a hair being removed from a glass of water.

It was something between a small room and a large closet, the faint light filtering in illuminating large sacks on the floor. Gently poking a sack, he could tell it was filled with sand. He then noticed a big plastic tube connecting them to the adjacent wall. That's where the sand came from that had filled the room on the day she returned. That was the secret compartment his mother was hiding.

Tamara flipped the light switch, and a naked bulb lit up the room in a buzzing yellow glow. A lone wooden closet stood before them, containing hiking shirts, a black fleece jacket, two pairs of pants—one blue and the other black with a slight tear at the top—a blue hydration pack with an orange cap, and a frayed bandana. A purple plastic basket with men's underwear sat nearby. Running his finger over the dusty yet neatly folded garments, Eli thought it strange that of all places, it was in this hidden nook that his messy mother had chosen to maintain such meticulous order. Continuing to scan the closet's contents, he noticed a small red wooden box next to a few notebooks, most of them black and one red. There was also a beanie hat featuring an image of a duck, and a large backpack with two words stitched to a patch of canvas on top: Robert McMurphy. *He was real*, Eli thought.

"Unbelievable," Tamara declared. "So she's the one who's been scattering his clothes across the desert all these years?"

Eli had no answer. He suspected her three-day disappearance had been deliberate—an attempt to hint at her connection to McMurphy. But what was she trying to say? He couldn't understand how his clothes had been lying there for so many years without anyone noticing. Not his father, not Naomi, not even himself. He'd once come across a study in which scientists had raised kittens from birth without exposing them to a horizontal line. When the kittens reached maturity, they couldn't see horizontal lines even when they were right in front of them. Their brains simply hadn't developed the ability to recognize them.

He felt lightheaded. Her peculiar behavior all those years, her mood swings, her summer stupors. He left the small room and returned to the study, where he heard keys jangling and the front door slowly swooshing open.

"She knows we're in here," he whispered to Tamara, who grabbed his hand and gestured at a thin cord in the corner of the nook, which looked like it might be part of a concealed alert system. At the sound of footsteps on the staircase, Eli pictured his mother's face when she opened the door and saw them, expecting it to be flushed, sweaty, and frightened.

And the face greeting him was indeed just that, but it didn't belong to his mother.

4.

Unlike his mother, his father rarely told Eli stories, and the few he did weren't tales of far-flung mostly fictional places like Chelm, but grounded in reality, fact-based, and often repetitive accounts. Among the paltry selection was Eli's favorite, about the day his mother launched a pen into the sky. Boaz described the pen landing on the windowsill of a house at the edge of the neighborhood, marring the facade with a big ink splotch. He noticed it the next day on his way to the grocery store, spotting the neighbor up on a ladder trying to wipe it off. From the top rung, the neighbor told him he intended to file a police complaint to find the perpetrator, but Boaz managed to dissuade him. Volunteering to help him clean the wall and citing a fictitious world-renowned-ornithologist-distant-relative, Boaz blamed the stain on a flock of migratory birds from Africa who were known to swoop down during their travels through Israel's blue skies, snatch things from people's hands—e.g., pens—and drop them from above just for kicks. He convinced the neighbor that the stain was the work of an evil flamingo or sinister crane. It always cracked Eli up, the idea that his father would concoct a zoological phenomenon just to protect his mother. He thought that everyone deserved to have a Boaz on their side, a serial helper-outer who'd top up the parking meter right before the inspector arrived, or stick out his foot to hold the elevator. But now, with his father standing before him flushed and embarrassed, Eli realized he'd had it wrong all those years. It was his mother who'd been protecting him.

"Hey there," Boaz said with an awkward wave, as if they just happened to bump into each other on the street, rather than in a hidden closet.

"Explain," Eli demanded.

Boaz placed his hand on his chest. "It's a little stuffy in here, let's go downstairs and talk over a cup of coffee."

"Explain," Eli replied. "Now."

"That stubborn streak you got from your mother." Boaz chuckled. Eli recognized that strained chuckle; it was his father's last line of defense when he felt overly exposed. It was Boaz's way of handling all the topics they weren't allowed to discuss, and there were quite a few. They avoided talking about politics, their debts, what happens after you die, or the fact that Naomi was making infinitely more money than his parents could ever fathom. They also avoided discussing the council head, who'd been promising for years to help his father out but never followed through, his mother's seasonal funk, or the fact that she'd been withering away living on the Cliff. It was Boaz's awkward chuckle that marked the boundaries of the family silence, and no one had kept those boundaries more faithfully than Eli. But no more.

"If you don't come clean right now, I'll tell," he said in English, his voice surprisingly steady.

His father raised an eyebrow. "Tell what? Tell who, Eli'le?"

"Everyone." Eli took his phone out of his pocket and began snapping photos of the room, then aimed the camera right at his father's embarrassed face. "I'm going to post these on every social media platform I know."

"Oh, be serious, Eli," Boaz raised his voice. "This isn't a game, there are a lot of people involved, a lot at stake, you can't just . . ." he faltered.

Eli kept his eyes on his screen, typing, "Look what I found! #searchingformcmurphy, #robertmcmurphy." He raised his phone defiantly, his thumb ready to hit post.

"Fine." Boaz sighed, and gestured at Tamara. "But this is a family matter, private."

Eli shook his head, but Tamara, who didn't understand Hebrew but grasped Boaz's request, placed a comforting hand on Eli's shoulder. "Good day, Mr. Lilienblum," she said formally before walking out.

They could hear her footsteps on the stairs, gradually fading away; when they were no longer audible, his father allowed himself to relax, his shoulders sagging. The front door clicked shut and Boaz leaned back against the wall and sank into a squat, his legs drawn in close and knees nearly touching.

Eli observed his father's futile attempt at calming himself through his meditative breathing exercise. "So you did see Robert McMurphy."

His father glided his hand over the floor, inspecting the dust. "I ran into him when he was staying on the Cliff." Boaz explained that back then—over a decade ago—he was so consumed with finding ways to dig himself out of debt that he barely noticed what was happening around him. One morning, a tall Irish man with a feral beard and unruly curls shambled up to the front desk, shivering cold, and inquired into their cheapest room. "He'd clearly spent the previous night sleeping outdoors," Boaz said, and Eli was surprised that this mythical, enigmatic figure was very much alive and real in his father's memory. "He was obviously struggling, and I didn't have it in me to send him back out into the cold. I told him he could sleep in the restaurant, which was just a storage room at the time, and charged him a few bucks."

"Did you tell him you actually needed the money?" Eli asked. "Did you tell him about the debts?"

"As a matter of fact, I did," said Boaz, and Eli wasn't surprised. He did not know the content of their conversation, but he understood that there was something about Robert McMurphy that made the people reveal themselves to him.

"And he didn't say much. He just wished he could find a way to help," said Boaz. "I know it's something people say, but I believed him. It really bothers him that he didn't have any more money to pay."

That was Boaz's only meeting with Robert McMurphy. "He left the key on the desk a few days later and that was it, he went back out into the cold." Somewhat guiltily, he confessed that much like the thousands of travelers before him, McMurphy had popped into his life for a fleeting moment before being completely erased from his mind.

Stretching his back against the wall, his father told him that the first McMurphy tourist arrived a few months after McMurphy's disappearance, a fellow Irishman who knew him from church. "He started posting things about 'the guy who disappeared in the desert as if the earth had swallowed him whole.' He spun the story into this giant mystery, and must have had quite an online following because people started pouring in, almost like a pilgrimage. That was the first time I realized the power a good story had on people." About three months after the first tourists came looking for McMurphy, the council head visited the lodge to talk about our tourism plan for next year. "That same morning our vacuum cleaner broke down, so I went to get a new one from the storage room, and when I was already halfway out the door with it, I noticed the bag in the corner." Boaz gestured at the blue-black bag in the room-closet, with Robert McMurphy's name stitched on it. "That's when I realized that the poor guy who'd been sleeping there was the one everyone was searching for."

Did it really take his father that long to connect the dots? Travelers from all over the world had been asking about the guy for months, and it only dawned on him when he saw the bag? A surge of anger running through him, Eli asked, "And it didn't even occur to you to inform the police?" As if stung by the question, his father shot up and stood in front of him, exclaiming, "Of course it occurred to me! It was the very first thing that crossed my mind!" He explained that the only reason he'd been dragging his feet was the meeting with the council head. He uttered the words "dragging my feet" as if he genuinely believed he'd be handing over the items to the police any day now, as if the intervening decade was nothing but a small technical hiccup.

Watching his father approach the door to the small room and run his hand over the singed lock, Eli tensed. It hit him. "That was you? That night in the crater?" he asked. Nodding, Boaz admitted that he had thought he was overreacting by changing locks. "But using the can opener to cut through the lock? I never would have thought of it," he admitted. "During the meeting with the council head, he said that whole story about the traveler disappearing really dropped into my lap like a miracle, because without the McMurphy tourists, the council wouldn't have extended my lease, and I knew—"

"That you don't just pass on a miracle." Eli finished his father's thought.

His father nodded again, then headed into the room-closet with Eli in tow. His eyes swept over the items on the shelves and lingered on the wooden red box. He brushed off the dust, cradled it with both hands, and opened it carefully. Inside the box was a yellowing postcard with the picture of the Cliff, the crater stretching into the horizon, and the houses off to the side. Boaz turned the postcard over and examined it under the light. The handwritten text was short.

> *Thank you for the warm hospitality, Mr. Lilienblum!*
> *I have an idea how to help you get back on your feet.*
> *More details coming soon . . .*
>
> *RM*

"You see, Eli, he planned this all along," Boaz said. "He didn't forget his bag in the cabin. He left it for me."

Eli read the last sentence over and over again. "Don't tell me you think he planned his disappearance to become a tourist attraction . . ."

"I don't think, I know," Boaz answered calmly.

Eli said it made no sense. "People who disappear usually don't become a myth. How could he have known this was what would happen?"

Boaz raised his hands in the air. "From a logical point of view, you're right," his father answered, "but McMurphy's story is not logical."

He said that all these years since, he thought about that single encounter with McMurphy over and over. "And every time I came to the same idea—that maybe Robert McMurphy was willing to disappear into the desert, to help another person."

If Eli hadn't met other people who described Robert McMurphy, he would have thought it was just his father's wishful thinking. But he met other people who gave similar descriptions that planted doubts in his mind. Was it really so implausible to imagine that someone who is willing to bear the pain of the entire world in their heart would create such a myth to help another human being?

Boaz said that the very next day, he drove all the way to the Irish embassy in Tel Aviv, hoping to obtain records with information about the missing traveler. The embassy staff cooperated, thinking that Boaz might assist in their own investigation. "The records clearly showed that McMurphy was an orphan who had no one—no parents, siblings, or relatives. A lone soul, and his father was his last connection to society."

"What are you talking about? His mother visited a year ago!" Eli exclaimed. "He was not a *lone soul.*"

"We didn't know that at the time." Boaz sighed with a shrug, explaining he pursued it himself for months, instead of simply relying on the records. He sent letters to both the foreign and interior ministries of Ireland, and to the municipality in McMurphy's hometown. He carried out his investigation with steadfast attention to detail, telling himself that the moment he found a living relative, he would send them all of McMurphy's belongings. But despite his thorough search, he came up empty-handed. "And as time passed, I couldn't shake the idea of McMurphy being a loner with no family looking for him, and I guess autosuggestion really is a powerful tool, because I honestly convinced myself that turning his story into a tourist attraction was the honorable thing to do, the only way to keep his memory alive. That this is what McMurphy would have wanted. To vanish. To become a shadow. A tale."

His father's account suddenly cast the modest McMurphy Museum, that small room dedicated to his memory, in a new light—no longer a mere tourist trap, but a genuine attempt at atonement by a man plagued by guilt. His father admitted he would bury an item in the desert every few months to create the illusion of an ongoing mystery. He even bought a secret jeep—a cash purchase—that he parked in the village's outskirts, using it exclusively for his nightly drives to the crater's depths, always careful to cover his tracks. "And all those times you went down to the crater with his things, it never occurred to you how wrong it was?"

"Why wasn't the Buddha a vegetarian?" his father replied with a question of his own, then explained that a traveler at the lodge had once told him that when Buddha was only starting out his journey with his followers, they used to panhandle on the streets with an empty bowl, living off whatever food was donated. "They ate what they were given; they didn't start checking every scrap to see if it met their moral standards," he said. And when Eli still looked perplexed, he clarified: "There are certain moral dilemmas which demand a well-fed mindset. And I felt that questioning the morality of the whole thing was a luxury I couldn't afford at the time."

"Until his mother showed up," Eli said.

"Until his mother showed up," Boaz repeated slowly, guiltily.

Out of nowhere, about a year ago, a pudgy woman in her sixties dragged a large suitcase into the lodge, looking like a displaced tourist. He didn't know who she was, but he knew that a woman her age usually didn't just come stay at such a lodge for no reason. Furthermore, she insisted on staying in the cheapest shared room alongside seven smelly-socked travelers. Then, on the third day, asking him for another towel, she told him matter-of-factly, "I'm Robert McMurphy's mother." His heart nearly stopped. Dropping everything he was doing, he led her into his office and sat with her for hours, trying to understand. "She admitted she had walked out on her family when her son was just a toddler, and remained absent from his life for many years." He said she was reluctant to go into detail, but said that she left Robert with his father and started a new life with another man, without looking back. During one of the very few conversations with Robert's father after she had left, he told her Robert was telling people his mother was dead. He even made sure to record it on official forms.

"And not only was she not insulted, she said she was actually relieved, taking it as a sign that her child had managed to move on without her. She said that any normal person with a shred of common sense could tell that Robert's behavior was a cry for help, but back then she just wasn't thinking straight." As time passed, regret began to gnaw at her, and when she finally made the decision to reconnect with her son, she discovered he had vanished. Swallowed up by the desert. His disappearance sparked an intense longing in her heart. "So she decided to come all the way here, alone, to try to retrace his steps through photos and eyewitness accounts," his father finished, and fell silent. Eli pictured McMurphy's mother scouring the desert in search of her son, and sensed that it was this very image that tormented his father. Suddenly his crime had a tangible face, a real, flesh-and-blood victim who was buried under his own myth. "What was her name?" Eli asked, compelled to know.

"Agatha," his father whispered, and Eli closed his eyes and imagined Agatha McMurphy trudging along the crater, drenched in sweat.

"You said, 'We didn't know at the time,'" Eli reminded him. "So Mom knew too."

His father looked puzzled. "I think I've been telling her story for too long. It's better you hear it directly from her."

Considering the weary man in front of him, Eli decided to hold back the many possible retorts swirling through his head. Hannah Bialika was right to say a man could be either compassionate or cruel, but she was wrong to consider them as mutually exclusive qualities. Sometimes people were both at the same time, depending on where you were standing.

Tamara was waiting for Eli on the ski ramp. He managed barely half a sentence before pausing to gather his chaotic thoughts. After a few moments he began telling her everything, slowly, like peeling back a bandage in the most painful way.

She touched his face gently. "We can wait, give it a few days. We don't have to do it today."

"Do what?" He didn't understand.

"Take McMurphy's things to the police."

The thought hadn't even crossed his mind. If they went to the authorities, would his father be arrested for tampering with evidence? Would his mother be considered an accomplice? And what would

Agatha McMurphy think of the couple who had lodged her on the Cliff while hiding the possessions of her missing son? His head was spinning.

"We'll give it a few days," Tamara said. Her hand was warm and comforting and he wished she'd leave it there forever.

li couldn't concentrate in the days after, especially not in the UX department's weekly meeting that revolved primarily around the findings of Paulina's survey of the Cliff's residents regarding the impact of cloud shapes on their moods. Roughly halfway through the meeting, Eli noticed that nobody else seemed engaged either. Their heads were buried in their phones.

"What are you reading?" Eli whispered to Yoel.

"About Cloudies' options," he replied through a clenched jaw.

"If you could please put your phones aside until the end of the meeting," Paulina requested, gesturing at Yoel and Eli. "We really need to decide between animal and geometric shapes like circles and triangles."

Ignoring her, Yoel whispered to Eli, "I'm finding it very hard to understand why certain people in this department were given considerably more options than me." He shot Rivka a dirty look.

"I don't understand," Eli grumbled. "Was the company bought by Google or something and no one told me?"

The department employees exchanged bewildered looks.

Evidently, the night before, they had received an enthusiastic email announcing a three-party deal among Cloudies, a major venture capital fund and a chemical company specializing in cooling technology. The chemical company would help them enhance their cloud composition, and the VC provide the necessary funding to continue the development process and recruit more employees—a collaborative effort that would hopefully get them going by the time Ben Gould visited.

He couldn't believe it. Naomi had struck a deal behind his back. Behind his mother's back. "How? When?"

His gaze drifting outside, Eli spotted Naomi in the aquarium room sitting with a few engineers and a man who, after a moment, he recognized as the VC representative. Without waiting for his colleagues' answers, he got up. The rep must have just cracked a joke because as soon as Eli opened the door, everyone at the table was roaring with laughter, with the rep's laugh being the loudest and most grating.

"Naomi, I need to talk to you," he said.

She looked at him with the expression of a schoolgirl who'd just heard the bell signaling the end of recess. "We'll be wrapping up here soon," she said, with a slight dip in her smile.

The rep rose and extended his hand to Eli. "I'm glad we're all part of the same team now," he said.

Without dignifying him with a look, Eli turned to his sister and barked, "Does he know that the contract he signed has no legal standing?" He never would have thought himself capable of embarrassing her like this, but the revelation about their father had eroded his trust in both of them. "I don't know what she signed, but you should know she doesn't have the authority," he addressed the rest of the room before turning back to her. "Nothing is finalized before you get Mom's approval."

Naomi stood up. "If you'll excuse us, I think my brother and I should step outside for a moment to resolve this misunderstanding," she said, gesturing for Eli to follow her.

"This isn't a misunderstanding, Naomi, it's a hostile takeover," Eli declared. He had no intention of stepping outside or anywhere else with her, lest she talk him into something he didn't want to do.

"The official company documents explicitly state that any changes in the business have to be greenlit by the founders," he said. "I'm a founder and I wasn't informed of this deal."

Naomi rolled her eyes. "Oh god, grow up, Eli. This isn't a *hostile takeover*." She air-quoted. "We need the consent of two out of the three founders to make decisions."

"But I didn't give my consent!" He threw his hands up.

"I know," Naomi said.

Did his mother approve the deal? No way. "She wouldn't have sold her idea to some greedy VC."

"But she did, Eli. Mom and I did the right thing," Naomi said, assuming her responsible-old-sibling tone.

Eli stormed out and went looking for his mother. She was neither in the offices nor at the other hangar. He headed toward the movie theater. She was nowhere in sight. Scanning the empty rows, he settled into a seat in the back and stared at the dark screen, taking a few moments for himself. It suddenly dawned on him that all those office meetings were nothing but an ongoing performance, a show put on by adults who convened daily in their smart clothes and hid the truth not only from others but also from themselves—that most of the time they had no idea what they were doing there.

He had known from day one that Cloudies was a show, but what he was only now coming to understand was that the whole business world was performing on that same stage—a world of inflated professional jargon meant to disguise the inherent unknowingness that existed in the lives of all those roaming the third planet from the sun. But even those who asserted with complete confidence that life was devoid of meaning didn't know it with absolute certainty. They were just as single-minded and ignorant as everyone else. Perhaps, Eli pondered, the only way not to err was to believe that life was meaningful, yes, but also meaningless. To wholeheartedly embrace these two contradictory beliefs. He had thought his mother lived by this principle. She would believe in an invention with religious fervor only to quickly abandon it and move on to the next one, because while everything in life was of the utmost importance, it was also never important enough.

He found her by the crater, not far from Hannah Bialika's house. She was standing near where he thought she'd be, wrapping her arms around herself to ward off the cool fall breeze.

"I know about McMurphy's things," he said.

She kept her gaze straight ahead.

"And to think I always thought you didn't want us in there because it was messy."

She laughed. Maybe that was his superpower, the ability to tear down his mother's defenses. "I went years without even thinking about that damn closet," his mother admitted. She said she always wondered if criminals deep down agonized over their crimes or made peace with them and just moved on. "I wish I could tell you my conscience was killing me the whole time, that I had palpitations, that my skin itched, but I'd be lying," she said, leveling her gaze at him. "I always thought that if you lived in the presence of an injustice, your heart wouldn't stop aching. But the truth is that you just learn to close your eyes. And later learn to open them without seeing." She told him it was only when McMurphy's mother visited the lodge the year before that something inside her broke. "Because suddenly our crime had a victim named Agatha McMurphy. And Agatha had the saddest, weariest face."

Looking out at the crater, he thought about the aging Irish woman and how her boarding the plane from Dublin to the Holy Land marked the moment his life started to crack—that was the story's Archimedean point. He wondered how many of history's turning points began that way, with no fuss or fanfare but only the gentlest tug, slowly pulling the rug out from under a family's life, then a village's, ever outward, until the whole world was caught off guard.

6

Something had loosened up in his mother since their talk by the crater. She confided in him that she had decided to sign the deal with the VC after realizing she wouldn't be able to get Cloudies to where it needed to be. "I don't know how to make it rain over an entire village," she admitted. "I can't even recreate the tiny amount of rain I managed to make that one time." Then she began to recount the period that followed their move to the Cliff, and he realized it was a story she had been carrying around for years.

"When your father got the offer to manage the lodge, I was studying aeronautical engineering at the Technion, but he said that dreams involved sacrifices," she repeated what she'd already told him at the hotel in Tel Aviv. "We both thought it was going to be temporary, that within a year or two the lodge would turn a profit and I'd resume my studies. But as you've already learned, the temporary has a way of becoming permanent."

She became a math teacher. This was pre-robotics-club days. And at the time, she was actually content being just an ordinary teacher, determined to be like everyone else, to follow the beaten track. But she couldn't do it—never quite found her place, neither inside nor outside the house. In retrospect, she never stood a chance. "It's ridiculous to think that life is a one-size-fits-all, that waking up in the morning, going to an office, exchanging a joke or two by the water dispenser before heading home to cook dinner for your family can work for everyone. I could barely manage my own life, so managing yours and your sister's too?" She reassured herself that even if it took time, she'd eventually grow into motherhood, that while it didn't come naturally to everyone, most people eventually found their way. She waited and waited, but nothing changed, and when that longed-for peace of mind never came, fear set in—a paralyzing dread that he and Naomi would come to see how lost she was. She did her best to hide her debilitating self-doubt, making up answers when he and Naomi came to her with questions such as who was the country's second president, or asking them what they were going to be when they grew up. It took everything she had to keep them from noticing how helplessly she tiptoed on the husk of this earth.

She seemed so lost. "I don't know, Mom, I think Naomi and I turned out okay," he said with a kind smile.

She smiled back. "It's just like with my inventions. You two came out great, but I'm not quite sure how it happened."

Gathering the nerve, he broached the subject occupying the largest space in his mind: Robert McMurphy. True to her fashion, she started with seemingly unrelated anecdotes—a story about Robert's childhood in Ireland, or the day they found his shoes in the desert—scattering a jigsaw puzzle of information for Eli to piece together. "When your father told me Robert's mother had checked into the lodge, I couldn't understand how language could accommodate such a sentence. And when it finally sank in, the first thing I felt was an overwhelming anxiety that the secret would explode into the open. But Agatha McMurphy didn't make any accusations, didn't even ask us any questions. She was just *there*. And in some ways, that made it even harder for me, realizing that she would be sleeping a mere few doors away from her son's clothes without ever knowing how close she'd gotten. I felt the thought poisoning my body." She said that all the questions she'd spent years suppressing started gnawing at her. Had Robert been a kindhearted or inconsiderate young man? What had his favorite food been? The last book he'd read? Small questions that rose up in random moments throughout the day. So one morning, while Agatha was visiting, she called in sick at school and—her students jumping with joy over the unexpected free period—went to the lodge to see McMurphy's mother. Finding the Irishwoman nestling a cup of tea on the porch, she approached and introduced herself as a local tour guide. With a tremulous voice, she offered to show her around. Boaz tried to talk her out of it but there was no use. She led Agatha, who donned a frayed green baseball hat with the logo of an Irish soccer team, on a tour of the area—guiding her along the crater. At each stop, she noticed Agatha's eyes narrow in scrutiny, as if hunting for signs that her son had passed through those very spots. Or as if he might even show up, materializing out of thin air. For two days, Sarai hung onto every word of the woman's tales about her son. To the world he was known as McMurphy, but to his mother he was simply Robert, the boy who once concealed himself in the corner of the schoolyard for an entire day, unaware that the game of hide-and-seek had ended; who had a three-year crush on a girl in his class and never told her; who leaped into the air so high when Shelbourne FC won the championship that he sprained his ankle upon landing. She also learned about the strained relationship between the mother and son, which had withered into nonexistence after her separation from his father. Agatha confided in Sarai that Robert was livid at her for tearing their family apart, and instead of bridging the gap, the distance had only widened it. Her visit in Israel had been a tragically belated attempt to reconnect with her estranged child. Agatha told Sarai that she knew that some things cannot be atoned for, but she could at least try to assuage her pain. She hoped to fill in the voids regarding her son, not knowing that Sarai was one of the only two in the world who could help. But Sarai didn't say a word.

The night Agatha left the Cliff, Sarai entered the small room with all of McMurphy's items for the first time. The room she tried to forget for years. Sarai looked mostly at Robert's notebooks, going over all the sketches of faces he had drawn.

As Sarai felt his compassion for the people he had sketched, she felt the weight of the injustice they had committed grow heavier. The moral transgression of not reporting that they'd found his belongings. The pain they were continuing to inflict. That night she vowed that she'd go with Boaz to the police. "To force ourselves to do the right thing," she said firmly, and fell silent. "So why didn't you?" Eli wondered.

The question visibly pained her. "Because too much of our lives had become entangled in that lie." While his father agreed with her that it was unfortunate, he was against the idea of going to the police, claiming that at that point the truth would do more harm than good. That it might prompt Agatha to take legal action and the police to launch an investigation into evidence tampering, not to mention discourage tourists from visiting. Once again he maintained that the best way to honor McMurphy's memory would be to allow his story to continue to captivate people around the world. "And I would have liked to tell you I was so angry I made him sleep on the sofa, that I insisted nothing was more important than a mother's need for solace; unfortunately, your father had not only passed on his dreams to me, but also his fears."

"Fears maybe, but dreams?" Eli said. "I mean, the lodge was his dream. It never became yours."

"What you said just now took me years to realize." She explained that for the first ten years of their relationship, she didn't know where she ended and his father began. They always spoke in the first-person plural: we want, we work, we dream. But she'd recently begun to suspect that this pronoun was an illusion, that within the collective "we" there were always hidden singulars. "Because sometimes, when one desires, the other gets swallowed up by it."

As winter settled over the Cliff, Eli withdrew further into himself and his silence. He listened to his mother's stories, and barely spoke to his father at all. Their conversation in the closet hung over them like a glaring sun—too blinding to look at but palpably present. With his mother he learned to communicate in a simple, unguarded manner, but with his father everything was more complicated. And besides, Boaz seemed to actively avoid him. And not just him, people in general. Even his mother. He spent fewer and fewer hours at the lodge, and started sleeping on an air mattress in his mother's study.

It wasn't only his mother who changed during that period; Cloudies did as well. Shortly after the VC's investment was received, a bus snaked its way across the village, pulled up at the entrance to the hangar, and unloaded Alice and Albert, the elderly chemists, along with a team of thirty other chemists and engineers they'd brought with them. Donning white coats, they efficiently took charge of the inventions hangar. Cloudies' original employees stood in awe on the sidelines as their new colleagues rearranged the research lab and set up tables, refrigerators, vials, beakers, and an extensive collection of chemicals meticulously cataloged in the cabinets. Naomi rented the chemists a few vacant Morgenstein houses, providing them a place to sleep at night after the long hours they had put in, working quietly as mice.

Eli was on a mission to unearth proof that the new collaboration was one big mistake, a greedy capitalist move that hijacked his mom's idealistic vision, but Alice and Albert didn't make it easy for him. Armed with good intentions and a genuine, profound love of science, the two breathed new life into the corporate culture. Cloudies took on a new sheen of professionalism, and even the employees from the Cliff appeared content with their new colleagues. As he overheard Paulina saying to a coworker, "With all due respect to Sarai's creativity, it's nice to finally feel we're being managed like a proper company." Taking advantage of the shifting dynamics, Naomi decided to reshape the company in her image: the VC rep received an office at the expense of the UX department, which was relocated into a smaller room; in an ode to real tech companies, English became the unofficial language of all internal email communications; and even Sagi, the kitchen manager, was promoted to the enigmatic role of product manager. Naomi had given him the office next to hers, and whispers of a budding romance rippled through the company like small-town gossip. Eli hoped the rumors were true. The notion of his sober and composed sister succumbing to the allure of a clandestine love affair in the tensest period in Cloudies' history made him smile. And that wasn't Naomi's only unusual move. One morning, to everyone's surprise, Hannah Bialika appeared at the office. As it turned out, Naomi had hired her as the company accountant. There was no doubt in Eli's mind that his sister had offered Hannah the role to keep her from spilling the beans about not having actually invested millions in the company. The last thing they needed was for people to start asking uncomfortable questions. Eli knew Hannah well enough to be sure she wasn't blind to Naomi's motives, but he figured she must have been thrilled to get back to what she loved most—crunching numbers. Plus, enjoying all the admiration from the employees as the savvy investor who was said to have pumped millions into the company was probably a nice bonus. Hannah wasted no time diving into the maze of spreadsheets, disentangling the mess while making sure the employees received their paychecks on time and that their pension funds were properly managed. Eli might not have been ready to say it out loud, but deep down, he was happy with the new company spirit. Even the seemingly mundane bureaucratic changes sparked something within him. They were a testament to the fact that behind every form and meticulously organized Excel sheet, there was someone genuinely committed to straightening things out.

7

A week and a half before Ben Gould's scheduled visit, Eli still had
no idea whether the cloud machine worked. The inventions hangar
where the chemists and engineers conducted their experiments
was surrounded by a makeshift canvas fence like some kind of Area 51.
Apart from Naomi and a handful of new employees, nobody was privy
to whether the company could pull off its grand promise of making it
rain all over the Cliff by Gould's arrival.

The village thrummed with anticipation as its residents readied
themselves for the arrival of the celebrated millionaire—the parks and
rec department planting winter-friendly flowers. Small decisions that
nevertheless felt high-risk, especially after the council's leader emphatically reminded everyone that Cloudies represented not merely the Cliff
but "the entire Jewish nation."

The impending delegation comprised not only Gould but also a
cohort of ten executives, around twenty journalists, and several heavy-
weights from Israel's thriving hi-tech sector, all requiring accommodations. Initially, there was a brief consideration of using the lodge for their
stay, but the idea of putting up one of the world's wealthiest men and his
entourage in a modest travel hostel was dismissed unanimously—not
even Boaz thought it was a good call. Naomi suggested "turning the
bug into a feature," by accommodating the visitors in the houses right
on the crater's edge, which offered the most spectacular view. She made
sure the houses were equipped with all modern conveniences and
comforts, and to gain the cooperation of the residents who'd need to
temporarily vacate their homes for this purpose, Cloudies offered
generous compensation along with plane tickets to their destination
of choice. The council embraced her idea, and many residents eagerly
seized the opportunity. In a matter of days, the row of houses on
the crater's edge transformed into a top-tier desert resort that gave the

impression it had been there for years. Each house featured a wooden hot tub out back, a golf cart ready to ferry guests around, and a seasonal room-service menu crafted by skilled chefs. Naomi announced her intention to stay in one of the houses until Gould's visit, her stated purpose being to inspect the place and ensure it met the high standards they had set. In reality, it was because the Lilienblum house had become an unbearable pressure cooker, and she desperately needed some peace and quiet. Boaz and Eli helped Naomi move her belongings to one of the houses, with Eli secretly hoping that Sagi would be joining her. He noticed his father gazing in awe at the impromptu luxury resort, witnessing how his daughter, in a spur-of-the-moment decision executed in just a few days, had achieved his life's dream. A dream that he had never managed to realize himself, and that would fade away mere hours after Ben Gould left the Cliff. At that moment, Eli thought that his mother had been right all along—some places were created only moments before they were visited, and dismantled once the visitors had departed.

But Naomi didn't just tackle the issue of accommodations. As she'd often expressed, she wanted to impress upon the visitors that Cloudies was a rose among thorns, a startup that had bloomed against all odds. To achieve this, she persuaded the council to delay garbage collection for two weeks and halt the watering of public gardens, resulting in the grass turning a withered yellow. When Eli shared the details of Naomi's plan with his mother, she couldn't help but laugh. "It won't be long before she makes the people living here disappear too," he remarked, to which Sarai replied that when it came to making things disappear, she could offer Naomi some valuable tips.

"So if she asked, you'd tell her why you disappeared?" he finally mustered the courage to ask.

"I can tell you as well," she replied.

Six months after Agatha's visit, she realized that she couldn't keep the secret any longer, and implored Boaz to go to the police with her and report the discovery of the Irish traveler's belongings. In an effort to ease his concerns, she even suggested that they claim to have stumbled upon the items that very day. Who would possibly suspect them of hiding the items all those years? This way, they could provide McMurphy's mother with the closure she had been longing for without incriminating themselves. She always assumed it was mostly fear of criminal liability that was keeping Boaz from coming forward, but even after she proposed her plan, he kept dragging his feet, insisting they continue to evaluate their options. She realized they'd strike oil in the crater before he made a move, and that his internal struggle and indecision were a performance he was putting on solely for her, his captive audience.

"So I told him he could continue to keep quiet if he wanted to, but I wasn't going to live with the secret for another second, and he said that if I felt so strongly about it, I really should go to the police. I thought he would try to stop me, but all he said was, 'Do whatever you need to do.'"

"So what happened next?" Tamara asked a few hours later, as they sat on the ski ramp, watching the afternoon sun streak the sky pink and orange. He told her that his mother wasn't brave enough to go to the police, so she came up with a different idea.

"To give the reverend back the money for the eggroll he bought McMurphy," Tamara guessed, and Eli nodded. His mother boarded a bus to Tel Aviv's central bus station. She decided that before meeting the reverend, she would use the exclusive access she had to McMurphy's journals, to embark on a brief journey to visit all the places he visited himself. Tamara wanted to know every minute detail: which bus she took (the 512), whether she had her phone on her (no), what she ate (two falafels, a salad, a few bourekas, and some snacks), and how she paid for everything (two thousand shekels in cash that was meant to go toward parts for her universal AC project). The moment she got off the bus, she started retracing his steps. She made pit stops at the grimy bathroom at the central bus station, Hilton Beach, a vegan Thai joint, and a tiny coffee spot he'd written about in his journal. While Sarai found it all fascinating, the highlight of her day was undoubtedly meeting the reverend. She introduced herself as McMurphy's mother because she couldn't think of any other way to explain her interest in him. She described the reverend as a kind and gentle man who served to remind her yet again that there had once been a Robert McMurphy in the world, and now there wasn't.

"But there's one thing I don't get," Tamara said.

Grinning, Eli replied, "If it's just one thing, then you clearly understand more than I do."

"Why didn't she just go home at the end of her visit? Why go to all that trouble with the cloud machine and the rain? Why all the show?"

Eli shrugged. He said that sometimes trying to find the logic behind his mother's actions was like trying to decipher a Rorschach inkblot. "It doesn't really matter, because everyone sees something different," he added.

Softly touching his arm, she said she was starting to understand that there was more to his mother's decisions than met the eye. He was afraid she would try again to persuade him to go to the police, to do justice by McMurphy, but she just kept running her hand over his arm, telling him it was amazing how protective he was of his parents. "Don't worry, I know you'd never go against their wishes," she assured him, her tone warm and soothing. They sat together until their eyelids grew heavy, but when Eli suggested they get some sleep, Tamara clung to him, tightened her grip, insisted they stay awake, explaining that creating a beautiful memory was worth more than an extra hour of sleep. It wasn't until around midnight that she finally agreed to part ways. He walked her back to the lodge, feeling lucky to have experienced such intimacy, for the chance to lose himself in someone.

When he arrived home, he saw she'd texted him: *I had a really nice time.*

The first unmistakable glimmers of love now began to flicker inside him. He almost wrote her something about it but held back, afraid of being too vulnerable and direct.

But when he woke up, and the glimmers were still there, and he knew he had to tell her in person. Stepping out into the sunlight, he spotted her by the square, with the bulky black duffle on her back and her eyes fixed at the village's front gate.

I was waiting for you, I wanted to say goodbye before I left," she said.

"Where are you going?"

"Mexico, to cover that music festival I told you about."

"But you said you were going to turn down the offer."

"I did say that, but then changed my mind," Tamara replied, lowering her gaze to the sidewalk.

She was right. There was no way to prepare for a tsunami crashing into you.

He put his hand on her arm, and she remained still. He noticed she was leaning under the weight of her bag, but when he reached out to relieve her of the burden, she tightened her grip around the strap.

"I don't get it, what happened, why now?"

"Because I know that waiting a few more days would just make this harder for you," she said, placing her hand on his chest.

"But, but what about us?"

"You're lovely, Eli, but my life is not on the Cliff, and what I realized in the last few weeks is that yours always will be."

"But we still haven't found McMurphy," he said, his tone part plea, part accusation.

"If you really thought I stayed all these months just because of McMurphy, think again," she said, and her confession hurt even more. "And besides, after what we discovered in that room, I realized I will never find him. Even if McMurphy was out there in the crater somewhere, the clues didn't lead to him, they led to other people," she explained. He winced at the thought of her implicating his parents, and she noticed. "Don't worry, I won't tell. I won't break my promise." Smiling, she gently ran her hand over his cheek. Despite his anger, he couldn't help but surrender to the warmth of her touch. He knew he wouldn't have another chance. "You're working so hard to maintain a semblance of normalcy, of an ordinary life, but honestly, Eli, I'm not sure that normalcy ever existed in your family. And even if it did, I'm not sure it did any of you any favors. Some shards aren't meant to be glued back together."

A gleaming white car drove by and came to a stop a few meters past the gate, honking twice. "That's my ride." She got up on her tiptoes, planted a peck on his cheek, turned on her heels, and dashed toward the waiting car, disappearing inside it.

Eli dragged himself to the office, shuffling past two orange-vested municipal workers busy hanging a large poster on the dusty bulletin board. He took a few steps back to examine Ben Gould's smiling face above the words "Welcome Mr. Gould!" in both Hebrew and English. He felt disconnected from everything happening around him, as if his internal clock had veered away from regular time and kept rewinding to the moment Tamara left the village.

Amidst the chaos of last-minute preparations for Gould's visit, his own swirling emotions went unnoticed. Around lunchtime, Hannah Bialika called him into her office and said she'd like to talk about something personal and exciting—"Your pension." She placed a hot cup of tea on the desk and pointed at a page filled with columns. Her eyes lit up with excitement as she explained the differences between a pension fund and executive insurance. "So, which road should we take to jumpstart your journey into the world of pensions?" When he didn't answer, she lowered the page onto the desk and considered him. "Gould's visit will be a success, don't you worry, your sister is doing a fantastic job. She reminds me of Mandy and me when we first started out. Success often comes—"

"Oh my god, I can't sit through another one of your Mandy stories," he cut her off. "I know it might be hard for you to believe, but most people have more than just money on their minds."

She fixed him with a calm, piercing gaze. "So, what's on yours?"

"Nothing."

"Tell me," she said, reaching out and gently resting her hand on his. The gesture stirred something within him. "Tamara. The volunteer from the lodge I've been seeing. She left this morning."

"Did you know she was about to leave?" she asked.

He admitted he didn't.

"Oy, you must be in a world of pain right now," she said, gazing down at her tea cup. Eli had expected Hannah to impart some sage wisdom drawn from her fifty-year marriage to Mandy. But she simply handed him the cup and said, "Hold it with both hands. The heat is healing."

Wrapping his hands around the cup, Eli was surprised to see that she was right. They stayed there for a long while, without talking about pension plans or heartbreaks. Without talking at all, just sitting together in silence, well after the tea had gone cold.

**THE
DAY
IT
RAINED**

1

The day it rained, Eli woke up late. Reaching for his phone, he saw there was still no text from Tamara. He then made his way to the bathroom to splash some water on his face. In the mirror over the sink, he spotted a hanger on his closet door, holding a light blue button-down shirt and pair of beige pants—both garments new. After drying his face, he walked over to the closet and found a yellow Post-it attached to the shirt, reading "For Eli." His sister. Reluctantly, he tried on the clothes, grumbling at his reflection when he saw how well they fit.

On his way downstairs he passed his mother in her study. It had been months since he'd last seen her there. He entered gingerly, as if trying not to scare a bird away. All of her old inventions were back in their places, and the walls and floor were once again white and spotless, with no sign of the spilled sand. The closet with McMurphy's belongings was open, and inside it Eli found his mother looking at one of the notebooks.

"Your father restored the room," she said. The computer was nestled in the corner of the study with the small fan nearby. The pipes, mirrors, and lightbulbs were back where they belonged, and not just back but arranged in the same chaotic order. She was wearing a flowery dress and those elegant brown loafers Naomi had forced on her. He suddenly noticed how long her hair had grown, and how crammed her study seemed with all the inventions.

Those four walls never really stood a chance at containing her, he thought. The room, which he'd always viewed as a reflection of her wildness, now felt stifling and narrow. Eli crowded together with his mother in the small space.

"It wasn't the sand that kept you away from the room," he said. "You didn't want to be near McMurphy's things."

She traced her finger along the red toy car. "What can I say, Eli? I could never hide anything from you."

His mother held the notebook, flipped through the pages filled with the faces McMurphy had drawn. Each of them had a different-similar pain delicately captured by his pen. Eli thought to himself what a wonder it was, if there really was a person in the world who could take on the pain of others by absorbing it himself. And what a price such a person must have paid.

"Wait," Eli said, placing his hand on the notebook. He turned back one page to find an empty one with a single sentence, written in Robert McMurphy's handwriting.

I wish I could turn all the pain and tears of the people I met into rain that would make the desert bloom.

Tamara was right. Behind all his mother's whims was a clear purpose. "So that's why you built the cloud machine in the first place," Eli said. "To give Robert's words a place in the world."

His mother looked at him, and just smiled.

They arrived at the hangar compound a few minutes behind schedule. Dozens of people were already present—reporters, Cloudies employees, and representatives from the hi-tech industry—all eagerly searching for Ben Gould. About a hundred pleather chairs were neatly lined up in front of the black stage, which featured a glass podium and a massive screen. He saw his father making sure the chairs were perfectly aligned, and next to him, Hannah Bialika rhapsodizing about pension plans to a captive employee. Meanwhile, a family of goats ambled along the crater's edge, casting curious glances at the faux-oak catering stands displaying assortments of cheese, bread, salads, and fresh-squeezed orange juice. At the rightmost stand was a sign in English that read "Traditional Cliff Cuisine," and upon approaching, he saw that it was something sushi-shaped, but instead of raw fish the rolls were filled with carrot tzimmes, and spicy tomatoes. He sampled a few pieces, which were unexpectedly not bad.

As reporters began to gather around his mother, he hurried to her side. Someone in the group inquired about her feelings on this big day, and she replied with a smile, "Fantastic!" and raised her daiquiri glass at Naomi. For a moment, he wondered if she was being sarcastic, but his mother didn't have a cynical bone in her body. There was no hint of disappointment or bitterness in her voice; she was genuinely happy for her daughter. Swept up in his mother's enthusiasm, he momentarily let go of his criticism and sorrow. He thought about Atlas unburdening the Earth's weight onto Hercules, and how far they had come from the sad little press conference in the rec center to this moment. Surely Morgenstein would have been proud to see what they had made of the place he designed. Perhaps even Ben-Gurion. Maybe Tamara too. If she had stayed, she would have seen that his relentless efforts to piece the shards together weren't in vain; they had meaning. Scanning the hangar as if willing her face to appear in the crowd, he suddenly felt a strong tug at his arm. "He's almost here!" Paulina exclaimed, cheeks flushed with excitement. She pulled him toward the entrance of the hangar, where Alice was already waiting with Naomi. His sister was sporting a black kimono-style jacket, hair pulled back, and those new round-rimmed glasses.

"I just hope we don't screw this up," she murmured, her eyes locked on the horizon.

"No, no way," she said as her mother approached with a fresh daiquiri. "Not going to happen. You're not greeting Ben Gould with a cocktail in your hand."

Sarai downed her drink in a single swig, then placed the glass on the ground, stepped closer to Naomi, and tucked a wayward curl behind her daughter's ear. "You look beautiful," she said. Naomi's lips curled into an awkward smile. Eli noticed there was something different about his sister's face.

"You're wearing glasses," he noted. "It's nice."

She blushed.

Everyone stood around waiting, but the guest of honor was nowhere to be seen. Eli knew he should be freaking out like the rest of the crowd, but his mind was drifting toward the remote lighthouse he and Tamara had promised to visit together someday. The sound of Naomi's phone ringing snapped him back to the Cliff. She replied with a few yeses followed by a cheerful "No problem, wonderful, wonderful," and hung up. "Gould. That motherfucker. He's going to be an hour and a half late."

"That's no good," Albert said apprehensively. "We factored in specific morning weather conditions. By noon the weather might change drastically, affecting the machine's performance in ways that—"

"We'll wait a year if we have to," Naomi interrupted him. Pointing at the crowd, she said, "Everything we've been doing here for months is meant to impress one person and one person only. And until that person shows up, we wait."

An hour and a half later, the Cloudies crowd reconvened outside by the entrance, slightly deflated. Three dots appeared on the horizon, gradually morphing into black luxury vehicles making their way onto the access road leading to the hangars. They pulled up in front of the towering chimney.

The first vehicle disgorged a team of dark suits. One of them approached the middle car and opened the door, and out stepped Ben Gould, flashing a triumphant smile. Unlike his sleek-suited personnel, Gould was wearing a skin-tight black T-shirt and black jeans. Blinded by the desert sun, he closed his eyes and donned his signature black sunglasses.

"We don't have this sun in San Francisco," he said with a grin. He was slightly shorter than Eli had pictured him.

Naomi shook his hand and introduced herself. Gould was a few years her senior, but they could easily have passed for classmates.

"The young prodigy CEO! No need for introductions, of course I know who you are. Call me Ben." While offering an apology for the delay, he swept his gaze across the crowd until it landed on Sarai. He made a beeline to her. "And you're the inventor from the video! What an honor," he said, pulling her hand in for a firm handshake.

Smile firmly plastered, Sarai readily surrendered to the man's charm, just like everyone else standing nearby—each receiving a handshake from Gould along with what appeared to be sincere inquiries about their roles in the company.

The tech billionaire mentioned that he was in dire need of coffee before the presentation, and Naomi quickly assured him they'd bring it right away. She added that his room was already waiting for him with coffee blends from nine different countries, all tailored to his taste buds. Gould paused for a moment and glanced at his smartwatch. "Actually, my schedule changed and I can't stay the night on the Cliff. I'll have to cut my entire visit short, so maybe we really should get this show on the road."

"No worries," Naomi replied calmly, feathers unruffled. Eli couldn't fathom how she managed to stay so composed. "We'll start right away." She led Gould and his team to the plush custom-made chairs they had commissioned from a talented carpenter in downtown Tel Aviv. When the announcer asked the audience to take their seats, the weary reporters suddenly perked up, and all eyes followed Gould as he took his place in the front row. The gravitational pull of the man and his money were palpable.

"Remind me, how much did I tweet I'd buy the company for?" Gould asked Naomi as he settled into the seat next to hers.

"Twenty million dollars."

Gould grinned. "All right then, let's see what you've got."

Naomi got up and headed for the white screen at the back of the stage, with Eli right behind her. "What an asshole," he muttered.

"Quod licet Iovi, non licet bovi," Namoi replied calmly. "Which loosely translates from Latin as 'Gods may do what cattle may not.'"

"That's a dumb saying."

"But accurate," Naomi said, squared her shoulders, and took to the stage.

2.

Eli took a front-row seat by his mother. Naomi flashed the audience a smile from the podium, and the logo of a white cloud against a black background appeared on the screen behind her.

"Welcome," she said, plucked the mic from its stand, and allowed a moment for the applause to die down. "Ladies and gentlemen," she continued, then paused for effect, staring at the floor as if in deep thought, "many inventions promise to change the world. But today, thanks to Sarai Lilienblum, my brilliant mother, you're about to witness an invention that will actually deliver on that promise." The audience erupted in applause. After expressing her gratitude to Ben Gould for gracing them with his presence, she took out her phone. On the screen behind her, the app's icon appeared—a cloud with the word "Cloudies" in English. She tapped it, and just like at the convention in Tel Aviv, pastel-colored icons of the sun, clouds, and rain popped up on the screen.

"For tens of thousands of years, people from every culture and corner of the world have prayed for rain. Starting today, those prayers can be answered with a simple click." She raised her hand high. "The only question left is—are you ready to witness a miracle?" she asked, prompting an enthusiastic whistle. Naomi came out from behind the podium to the front of the stage. "Then let's start the revolution!" she exclaimed, tapping the rain icon. Instantly, the chimney roared to life and the screen filled with a view of the room at the chimney's base. The camera zoomed in, revealing massive mounds of sand being sucked up by a large air hose. It then panned out to focus on the chimney itself. After a brief moment, a long, slender plume of cloud billowed out, slowly floating toward the sky above the hangar. The camera shut off and the audience gazed upward, their eyes tracking the cloud as it drifted toward the houses on the Cliff. The chimney made an especially loud grumble, and Eli suspected his sister had amped up the surround sound to enhance the audience's experience. It seemed to have worked. Phones in hand, people rose from their seats and started recording the cloud formation, oohing and aahing. Eli scanned the crowd until his gaze settled on Ben Gould, beaming with satisfaction under the gradually condensing cloud. The cloud logo reappeared on the screen, now accompanied by a stopwatch counting down from fifteen minutes. "When the timer hits zero," Naomi declared, "it will start raining." She turned to the front row. "Mr. Gould, if you peek under your seat, you'll find something you're going to need very soon."

Gould reached under his seat, stood up, and produced a large red umbrella.

"Now, that's no ordinary umbrella," Naomi effused, "that's an umbrella built by the smartest woman I know. She designed an automated, self-opening sensor-controlled device that deploys the moment it starts raining, and here at Cloudies we've decided to give one to each and every one of you!" Eli scanned the crowd as people started pulling out their big red gifts from under their seats. Finding his own waiting there, he turned to his mother, seated beside him. Smiling, she raised her glass in gratitude.

The clouds were growing bigger by the second.

"Hey, look over there!" someone called out. Eli obliged and observed a cluster of bunny-shaped clouds. Narrowing his eyes, he noticed the delicate wisps and cotton-candy texture. He searched the crowd for Paulina, Rivka, and Yossi, and saw them staring at the sky with pride. He couldn't help but feel moved. It was thrilling to witness ideas that had been discussed to death at UX department meetings come to life before their eyes.

"If I may," Naomi said, redirecting the audience's attention back to her, "I'd like to take these last few minutes before the rain arrives to introduce someone special. She's the brains behind the game-changing invention that's about to reshape reality in dry regions. Please give it up for the amazing entrepreneur, my mother, Sarai Lilienblum."

"Go on," Eli whispered to her. His mother got up and shuffled awkwardly to the stage. Naomi took their mother's hand and raised it to thunderous applause. A slight smile appeared on Sarai's face, and Eli suspected that she might actually be enjoying it.

Amidst this pure elation, Ben Gould sprang onto the stage, sidling up to the mother and daughter duo. He splayed his arms wide, palms skyward, and started clapping loudly, amping up the crowd. Eli couldn't stand this man who had to be the center of attention at all times. Gould took off his sunglasses, shot an impressed smile at Sarai, and turned to the audience. "I have to admit, when I sent out that tweet, I never actually thought I'd end up here four months later," he said, basking in the applause now directed his way. "In a few minutes, we might see the miracle of rain production, or not. Either way, the very idea of a hi-tech company here, in the middle of the desert, is a serious accomplishment in itself. Seeing it all happen here, surrounded by goats and other animals I can't even name, that's what the tech world is all about—creating real social impact, even in the most remote places on Earth."

With just seven minutes left on the stopwatch, the clouds began looming over a big chunk of the Cliff, taking on that silvery-gray tint Paulina insisted on. Several reporters raised their hands, and Gould pointed to a young journalist in the back row. "Let's get that guy a mic, see if we can sneak in a few questions before the storm."

Naomi leaned in and whispered something in his ear, visible to Eli and the rest of the audience. Gould responded with a dismissive wave, and his response was picked up by the microphone—"Worst case we take a few questions in the rain, right?" Naomi nodded with a smile and signaled to Sagi to hand the reporter a microphone. Clearing his throat, the young journalist asked, "Mr. Gould, do you believe climate engineering will be the next major frontier in the global tech industry?"

"Absolutely. There's no reason we can't crack climate modification to tackle the biggest calamity of the twenty-first century—climate change."

"And Mr. Gould, do you plan to follow through on your commitment to purchase Cloudies for twenty million dollars?"

"If we get a solid ten minutes of rain here, I'll absolutely follow through. I just hope the bank app can handle the transfer."

As the audience burst into laughter and applause, the stopwatch showed two and a half minutes left. Naomi tapped Gould's shoulder. "Perhaps we wrap up the questions and let them enjoy the rain? It's going to be a once-in-a-lifetime experience."

"Oh, I very much hope it'll happen more than just once!" Gould replied with a wry grin, then turned back to the reporters. "You've all been aiming your questions at me, when there are two extraordinary women right here by my side. Does anyone have a closing question for them?"

A reporter sporting red-framed glasses stood up, and with the microphone in one hand and her phone in the other, directed her question at Naomi. "Are you familiar with a Luciano Rodrigo Ancelotti?" she asked, and glanced down at her phone. "I'm sorry, not Rodrigo, Rodríguez Ancelotti."

Eli blanched. The question hit him like a sucker punch, leaving him astounded and stupefied. His sister, on the other hand, remained unfazed. "It doesn't ring a bell," she replied calmly. "And with such an unusual name, I'm pretty sure I would've remembered." She chuckled, then gestured at the screen. "We've got sixty seconds left, so pay attention. When the stopwatch hits zero, you'll see the rain starting to fall from your left, over the Cliff's houses, and it will—"

"General Luciano Rodríguez Ancelotti the Third!" another reporter shouted out from the crowd. "Are you telling us you've never heard of him? So you're denying the headline that was just published on the British website News-Tech a few minutes ago?"

"I can't deny something I know nothing about," she replied, her hand balling into a fist.

"What was the headline?" Gould asked curiously.

"We can discuss all that after the rain," Naomi insisted. "It's going to start any second—"

"The headline is 'Promising Israeli Startup Suspected in Major Phishing Scam,'" the reporter read from her phone.

Gould looked at the reporter while Naomi gazed out at the Cliff. Right at that moment, the rain began to fall.

It started as a gentle drizzle over the distant wooden houses of the Cliff, and as the pattering of raindrops gradually intensified, the reporter raised her voice and read the article's opening paragraph: "'An insider familiar with Cloudies' operations has presented compelling evidence linking Sarai Lilienblum's promising startup to a large-scale email scam involving a group of travelers who stayed at the hostel owned by the company's founders. According to the source, the email scam was devised to shore up the company's finances in the face of cash flow challenges.'"

It had to be one of the travelers who worked on the email scam, Eli thought. *The Icelander?*

The rain was creeping closer. "Honestly, I have no clue what you're taking about," Naomi countered. "I don't have to tell you about fake news. Someone in your line of work must know the media loves making up stories for clickbait. After all—"

The sound of a champagne bottle popping interrupted her midsentence, and her red umbrella shot open. Umbrellas started sprouting all around, creating a canopy of red circles over the crowd, the atmosphere a mix of pure excitement and fear of accidentally poking a neighbor's eye out. A few seconds later, the first raindrops gently landed on their upturned umbrellas. Eli leaped onto the stage and snatched the microphone from his sister's hand. "As you can all see, it's raining, so we recommend continuing our conference indoors," he suggested, pointing toward the nearby office hangar. "We have desserts and hot beverages waiting for you." He motioned for Paulina to lead the way. The bespectacled reporter tried to protest, but the crowd was already heading indoors. Eli glanced at his sister standing mere inches from him on the stage, her eyes cold and unblinking.

3

"T his way," Eli motioned, guiding Gould and his crew toward the offices. Naomi walked ahead, avoiding eye contact with the reporters. "I'm assuming you can explain," Gould said, and Eli nodded. "Of course."

"Great, then I'd love to hear it," Gould said, looking up at the intensifying rain. Raindrops pelted their umbrellas and slid off onto the muddy ground. Eli signaled to Paulina to take his place as tour guide, and she stepped in, relieving Gould of his umbrella and holding it high above his head. "Mr. Gould, reach out and feel the rain," she urged. "We worked hard to get the size just right."

Eli picked up his pace, catching up to Naomi. "The Icelander," he snarled, but Naomi didn't respond. She didn't even look at him.

"Is that snow?" Gould asked, and Eli turned to see a growing pile of white snowflakes in Gould's palm. Paulina smiled and said, "I've never seen snow up close, so I couldn't tell you." Gould was surprised to hear that it was her first snow sighting, and as he began to ask more questions, Eli stuck his hand out from under the umbrella. Like Paulina, he had never experienced snow in real life either, but within moments, he knew Gould was right. He looked at his hand, where large drops of water mixed with cold, white flakes, softer than hail. He looked up; the flakes were gradually filling the sky.

"Fuck," Naomi said. "Out of the frying pan and into the fire."

It was a horrible but breathtaking bug. Eli's gaze traced the swirl of snowflakes as they floated downward from the sky and settled softly on the ground. Despite the warm temperature, the snow resisted melting.

"I'm pretty sure that's snow," Gould said, while Naomi quickened her pace, putting more distance between them. The snowflakes landed on the rooftops and wafted into the crater.

"Tell me," Eli turned to Gould and pointed at his smartwatch, "what time is it?"

"Twelve twenty-seven."

"So the snow decided to show up three minutes early," Eli said calmly. "It wasn't supposed to start until we got to the offices."

Gould raised an eyebrow. "Is that so?" he mumbled, extending his hand from under the red umbrella. "So you're telling me you're actually capable of producing both rain and snow?"

"You bet!" Eli exclaimed. "You thought this giant operation was dedicated to one feature? That would be a waste, wouldn't it?" Eli elbowed his sister, but instead of backing him up or at least showing some admiration for his ingenuity, she remained silent and withdrawn. Watching the snowflakes settle on roofs across the Cliff, Eli tried to read Gould's thoughts about the "feature" he had just made up, but the mogul's expression was as blank as his sister's.

Naomi was the first to reach the offices. As she hurried to the aquarium in the middle of the hangar, Eli took it upon himself to secure a private room for Gould and his entourage. Pointing out that it was the office with the best view, Eli raised the blinds while Gould settled into an executive leather chair, mesmerized by the snowfall. Eli assured Gould they would be resuming the press conference any moment, and that in the meantime he and his people were welcome to enjoy the vista.

"Very well," Gould said with a nod. "Just to reiterate, the deal was rain, not snow. But let's start with you giving answers to the reporters."

"Of course, of course," Eli replied, mustering the most authoritative and composed voice he could manage.

"Good," Gould replied. "And keep in mind that I need to start heading back to Tel Aviv in an hour."

Eli nodded, swallowing his overwhelming sense of helplessness at the unfolding crisis. Exiting the office, he sought out Sagi and asked him to distract the reporters.

"What's the deal with that article the reporter mentioned?" Sagi asked. "That's exactly what I'm trying to figure out," Eli replied, and headed to the aquarium, where he found his sister by herself, slumped over her phone.

"Sit up straight, everyone can see you," he said.

Slowly pushing herself upright against the backrest of her chair, she replied, "The article is even worse than the headline."

"I told you it was going to blow up in our faces."

"Oh, Eli, I knew that, I just thought it would happen *after* we closed this goddamn deal and we'd have time to think about how to clean up the mess."

"So, how do we clean it up?"

She shrugged. "I honestly have no idea."

At that moment, Alice and Albert opened the door.

"I promise you, that article is a load of—" Eli began, but Alice cut him off. "We're not here because of the article," she said. "We explicitly told you we couldn't stray from the schedule! Did we or did we not explain to you that we'd factored in the specific morning weather conditions?"

"There's a problem with the thermoregulation," Albert grumbled. "And it's causing the precipitation to be a lot colder than we planned. I suspect that's why it's snowing right now. God, snow. Who would have thought?"

"Then just turn it off," Eli replied.

"There's no way to turn it off."

"How can that be?"

"It's a calculated risk we decided to take," Naomi intervened.

"There has to be an off switch, a plug to pull," Eli insisted.

"If it was only one machine, then maybe, but when it's three hundred forty-six, then, no."

"What are you talking about?" Eli came close to shouting, pointing outside. "There's only one chimney. One."

"And inside that chimney, there are three hundred forty-six cloud-producing vacuum cleaners," she replied matter-of-factly, going on to elaborate that all their attempts to improve upon their mother's invention had failed, the only successful approach having been to faithfully replicate the technical specifications of Sarai's small cloud-making contraption. It was the same model as the old red vacuum seen in the video. Even a slight change in the plastic's color caused the machine to malfunction. "We realized that on such a tight schedule there was no way we were going to crack the tech needed for a large machine," she continued. "So we just mass-produced hundreds of small cloud machines, exact replicas based on her original blueprint. We hunted down every vacuum cleaner of that exact model, followed her tech specs to a T, and voilà, rain. We tossed it all into the massive chimney, and that was that."

"The catch is that we don't have complete control over the system, because we don't fully understand how it works," Alice jumped in. "Once the machines start going, we don't know how to turn them off. They'll keep making clouds until the sand inside each one of them runs out."

"How long will that take?"

"According to our math, it should be a few hours," Alice replied. "But your mother's inventions have a habit of not playing by the rules."

"We need to talk to Mom," Eli said, peering through the glass walls of the aquarium at the reporters huddled together, sharing their phone screens and swapping details about the alleged scandal. "They're not even looking at the snow," he muttered, unable to fathom how they could choose a newspaper story over a downright miracle. Just moments ago they were in awe of Cloudies, eating out of the palm of his sister's hand, dying to see the chimney in action, and now they were fighting for front-row seats to the company's downfall. Eli glanced out the window. The houses of the Cliff were hardly visible under the white snow that blanketed the muddy ground.

"Hey, do you think the snow might block the access road?" he asked, and when no one answered, stalked out of the aquarium.

The reporters swooped down on him, firing one question after another. (Mr. Lilienblum, care to comment on the News-Tech article? Did you know about the scam? Do you think Mr. Gould will uphold his promise to buy the company despite these revelations?)

"I promise we'll get to all your questions properly," he said, trying to pave his way out, but the reporters had him cornered. Just then, Naomi emerged from behind him, diverting their attention to her. (Ms. Lilienblum, have you contacted a lawyer? Do you plan to step down due to the publication?) She moved forward reluctantly, as if propelled by an external force—which, as it turned out, she was; Eli saw his father standing behind her, pushing her toward the exit. When Boaz spotted Eli, he reached out and pulled both his kids toward safety. Joining the extraction efforts, Paulina swung open the door, and after Naomi, Eli, and Boaz got out, she quickly locked it, leaving the three of them in the snow.

While Paulina blocked the door, trapping the reporters, the three Lilienblums found themselves in the midst of the snowstorm. Everything beyond the hangar was a world of white and stillness, and only a faint tapping on one of the windows disrupted the silence. It was the VC representative, angrily gesturing for them to return indoors. Eli gave him a quick glance before shifting back to the swirling snow.

"Wait for me here," Boaz instructed them, and began walking toward the compound gate.

Eli's lightweight clothing offered little defense against the cold, and he was shivering violently.

"What a clusterfuck." Naomi sighed, and after a moment's pause, Eli replied, "Well, at least it's a beautiful clusterfuck." He wished Tamara was there to see it.

They heard an engine rumbling through the storm, and soon after, Eli spotted a battered white jeep approaching, their father behind the wheel.

Eli figured it was the secret vehicle Boaz had used for his nightly escapades of scattering McMurphy's belongings around the crater.

The passenger seat window rolled down, revealing their mother. "Hop in."

"Are you out of your mind? We can't just run away," Naomi said. "We have to stay and sort out this mess."

"Get in," their father urged. "There's a solution. Just get in before the snow buries us." Eli climbed into the jeep, with Naomi following hesitantly. Snowflakes piled up on the windshield, the wipers struggling to cope. Boaz switched on the headlights and drove at a crawl.

"All right, start explaining," Naomi demanded.

"I can barely see the road. I'll explain when we get home."

The relatively brief journey between the hangar and their house turned into a tediously long drive. Eli felt as though they were driving toward an ever-receding white wall. As they neared their home, he noticed that the main square was completely covered in white and the streets were deserted. Draped in snow, their house finally looked like a proper ski chalet.

Boaz parked by their fence.

"Now tell me, what's the plan?" Naomi asked impatiently.

Boaz unbuckled his seat belt, ran his hand over his forehead, and peered at her through the rearview mirror. "Honestly? I just wanted to get you out of there."

"No, absolutely not!" she shouted. "Take me back right now."

"Sorry, no way. I'm not driving in this snow again," Boaz replied quietly.

"So dozens of people got stuck in a snowstorm, and we ran away and left them stranded?!" she seethed. "Do you even comprehend the repercussions? The article is going to be the least of our worries."

She took out her phone and tried calling Sagi, but there was no signal.

Flinging open the car door, she stepped out into the storm and started trudging through the snow back in the direction of the village's main gate. Eli got out and followed her, their progress painstakingly slow in the deep snow. He had never experienced such extreme cold, and every inch of his skin stung. He called out to her to come back, to think everything over calmly. "If I don't go back there right now," she yelled, "my career is over."

"A career doesn't seem like a good enough reason to turn into a human popsicle," Eli shouted, plodding after her.

Stomping ahead, she sank up to her knees in the plush white snow, firmly stuck. Finally catching up to her, Eli wrapped his arms around his sister and helped dislodge her from the snowy trap; together, they turned back and began the slow, silent journey home.

The four Lilienblums funneled into the kitchen. Boaz fetched a stack of blankets and sweaters and made four cups of tea, which they each cradled for warmth. Naomi tried calling Sagi from all four phones, but it was no use.

"Too bad we didn't install the sauna in Morgenstein's blueprints," Sarai deadpanned, to which Boaz and Eli exchanged grins.

Naomi was oblivious to these subtle interactions. She seemed adrift in her helplessness, and while he had warned her time and again that it would end badly, Eli felt not one iota of schadenfreude, only compassion.

He tried using the phone's internet, but there was still no signal. Opening his inbox almost mechanically, he was greeted by two texts sent over an hour and a half ago, both from Tamara. In that moment, it felt as though the entire world had condensed into the confines of his phone screen. The first message was a hyperlink to the News-Tech story with the headline detailing an investigation into fraud by a promising Israeli tech company. The next text from her consisted of just three words—*Are you okay?*

He clicked the link but kept getting a retry message. He texted back a succession of question marks, but the message refused to go through. Looking up from his screen, he saw his parents and sister lost in thought, and hoped they didn't notice the panic and confusion consuming him.

4.

No way. Couldn't be.

He replayed their recent conversation in his mind, the one when she assured him—*Don't worry, I won't tell. I won't break my promise. Even though I think you're making a mistake.*

"That article is a disaster," he muttered, "a colossal disaster."

"I'm sure Ben Gould will fix it," his father said confidently. "People like him have all the connections and resources to handle false allegations."

"Gould isn't going to buy Cloudies," Naomi said, hugging her tea cup with a furrowed brow. "Even if, in theory, he could handle the article, why would he want to? Gould is after a Cinderella story."

"Then fix the flaws!" Boaz cried out. "We'll take them to court. It's absurd to think that a news site can get away with publishing just any bogus gossip that—"

"Seriously, are you that naive? Don't you understand how this works?" Naomi snorted. "Even if we could prove the article is false, people will always have doubts. What they'll remember is the accusation, not some retraction buried in the back pages." Sarai and Boaz looked at their daughter with a mix of shock and sympathy. His father searched for his mother's eyes, but they remained fixed on Naomi.

A few minutes later the power went out. With the pale glow from the kitchen window the only source of light, the house instantly felt colder. Boaz gathered all the warm clothes he could find—Eli snagging a green beanie and thick red scarf and Naomi two pairs of tights and purple earmuffs—while their mother poured another round of steaming tea, adding thin slices of lemon.

They sat in the kitchen for three long hours, silently watching the storm quiet down to a sigh. "I think it stopped," Boaz said, and carefully cracked open the front door, causing a pile of snow to collapse onto the floor. Eli looked up; the sky was starting to darken. The streetlights came on, blinking thrice until finally steadying. The roofs groaned under the weight of the snow, and the roads had become an icy white canvas. While the snow covered every inch of the village, far on the horizon he could see the sharp outline where the desert had remained its sandy self. It wasn't a gradient color scheme, but more like something out of the children's game Land, Sea, Air—a clear, definitive line; snow on one side, desert on the other.

Cell service returned, detonating an explosion of angry voice messages and texts from Cloudies employees, reporters, and stranded catering staff on Naomi's phone. She called Ben Gould's assistant, who told her he had holed up in the conference room alone, silently staring out the window. Naomi asked the assistant to pass on to Gould the message that she was absolutely on top of the situation and committed to getting him out of there as soon as possible. She wanted to arrange for a fleet of helicopters to extract everyone from the hangar, no matter the cost, but a quick check revealed that the civil aviation authority had labeled the area a no-fly zone due to concerns about the artificial climate system triggering unpredictable and uncontrollable weather events. She then looked into the possibility of renting snowplows to clear the roads, but there was not a single snowplow to be found in the entire southern district of Israel. She reached out to the council head, who was stranded in Cloudies' hangar along with everyone else. He called back a few minutes later, informing her that he had sent for snowplows from Mount Hermon and had also contacted the southern base commander of the army's engineering corps to mobilize every bulldozer, tractor, and other engineering tool in his possession. The first convoy of earth-moving machines arrived within an hour. It was already dark outside, and Eli was mesmerized by the lights of the heavy equipment carving their way through the wall of snow.

"It's going to take them hours to reach the compound," Eli observed. Naomi shot him a look of despair, trudged upstairs to her bedroom, and slammed the door shut. Sarai, turning on the kettle for another round of tea, motioned for Eli to go after his sister.

Armed with a cup of tea, Eli carefully climbed the stairs and knocked on his sister's door. After a few unresponsive moments, he gave up, retreated to his own room, and plopped himself on the bed. He stared at the wall separating them, then closed his eyes and waited to hear her making reassuring calls to their employees or the reporters, but all he heard were heavy, labored breaths.

"Well, I guess I won't be the next Steve Jobs," she said through the wall, and Eli wasn't sure she was being facetious.

"You had no choice," he said.

"Of course I did. I was just confident I could sort it all out in time."

"There was no other way, Naomi. I was there," he said, gazing out the window at their neighbors' snow-covered roof. "You had to find a discreet way to get funding until the VC's investment came through. If word had gotten out that Hannah didn't actually have the money, we would have become the laughingstock of the hi-tech world."

"We should have turned down Hannah's offer when we found out she didn't have the money. We should have looked elsewhere."

"The company wouldn't have survived until we found another investor," he said with certainty, surprised by how strongly he felt about it. "If we had played by the rules, we would have had only two options—either become a serious, conventional company, which would've meant Mom leaving, or stick with Mom's wild ideas and achieve nothing. You're the one who kept this company alive because you knew when to bend the rules. It's all because of you that we have a cloud machine that made it rain on an entire village, like we promised."

"Only it's not rain, it's snow."

"Come on, are we really going to split hairs? So we put out a press release saying it was rain, no one will even notice," he said, hearing her laughter on the other side of the wall.

Tamara's face flitted before his eyes, stirring a whirlwind of anger and longing. He still didn't know whether she was the leak behind the article, or had simply sent him the link to say that she knew and was worried about him. Once again, he realized that Mandy Bialika was right—people were both compassionate and cruel beings. Tamara had yet to reply to his barrage of question marks, so he sent her one more and closed his eyes.

He was jolted awake by the deafening drilling and beeping sounds outside his window. The bulldozers were hard at work, clearing a path to the main square. Eli rushed downstairs and stepped outside, where he found his father standing beside a bulldozer, directing the operator on where to push the snow. Back inside, Naomi was at the kitchen table on speakerphone with the VC rep, telling him her plan to catch a ride on a snowplow to the hangar.

"Absolutely not!" the rep shouted, going on to describe how furious everyone at the hangar was at her.

"The responsible thing is to show up and confront the criticism," she replied.

"That would be the dumb thing to do, and I promise that if you decide to do it anyway, we'll pull our investment," he yelled. "Just keep your head down, wait until morning, and pray that after everyone gets a good night's sleep, they'll be a bit less angry."

While she'd never admit it, the clear instructions had a calming effect on Naomi, like a weight lifted off her shoulders, even if only until morning.

By the time the snow plows arrived from Mount Hermon, the village's access route had already been cleared. Boaz wasted no time hopping onto one of the plows, riding it all the way to the hangar compound, while some military equipment continued its snow-clearing efforts within the village itself. At eleven P.M. he texted his children that he'd reached the entrance to the compound, although it would be another full hour before he made it to the offices. Two spotless buses were on standby to rescue the stranded crowd, offering warm blankets for the journey back to Tel Aviv. While most guests opted to board them, assured that their cars would soon be excavated from the snow and sent their way, others insisted on spending the night on the Cliff and picking up their cars themselves in the morning. Paulina and a handful of dedicated Cloudies employees managed the arrangements for those who decided to stay at the boutique tourist resort on the crater's edge, despite the thick layer of snow obscuring any semblance of desert luxury. While a stretch limo was being arranged to chauffeur Gould back to his hotel in Tel Aviv, around midnight, Naomi's phone lit up with an unexpected text from Paulina.

"Gould decided to stay the night. He wants to see you first thing tomorrow morning."

5.

The snowplows toiled until the crack of dawn, leaving the roads clear and clean amidst the soft white landscape. As Eli and Naomi made their way by foot to the ersatz tourist resort, many of the villagers were outside, busy shoveling snow from their doorsteps and roofs. While some were sour-faced, others seemed buoyed by the snow, especially the children. Eli pictured Morgenstein smiling, knowing that the people of the Cliff had somehow bent nature's rules, finally bringing the houses he had designed in harmony with the climate. The Cliff's imperfections were still there—the peeling walls, cracked sidewalks, and funny-looking houses, but for the first time, Eli saw clearly what a beautiful place it was.

Waiting for them by one of the houses co-opted for the resort, Paulina informed them the last of the reporters had just left. A few employees were busy tidying up the houses, and the golf carts rented for the guests were still blanketed in snow, as were the hot tubs on every porch.

"Where is he?" Naomi sighed. Paulina pointed toward a narrow path carved through the snow, leading to the crater's edge. At the far end of the partially obscured trail sat Gould, alone on a white plastic chair, looking out at the crater through his sunglasses, espresso in hand.

"We need to talk about what happened," Paulina began, "yesterday and this morning, it's—"

"Wait, let me handle Gould first," Naomi cut her off.

Paulina persisted, saying that with all due respect she couldn't just leave dozens of employees in the dark, not after everything that happened and the stories on the news; but Naomi's attention was fixed on the trail. "Want me to come with you?" Eli asked, and his sister bit her bottom lip. "Why not," she replied.

Eli took the first step on the narrow path leading up to Ben Gould, with Naomi lagging behind. When they reached the end of the trail,

Gould raised his sunglasses and considered them silently. Despite the snow, he was wearing running shorts and a tank top.

"You know, Mr. Gould," Eli broke the silence, "my gut tells me that yesterday wasn't the best presentation you've ever seen."

"You've got good instincts." Gould chuckled. "I typically tell folks that the worst outcome of a poor presentation is some mild disappointment, but after last night, I think I have to amend my answer."

"Cloudies would be delighted to arrange for a limo and hotel in Tel Aviv for you," Naomi responded. "I'm so sorry, we'll do everything in our power to make up for your terrible experience."

"First of all, your obsession with limos? Mind-boggling. It's a rich-people relic from the eighties. We Uber nowadays. Second, the fanciest hotel room in the Middle East wouldn't make up for the total lack of professionalism I witnessed yesterday." Gould casually set his espresso down on the muddy ground. "And speaking of which, I honestly can't fathom why you believed that serving hummus-stuffed sushi rolls and other such nonsense would make me want to invest in your misguided venture." The guest of honor glared at Naomi. "However—yesterday's debacle doesn't change the simple fact that you have a good invention. The only problem is your business model."

"Respectfully, Mr. Gould, I actually think there's huge financial potential here," Eli blurted out, even though he wasn't quite sure where Gould was going.

"You're wrong. The people most in need of the services of a company that turns sand into rain are precisely the people who can't afford them. And while it might not be very woke of me, if they can't pay, I don't play."

The mogul continued, explaining that he had had a symposium scheduled in Greece for December, so he thought he might as well pop by for a quick visit. Eli then realized that the tight four-month deadline set in the tweet was nothing more than a vacant morning slot and a publicity stunt. Gould had never intended to cross the Atlantic just for them. He was in the neighborhood and decided to squeeze in another event.

"But funnily enough," Gould continued, "something about your botched presentation made me realize you do have something real to offer. What I saw wasn't a rain-making device, it was a system capable of manipulating local climates. And that kind of invention, well, there's a hell of a lot of untapped potential right there."

Naomi was nodding in slow motion, as clueless as her brother about what was coming.

"I realized two important things about your mother's invention yesterday. The first—your machine isn't limited to rain production, it's capable of producing artificial climate systems that include other winter modes like snow," he said, motioning toward the crater, at the abrupt transition from snow to desert. "And the second thing is that the artificial storm can be confined to a specific area, which is not only impressive but also incredibly useful. Climate change is the twenty-first century's biggest problem, and up until now all attempts to address it have involved global, worldwide solutions. Billions of people, tens of thousands of corporations, and hundreds of governments all collaborating to take on one challenge, in an extremely complicated endeavor. But your invention can be a serious game-changer," he announced.

It dawned on Eli that what he was witnessing at that very moment was an impressive display of Gould's renowned ability to spot diamonds where others saw only mud.

"Your invention could transform climate change from a global problem to a localized concern. If the residents of Rome find themselves sweating through an unprecedentedly hot day in the middle of July, they won't have to wait a few decades for some elusive solution that may never come, they can just cool the city with a few clouds instead."

"That does sound good," Naomi said.

"Good?" Gould raised his voice. "It's freakin' amazing! You've taken humanity's biggest challenge and broken it down into a lot of small, readily solvable problems. Imagine a few years from now, every town with the ability to provide its residents with a mild summer. Maybe even every neighborhood. It will be the biggest thing since the iPhone."

Naomi's eyes sparkled with sudden clarity. "The blue ocean strategy," she burst out, any trace of despair wiped from her face.

"Sounds like an amazing vision, Mr. Gould," Eli said, secretly hoping that his unfamiliarity with the blue ocean strategy or its relevance to their desert wasn't too obvious. "Truly amazing. But how does it solve climate change? Correct me if I'm mistaken, but even if we help people in Rome avoid a heatwave, the earth will still keep warming up. It seems that would be treating the symptom rather than the root problem."

"Remind me who you are again?" Gould asked, and Eli couldn't tell whether it was a genuine question or a belittling tactic.

"Eli Lilienblum, cofounder."

Gould narrowed his eyes at him. "Actually, Eli, you're not entirely wrong. We won't be solving climate change. But to be frank, I don't really care." Eli noticed that Naomi was equally taken aback by his response. Gould explained that as an entrepreneur the only thing that ever interested him was the end user. "With all due respect to climate change, what I care about is making someone feel a little less miserable when it's a hundred and ten degrees outside. The future of planet Earth, which I'm not saying isn't important, is for scholars and activists to tackle. Not me."

Eli wanted nothing more than to say that he was sick and tired of how cynical it was, all these people trying to pass as eccentric philanthropists working for the betterment of humanity when in reality there was nothing further from the truth. He had plenty of things to say, but he bit his tongue, for the sole reason that Naomi shot him a look that said, "Don't screw this up for us now," and he knew his sister was right. They were knee-deep in debt, with millions to be repaid, and for the time being, that took precedence over the fate of planet Earth.

"Okay, I get it," Eli said, offering his sister a reassuring look. "But does it honestly matter if we choose to call it a cloud-creating system or a climate system?"

Gould grinned. "It's a subtle but crucial distinction. Water scarcity is mostly a Third World problem, but climate change is everyone's problem—including the First World's. And given that the First World is our target audience, that's how we market it."

Eli scanned Naomi's face for anger and disdain toward Gould's statements, given her claims of infiltrating the hi-tech world to dismantle it from within, but her expression remained blank.

"In short, guys, we're going to do big things together," Gould announced, rising from his seat to give them each a pat on the back. "And now that the matter of the article has been resolved, as far as I'm concerned, we can move forward."

Eli and Naomi exchanged uncertain glances.

"Wait, resolved? News-Tech retracted their accusations?" Naomi asked.

"Well, the culprit confessed." Gould sighed, throwing his hands up. Then he stared at them. "Fuck, you actually don't know."

AFTER
THE
RAIN

I n the unassuming Arial 12 font, beside an image of a quintessential Cliff house, News-Tech's headline read, "Inventor Sarai Lilienblum's Husband Confesses to Massive Fraud," with the accompanying byline expounding, "Boaz Lilienblum, Local Hostel Proprietor, Admits to Orchestrating Months-long International Email Scam."

Boaz told the investigators that he hadn't trusted Hannah Bialika from the get-go, suspecting she wouldn't come through with her investment, "what with all the rumors about the old shrew pilfering toilet paper from restaurants." Those gnawing doubts prompted him not only to take out a loan to fund the company, but also to concoct the covert phishing scam in a secret room at the back of the restaurant. A contingency plan, he explained, in the event Bialika faltered in her financial commitments—which, as fate would have it, she did. He provided the investigators with four folders of detailed documents proving he was the one who recruited the volunteers, oversaw their work, and managed the finances. He was on top of every detail, including the password for every fictitious email account he'd opened. He showed the investigators that given Cloudies' chaotic management, he had little trouble making the company accountants believe that the money came directly from Hannah Bialika.

Boaz's story was reasonable and convincing. There was only one problem—Eli knew it wasn't true. He had been right there at the birth of General Luciano Rodríguez Ancelotti III, his sister's brainchild. With his own eyes he saw her lay the groundwork for the entire scheme. But when confronting her that night with the facts, she shot him an indifferent look and said, "I feel bad about what Dad did, but I had no part in it."

His sister and father had been in cahoots all along. He not only knew about her secret funding plan from the very start, he actually ran the show. The volunteers corroborated Boaz's story, saying that he was their sole supervisor. Eli realized that, having anticipated the inevitable implosion, his sister had carefully set things up so that not a single piece of shrapnel would fly her way. Even when Eli threatened to go to the police and report the fraud, she told him she had no hand in the matter, casually adding, "And I assure you, other than your word, they won't find a shred of proof tying me to this." And she was right. Despite their many conversations about it, there was no evidence pointing to her involvement in the email scam. All roads led to Boaz Lilienblum, who took the fall. Had the police done their job and dug a little deeper, they might have stumbled upon information that challenged his story, but it was a story that seemed to suit everyone. Boaz's confession allowed Naomi and Cloudies to escape unscathed, enabling the company to carry on with its usual activities; the police department reveled in the glory of a speedy and successful investigation; the Startup Nation celebrated another tech victory; and Ben Gould was relieved to be rid of all the unpleasantness.

When Boaz was arrested that day, Cloudies issued a statement, clarifying that they had no prior knowledge of the wrongdoings. They emphasized that Boaz Lilienblum had never held an official role at the company and announced their intention to appoint Naomi as CEO instead of her mother, suggesting a move away from the chaotic era of Sarai's management.

A day after his arrest, Boaz called his son. "I know you must be confused and worried, but I've made my peace with it. I've done some things in my life, Eli, and now it's time to pay."

Eli suspected that what truly burdened his father was the guilt of authoring the Robert McMurphy myth, and a few days later, his suspicion was confirmed when the final puzzle piece fell into place.

The volunteer search-and-rescue unit received an alert regarding two stranded travelers trapped inside a crater. Racing to the crater in his black jeep, the rescuer found two travelers who led him to a hidden ravine between the bushes and pointed at a black duffle bag lying on the ground. Robert McMurphy's bag. Inside it they found his clothes, journals, and notes. All the equipment that had been hidden for years in the house of the Lilienblum's suddenly appeared in the desert.

In the following weeks, the rescue unit went through all the items, examining them meticulously, hoping to find some new clues. Paulina, who joined the effort as a volunteer, examined the notebooks. She always dreamed of being a yachtswoman, and used her fondness for nautical charts to notice that not all the numbers that Robert McMurphy wrote were completely random. Some of them indicated coordinates of locations. Locations that Robert McMurphy visited during his travels in Israel.

Four of the locations were inside the crater, and a rescue mission was sent to each of them. Eli was sure that this would be another failed attempt in a long history of failures.

But he was wrong.

Within the heart tangle of thorny bushes, near a small and hidden wadi, they found the thing they had been looking for all these years.

A DNA sample confirmed the police's suspicions. The rescue team had found the remains of their first missing person, Robert McMurphy.

The reverend was notified of the discovery, and thanks to an anonymous donation to the church, and at the request of McMurphy's mother, he purchased McMurphy a burial plot in Jerusalem. For the second time in her life, Agatha traveled to Israel, this time with a small group of parishioners from her church, to hold a modest funeral for her son.

"And lo, on this day, the land was filled with grace and acceptance," the reverend wrote Eli after the funeral service. When he showed Sarai the message, her eyes lingered on the words for a long while, and he sensed that it wasn't just the land but also his mother's heart.

Two weeks after his father's arrest, a deal was signed between Ben Gould's representatives and Cloudies, solidifying Gould's acquisition of the company and honoring his tweeted commitment. Gould's power of persuasion was so extraordinary that it left Eli wondering whether the figure was too low for a pioneering climate-tech company, but he knew that with the shadow of criminality looming over the company and the mounting debt, there was no alternative. He further realized that Hannah Bialika had been right when she said the economic system didn't reward creative minds, but those who knew how to capitalize on the creativity of others.

Twenty million dollars fell far short of fulfilling the employees' fantasies. A large portion of the funds found their way to the VC's vault, padded Albert and Alice's pockets, and got gobbled up by the tax authorities. Out of the money retained by the company, Naomi paid a hefty compensation to the victims of the email fraud (once they'd signed a liability release from Cloudies, absolving the company of wrongdoing and waiving any further claims). The balance was divided among the company's dozens of employees, resulting in a one-time bonus that could reach up to fifty thousand dollars per employee, depending on the number of options negotiated in their contracts. While a substantial sum, it wasn't the kind of money that would enable them to retire at forty-five and move to the Caribbean, as many had hoped for.

The only person to receive a bigger chunk of the money was Hannah Bialika. Despite not delivering on her full investment promise, she was still the one who had injected the initial half million shekels that jump-started the company. Now finally possessing the financial means to move out of her giant house, she opted to stay there, as well as in her role as Cloudies' accountant. A remarkable shift occurred in how the residents of the Cliff viewed Hannah Bialika; no longer seen as a grumpy recluse, she transformed into a revered philanthropist. Embracing this new image of hers, she even welcomed guests into her home, personally guiding them on tours, and slowly but surely the mansion became a tourist attraction. During the council meeting held at winter's end, the council head said that thanks to the Bialika house, the Cliff was now drawing a different kind of tourist—more sophisticated, mature travelers for whom the modest accommodations of the lodge wouldn't suffice. That being the case, it was time they considered allocating a sizeable sum toward the development of a luxury tourist resort, drawing inspiration from the successful impromptu model put in place during Ben Gould's visit. "It would mean diverting funds from the council's support for the lodge," the council head acknowledged, "but as we know, there's always a price to pay to make the desert bloom." Boaz was released from custody two weeks later and didn't oppose the new tourism plans. He informed the council head that he'd already intended to sell the lodge to free up time to prepare for his trial.

The money left in the Lilienblums' bank account after selling both Cloudies and the lodge afforded each family member the freedom to pause and reconsider the course of their lives. To Eli's surprise, Boaz didn't return to the Cliff. Instead, he rented a modest apartment in Be'er Sheva, ostensibly to be closer to the courthouse, but Eli had a hunch he was doing it to give his mother the space she yearned for, and that he perhaps needed himself. With no more secrets left to out, they needed to see whether this new void could be filled, or if they had drifted too far apart.

Naomi moved back to Tel Aviv, where she set up the company's executive headquarters. The revelation that she had always intended for their father to bear the blame for the email scam, even with his full consent, eroded his trust in her, and he began to doubt whether she had genuinely set out to be the tech industry's Trojan horse, or if it had just been a ploy to gain his trust. The only hint suggesting some truth to her story was her uncompromising stance during the negotiations with Gould's lawyers that the R&D center remain on the Cliff, with all its employees retaining their roles. In addition, Naomi negotiated a clause into the sales agreement that secured their mother the title of company president—a prestigious position devoid of any real substance or responsibility, just as Sarai had always wanted.

Sarai mentioned going back to teach the high school robotics club, but Eli knew her heart wouldn't be in it. One evening, he handed her a letter from the Technion, which she had to read three times before grasping its contents.

"You enrolled me in the winter semester of aerospace engineering?" she asked with a befuddled look. "Only in the courses you needed to finish your degree," he replied with a grin. He said the head of the engineering department was so excited about the prospect of Sarai

Lilienblum, inventor extraordinaire, as their student again, that he agreed to convert the missing credits to lab-work hours. "Apparently, the professors there are already fighting over who gets to host you in their lab first."

A hint of panic in her voice, she dismissed the idea as unrealistic, explaining that she'd already given the high school her word, and that on top of everything else, she was too drained to uproot her whole life and relocate up north to Haifa. "Everything's been taken care of," he reassured her. "I spoke to the high school principal, and he agreed to give you a sabbatical. And I found a small hotel right by the Technion where you could stay. Give it a chance, see how it feels. What do you have to lose?"

With Eli at the wheel of the battered white Mazda, they crossed the desert, plains, and mountains on the snaking way to Haifa. His mother looked out the window at the evolving landscape growing greener with each passing moment.

"Do you think there's someone building Haifa right now just for our visit?"

"I'm sure of it," she replied.

Munching on apple slices while flipping through radio stations, she suddenly heard her daughter's voice. It was an economics program, and Naomi was being interviewed in honor of the inauguration of Cloudies' Tel Aviv headquarters. Eli touched her hand, lest she accidently turn the dial.

Naomi announced that Cloudies would be expanding its workforce by hiring an additional hundred engineers and chemists, while assuring that "the employees from the Cliff will maintain their pivotal roles within the company." Asking Naomi about her father's fraudulent activities, the host noted that the public had yet to hear her personal stance on the issue. "Needless to say, it's a tough spot to be in. My father has always been and will always be an important part of my life, but even if he didn't mean any harm, fraud is no laughing matter. As CEO, I won't stand for it, plain and simple."

"If he's found guilty, do you think he should go to jail?"

After a brief pause, Naomi said that no one wanted to see their parents behind bars, but that there was no excuse for taking the law into one's own hands, "and if someone chooses to do so, they have to face the consequences."

He heard a hint of sorrow in his sister's voice. He glanced at his mother beside him, trying to read her thoughts. Was she as angry at Naomi as he was? He couldn't tell whether his sister was genuinely sorry for their father, or in denial, trying to ease her conscience by convincing herself that he had been the brains behind the operation. The fact that Eli couldn't understand even those closest to him made him feel frustrated and lonely.

It was nearing evening when they pulled up to the hotel in Haifa. Taking charge, Eli hauled his mother's suitcase into the lobby and handled the check-in. Sarai asked the concierge if there was a hair dryer in the bathroom, and was assured that her room was equipped with all necessary amenities. Smiling, Eli pictured his mother disassembling the dryer to repurpose its components. Before parting ways, she asked about his plans, and he told her he'd be heading back to the Cliff to take care of a few things related to the lodge's sale. "And after that?" she asked.

"I'm not sure."

"The Cliff is a very nice place, Eli, but if you don't start using your share of the sale to explore even a fraction of this world, I'll personally drag you to the airport myself."

"Where do you want me to go?"

"I'm sure there's at least one place on this giant planet you'd like to visit."

It was nearly dark by the time he arrived, his backpack digging into his shoulders after the long flight and bus ride. Illuminated by the soft glow of the setting sun, the lighthouse emerged into view, a striking structure—taller than he had imagined—striped blue and white. Just as she had described.

At the front desk, an older woman with cropped white hair and purple-rimmed glasses asked if he had found the place okay. He admitted it had been a challenge, that the lighthouse didn't appear on any map, but fortunately the bus driver knew the place and where to drop him off. She offered him some cake, which he politely declined, but somehow ended up eating. It was good. He handed her his passport, and while photocopying it, she remarked that Eli was a nice name and asked him if he had arrived in Spain that day. He said he had, and she told him it showed, that something in his body had yet to uncoil. "It's a good thing, it means you're excited. Now go up there before you miss the sunset."

He went up the spiral staircase, joining a handful of fellow travelers on the lighthouse's top floor. A young couple stood hand in hand by the giant wooden-framed window, watching the sun slowly sink into the ocean. He waited until it touched the water and snapped a photo, then sent it to his mother along with a short update on his arrival. Relieved to hear he'd arrived safely, she reported that she was writing from the materials science lab, where she'd accidentally blown up a supply closet the day before, but was otherwise loving every moment of it. Eli then found himself staring at the photo of Tamara in her triangle jacket that appeared next to her texts. After a brief hesitation, he decided to send her a photo as well.

She replied a moment later:

For real? You're at the lighthouse? You've come a long way.

(Btw I didn't leak the story to News-Tech, in case you were wondering.)

And after a few more moments added:

I think it's time we meet.

He didn't know whether to believe her; he had to see her in person and look her in the eye to know. Right away, a wry smile crossed his face as he admitted to himself that it was no more than a clunky excuse, and that the truth was much simpler.

When the sun had gone down and the world dimmed, Eli went downstairs, the sound of upbeat music growing stronger with every step. In the small lobby, a few hotel guests were dancing.

"Is that salsa?" he asked the older woman at the front desk.

"Yes, salsa," she replied, stretching every syllable, then rose and offered him her hand.

He didn't know how to dance salsa. He didn't know how to dance at all. And yet, he reached out and let her guide him to the middle of the lobby, where she began to sway to the beat of the music. He tried to mirror her movements, acutely aware of how stiff and awkward he looked. Stumbling along, he saw that his clumsiness made her laugh. It made him laugh too.

Eli Lilienblum smiled, giving in to the music, surrendering himself to this strange new experience in which he allowed himself to lift one leg into the air, without knowing where it would land.

Acknowledgments

My deepest gratitude to my editor, Ben Schrank, whose brilliant suggestions and insights helped me see my work through a new lens, allowing me to truly understand the Lilienblum family and their world. Thank you for your unwavering belief in me and this book, and to Rachael Small and the entire team at Astra for creating such a warm and supportive home.

Endless thanks to my agent, Deborah Harris, who was the first to believe in me and Mrs. Lilienblum, and for being a steady anchor in turbulent times. Nothing would have been possible without your infinite driving force. Special thanks to Jessica, Hadar, Talia, and everyone at The Deborah Harris Agency for their constant support, and to Daniella Zamir for her exquisite translation, and to Dalia Rosenfeld who edited it.

Thank you to Dr. Daphna Shohamy and my friends in the lab, for teaching me every day about the brain, stories, and most importantly, humans. Thanks to Sagi and Eyal—your insightful comments were invaluable. And to Sylvie Rabineau and Jill Gillett, whose passion for stories and people has taken me and my work to places I never dared dream.

Thank you to my parents, Meir and Shelly, who came to my first event as an author with three cameras, and who since then continue to embarrass and support me, and to my sisters Michal and Sharon, who have always been there with endless love. To Neria, who has crossed continents with me since Havana, always chasing the next adventure. And finally, to General Luciano Rodríguez Ancelotti III, whose dear friendship and character is, in so many ways, the soul within this book—I hope we meet again soon, here or on the other side.

About the Author

Iddo Gefen was born in 1992 in Tel Aviv and is currently based in New York City. He is an author and a PhD student in cognitive psychology at Columbia University and the Zuckerman Institute for neuroscience, researching the relationship between narrative understanding, human memory, and decision-making. His first book, *Jerusalem Beach*, was the recipient of the 2023 Sami Rohr Prize for Jewish Literature.

About the Translator

Daniella Zamir is an Israeli literary translator of contemporary fiction. She is the winner of the CWA International Dagger for her translation of *A Long Night in Paris* by Dov Alfon. In 2023 she won the Sami Rohr Prize for Jewish Literature for her translation of *Jerusalem Beach* by Iddo Gefen.